THE GHOST
and The
GRAVEYARD

Genevieve Jack

Carpe Luna Publishing

The Ghost and The Graveyard:
The Knight Games series, Book 1

Published by Carpe Luna, Ltd.,
PO Box 5932,
Bloomington, IL 61701
www.carpeluna.com

SECOND EDITION: AUGUST 2013

ISBN: 978-1-940675-06-0

*Cover design by Adam Bedore at Anjin Design,
photo by Hot Damn Designs.
www.anjindesign.com*

*Formatting by Polgarus Studio.
www.polgarusstudio.com*

v 3.0

BOOKS BY GENEVIEVE JACK

Knight Games Series

The Ghost and The Graveyard

Kick The Candle

Queen of the Hill

(and more to come!)

Contents

CHAPTER 1
I Get What I Pay For

Welcome to Red Grove. Population 200

"Now, two hundred and one," I murmured as I passed the painted wooden sign in my trusty red Jeep. Small towns like Red Grove always made me think of horror movies, as if a gap-toothed, overall-wearing butcher might hobble out of his deep woods shanty, pitchfork in hand, at any moment. The town had an off-the-charts creepy factor. On my right, a dark forest worthy of the Brothers Grimm. On my left, a cemetery edged in a weathered wrought iron fence. I think there were more than two hundred headstones. More dead than living. Nice.

There must be some mistake. I came here to start over. Could a new life be hiding behind the unappealing rural exterior? My promised house remained a mystery. I double-checked the notebook with my father's scrawled directions resting on the passenger's seat next to me. Technically, I'd lived in Red Grove as a child, but we'd moved before I turned two. I didn't remember the town or the residents, living or dead.

I shifted my attention back to my driving. *Holy shit!* I overcorrected the wheel, and my foot drifted from the gas.

The man on the side of the road was so attractive I could've died—literally. He was planting something. A tree, I think. Every time his shovel hit the dirt, a ripple coursed through his shoulders and down his stomach. I raised an eyebrow at the glint of sun on tanned, shirtless skin. Dark hair, low-slung jeans. I tried not to gawk, but the best I could do was to keep my head inside the window.

I was thinking he belonged in a museum, a chiseled-by-the-gods man museum, when my brain was hijacked. I forgot about the road. I forgot where I was going. A fantasy hit me so fast and hard, it could've been a memory.

We were in the shower. I stood behind him, my arms wrapped around his torso, rubbing lather circles down his chest, over his rock-hard abs, and lower. In my daydream, he moaned my name, and I was considering ways to wrap myself around him without breaking the rhythm. The scene was so vivid, the lavender scent of soap filled the cab of my Jeep.

The *rat-tat-tat* of pebbles hitting the undercarriage wrenched me from my reverie. I slammed on the brakes, sending my vehicle into a reckless skid toward the edge of a stone bridge straight out of a Thomas Kinkade print. Whether by ace driving skills, gravity, or sheer dumb luck, I stalled at the precipice, all white knuckles and shivering limbs. Eyeing the boulders in the brook below me, I suppressed a lingering fear of plummeting to my doom.

"Hey, are you okay?" the man called. He dropped his shovel and headed toward me, his eyes narrowing in concern.

With a gasp, I clutched at the front of my shirt, relieved I was still dressed. What the hell? Sure, he was attractive, but I'd never had that kind of reaction to anyone before. The fantasy was so...*real*. I tried to shake the vision of him naked from my head.

No way could I explain what just happened. I couldn't possibly tell him about my fantasy, and I wasn't a good enough liar to make up an alternate story on the fly. The hot sting of a blush crept across my face.

"I'm okay. Thanks!" I gave a friendly wave out my window.

He nodded but didn't stop walking toward my car.

Before he could reach me, I accelerated back on course, leaving him staring in my direction. I wasn't trying to be rude. Besides the obvious embarrassment, I had no business talking to a man who looked like that. I had no business talking to *any* man. Not until I took control of my life again.

I reached the end of the road and pulled into the driveway of the house I hoped would be my salvation, my financial rebirth. The truth? I had bigger things to worry about than a man on the side of the road, no matter how gorgeous. It was time to face my future.

Wedged behind the tailgate of my Jeep was one large moving box. I sighed. My entire life fit inside a cardboard cube with the logo of a defunct trucking company. Technically, the box wasn't even mine; I'd borrowed it from my friend Michelle.

The wrinkled cardboard flaps bowed like judgmental eyebrows, and I slapped them down with unnecessary vigor. I reached for the mammoth cargo, too big to carry from the bottom without completely blocking my face and without those convenient cutout handles you find on cases of beer. I hoisted the box using the pressure hold, bear-hugging the cardboard to my chest and resting the bottom on my knee. It weighed a ton. While I shuffled up the stone pathway to the porch, the leaden box slid down my body centimeter by centimeter. By the time I reached the bottom step, I was hobbling toward the door, holding the box up with my flexed foot.

That's when my hip started vibrating. With one final heave and a contortion of my limbs that must've looked like I was having a seizure, I propelled the box onto the porch and ripped the phone from my pocket. I thumbed the answer button while I kicked the cardboard monster toward the door.

"Hello," I said, in a tone that clearly meant goodbye.

"Grateful? Is that you?"

I lowered the phone from my ear to see Michelle Murphy's margarita-fueled grin staring back at me from the screen, a photo I'd taken of her two spring breaks ago before my financial apocalypse. I put on my happy voice. "Yeah, it's me. Sorry, you just caught me trying to launch the moving box from hell onto the porch."

"I should've helped you move."

"It's one box. I think I can handle it."

"Right... That bastard."

"It's my own damn fault. I handed him the money. Who gives a boyfriend that kind of money?" I rolled my eyes at my own stupidity.

"You can't blame yourself. It's not your fault for trusting someone you loved. I'm telling you, you're a victim! Your situation is a manifestation of the blonde paradox."

Michelle and I attended nursing school together. After we graduated, I'd had enough of academia. She, on the other hand, decided to pursue a master's degree in mental health nursing. Now she thinks she knows everything about relationships and psychoanalyzes all of my problems.

Her blonde paradox theory is based on two recent research studies—the type you read about in magazines at grocery store checkouts. The first study found women who look like Barbie—blonde, blue eyed, big boobs—are more attractive to men. Something about these features signifies a more fertile womb to the caveman brain. I loosely fit this description. I do have blue eyes, but my hair is more of a honey blonde than platinum. My boobs are on the large side, but it's because I'm about fifteen pounds heavier than my goal weight. However, Michelle thinks I am close enough to ignite evolutionary passions and this explains why I never lack masculine attention.

But here's the rub. The second study found that men shown pictures of Barbie-ish women scored lower on intelligence tests. Turns out people who believe the "blondes are dumb" stereotype actually take on the projected characteristics of their prejudicial target. Thus the paradox. I attract more men than the average woman, but they degrade into idiots in my mere presence.

The theory does explain some things. Like why I ended up with my snake-belly of an ex-boyfriend, Gary, while Michelle, five foot two and a hundred-sixty pounds of dark-headed attitude, is married with a baby.

"So, what should I do? Dye my hair?" I asked.

"Or contacts. Green might be nice."

"You can't be serious."

"No. I'm not. You're a wonderful person. You just need to find someone who will love you for you, the whole package. I know he's out there, somewhere."

"I hope you're right. I can't take another Gary," I said.

Silence. Michelle was probably holding her tongue so she wouldn't say, "I told you so." Smart woman. "So what's the free house look like? Is it as bad as you expected?" she finally asked.

"No. Super cute! I can't believe this place hasn't sold. Definite curb appeal, the architecture looks old but freshly painted. Hold on, I'm going inside."

I fumbled in my pocket for the key and turned it in the brass lock. The door opened, and the sun cast a square of light on the floor around my silhouette. I patted the wall for the light switch and soon an elegant chandelier glowed from above.

"Wow, Michelle, it's fabulous! You have got to see this. Hardwood floors, two-story foyer, curved staircase." I walked into the kitchen. "*Holy crow*, stainless steel appliances!"

Michelle squealed on the other end of the phone. We were both expecting a dump. I mean, after I had to crawl to my real estate agent dad for help, I kind of thought the unsellable place he gave me to stay would be a punishment. Compared to my last apartment—or worse, the dorm room Michelle and I lived in at college—this place was a palace.

"Hold on, I'm going to check out the rest." I walked to the front of the house and opened the curtains, bathing the main floor in natural light. The place had an elegant dining room and a family room with a flat-screen television. The living room's floral print screamed *old lady*, but I wasn't complaining. The furniture looked new. I talked Michelle through the tour, bounding up the stairs two at a time to check out the bedrooms. Besides a little dust, the place was meticulously maintained.

On the second-floor landing, I attempted to toss back the curtains to have a look at my new backyard, but the rings caught on the antique cast-iron rod. I wrestled with the damask, catching a glimpse of what was beyond the glass. My heart sank into my gut, and distracted, I dropped my phone. I tried to catch it with my other hand, but it bounced off my palm. Thankfully, the thick carpet of the landing saved me from certain communication purgatory.

"Grateful? You still there?"

I scrambled to return the phone to my ear. "I think I figured out why this house hasn't sold yet," I said.

"Why? Is the yard small?"

Turning back toward the window, I gave the curtains one last firm yank. They gave way, rewarding me with a clear view. The yard sloped from the house toward a weathered, wrought iron fence that bordered the property. Behind the fence, row after row of tombstones stretched across the landscape, with the odd mausoleum thrown in for good measure. The graveyard I'd seen driving into Red Grove extended all the way to my back door.

"My backyard is a cemetery," I deadpanned.

"Seriously? Is that even legal?"

"I've gotta go, Michelle," I said. "I need to take this up with my realtor."

"Okay. Say hi to your dad for me."

* * * * *

I paced the floral living room, trying to keep my voice from climbing to the octave of hysteria. I was pretty close. Any higher and dogs would come running. "Dad, you could have told me."

"Sweetheart, it's nothing. Keep the drapes closed and no one will ever know."

"Don't you think an important piece of information to share with a potential homeowner is the number of dead people buried in the backyard?"

"Now, don't overreact. First of all, may I remind you, you are not the homeowner but a custodian, so to speak. And think of it this way—your neighbors are a quiet, keep-to-themselves type of people." I heard a muffled chuckle.

"I can hear you laughing," I said. "I've told you before, putting your hand over the receiver does not work. Can't you understand why this might freak me out a little? I'm here all alone."

"I'm telling you, a few nights there, and you'll forget why you were ever worried," Dad said. "Plus, if you get scared, the caretaker of the cemetery lives just over the bridge from you. Come to think of it, he would probably give you a tour if you wanted. Maybe that would put you at ease."

"Oh sure, a tour of the cemetery with some old, creepy caretaker is just what I need to feel at home!" My voice was rising again. I was painfully close to looking the gift horse in the mouth.

"Grateful, I love you."

"I know, Dad."

"I wouldn't put you in harm's way."

"I know, Dad."

"I stocked the refrigerator for you…"

Like that mattered. We were talking about dead people here.

"…and the wine cellar."

"This place has a wine cellar?"

"In the basement."

"Awww, you're the best." I guess Daddy's charm was harder to resist than I thought.

"So you'll give it a few nights?"

"Sure."

There are few things in this world I won't do for a really fine bottle of Shiraz, and fewer still I won't do for my dad. I wouldn't let a bunch of dead people ruin my chances at a new life. Dad was right. I could do this.

I ended the call and raced to the little door behind the kitchen I assumed led to the basement. To my pleasant surprise it was a finished walkout; too bad if you walked out it would be straight toward the dead people. I tried to ignore the view and veered toward the wine cellar. As big as a bedroom, the section for reds had a separate door from the whites to keep each wine at the optimal temperature. Looking over the rows of bottles, their labels turned upward, my mood significantly improved. Dad hadn't let me down—my favorite label was at eye level. I grabbed the familiar bottle of Shiraz from the reds and headed upstairs.

Dad had come through on the food as well. I found a Styrofoam clamshell from Valentine's, my favorite restaurant. Salmon fillet, some red potatoes, and fresh asparagus. I scraped the contents onto a plate and popped the vittles into the microwave. Cooking with wine is my specialty, so I grabbed a glass and reached for my old friend, Mr. Shiraz. Unfortunately, the bottle in my hand was Pinot Gris.

"Weird," I said to myself. I could have sworn I'd grabbed the red. Odder still, the white was cold. I didn't remember going into the refrigerated section at all.

I revisited the cellar. The bottle of red I'd wanted was back in its spot. I replaced the white in the cooler and then ran back upstairs with my Shiraz, double-checking the label. Man, I was losing my mind. I blamed the stress of moving.

In the dining room, I uncorked the bottle and poured myself a glass, admiring the clarity and subtle scent of berries. I drained the vino with an unladylike swig. Who cared anyway? Like my dad said, the neighbors wouldn't be talking.

The doorbell rang. I jolted, almost dropping my glass. Who the hell could that be? I set the glass down and approached the door cautiously. The bell rang again.

"Can I help you?" I yelled through the etched glass oval of the door. A man's silhouette sliced the twilight. There was no way I was opening up without some credentials.

The man's muffled voice filtered through the door. "Hello? I'm Rick Ordenes, from up the street. Your dad asked me to stop by and welcome you to Red Grove."

"Up the street?" I hadn't noticed any neighbors.

"Yes, I live across the bridge. I'm the caretaker."

"Oh. Hold on." It was nice of my dad to send the old guy over to check on me. I unlocked the deadbolt and opened the door.

And came face to face with the chiseled Adonis from the side of the road.

CHAPTER 2
I Break My Own Rules

"Is this yours?" he asked, effortlessly holding the huge box I'd forgotten on the porch.

"Yeah." With some effort, I lifted my cardboard nemesis from his hands and dropped the sucker ungracefully into the corner of the foyer. "Thank you."

"You're welcome."

Even more striking up close, I wanted to snap his picture to post on Facebook along with the status: *Getta load of my new neighbor.* Outlined in my doorway by the orangey-purple sunset, even the sky seemed to blush at the sight of him. And what a sight he was. Taller than me, his dark, wavy hair curled at the base of his neck in a style I'd call well-managed chaos. His straight white smile contrasted nicely with his golden complexion and Mediterranean features. Masculine with a long-muscled grace, he reminded me of a matador or flamenco dancer. Almost regal.

"Rick Ordenes." He extended his hand. "I'm the caretaker."

I accepted his handshake. Firm, strong. Good eye contact. He definitely passed Handshake 101. "Has anyone ever told you, you don't look like the typical cemetery caretaker?"

"What does a typical caretaker look like?"

"I don't know. I was expecting old and gray."

He laughed. "Believe it or not, it takes *resilience* to do my job. An aged man would struggle with the work."

"I never thought of it that way." I hoped I hadn't offended him.

He raised an eyebrow. "You're not what I expected, either."

"Oh, you mean based on my father's description," I said, grinning. "He probably still describes me in pigtails."

He shook his head. "Actually, he didn't even tell me your name."

"Oh, um, I'm Grateful."

"You're grateful he didn't tell me?"

"No! I mean, that's my name. Grateful. Grateful Knight. I know, it's a strange name, considering my father wasn't even a hippie." I shrugged.

A slow smile spread across his lips, and his gray eyes twinkled. "Grateful is a lovely name. I suppose it's fitting that a rare beauty have an equally rare name."

The compliment captivated me. Not just the words themselves but the way he said them. With a hint of a Spanish accent, they tumbled over his full lips in a silky smooth ripple, like moonlight spilling over still water. I caught myself staring at his mouth.

My cheeks warmed. Oh. My. God. Had I reverted to an awkward fifteen-year-old blushing at the hint of male attention? I mentally slapped myself.

"Would you like to come in?" I opened the door a little wider.

"Are you inviting me?"

I blinked in his direction. "Um, yes. Where I come from, 'Would you like to come in?' is an invitation."

"In my experience, it's always best to make sure," he said, teasing me with a delectable lopsided grin. Bending, he retrieved a vase of the ugliest wildflowers I'd ever seen from beside the door and handed them to me. "Sage and garlic, to ward off evil spirits." He stepped into the house, eyes darting around the foyer with the curiosity of a tourist.

"Oh, thanks. How thoughtful. My dad must have told you the cemetery kind of freaks me out."

He ignored my comment but turned the full weight of his attention on me. "Do you go by Grateful, or something shorter?"

"Yes, Grateful. You can't really shorten Grateful. Unless I went by a single letter like G, and I'm not a music mogul or one of the Men in Black, so Grateful it is." I led the way into the dining room, where I placed the vase at the center of the table. "And you? Is Rick short for Richard?" Or maybe, wanton sex god?

"Enrique. My parents were Spanish. But call me Rick."

Our eyes met. An awkward pause ensued while we soaked each other in. A magnetic field had formed between us, coaxing me toward him. I refrained, but barely. Delicious warmth unfolded deep within me. I was surprised the drapes didn't melt down the walls from the heat between us, and I couldn't stop my mind from replaying the shower scene I'd imagined driving in. *Damn!* What was wrong with me? I sucked my bottom lip between my teeth and turned away so that he wouldn't see my face redden once again.

"It smells good in here. Were you cooking?" he asked, breaking the tension.

"Yes, actually. I just sat down to eat."

"Oh, I've interrupted your dinner. Please, continue."

"Have you had something? I could whip up a plate for you?" I had no idea what I would do if he said yes. I couldn't actually cook, and I wasn't sure my dad had left sandwich fixings.

"I've eaten, thank you. But, please..." He pointed toward the kitchen.

"Okay. But don't feel like you have to leave." I retrieved my plate from the microwave and took a seat at the dining room table across from him.

"Can I pour you a glass of wine?" I asked.

"Yes. What do you have there?"

"Shiraz—" I froze as I looked at the bottle in front of me. A circle of red still stained the bottom of my glass, but next to it was not the Shiraz I'd opened. Instead, the Pinot Gris faced me, sealed and dripping with condensation. My scalp prickled.

"What's wrong? You're as white as a ghost." Rick moved to my side.

"Th-This is not the wine I was drinking. Look." I showed him the top of the bottle. "It's sealed. I put this bottle away in the cellar."

Surely Rick would think I was crazy, but I was too majorly creeped out to maintain the I'm-perfectly-normal facade.

He gingerly took the bottle from my hands, as if the dark green glass might sprout legs at any moment. Tilting his face toward the ceiling, he squinted and his lips pressed into a flat line. "I was hoping this wouldn't start so soon."

"What wouldn't start?"

Rick leaned forward and whispered into my ear. "I don't want to alarm you, but I think this house is haunted."

I waited all of three seconds to break into laughter. "Oh, come on. Haunted?"

The corner of his mouth lifted. "You don't believe the house could be haunted?"

"No. Not really. I mean, the wine is weird, but there has to be a rational explanation."

"There is only one way to know the truth." His face was inches from mine now, and I caught him glancing down the V-neck of my T-shirt.

"Blonde paradox," I whispered under my breath.

"Excuse me?"

"Oh, I just asked what—what is the way to know the truth?"

He held up the bottle and focused his dark eyes on me as if it was ninety degrees and I was a tall glass of ice water. I wriggled in my chair from the intensity. Pressing one hand to his chest, he said, "We must drink this ghostly wine late into the night, and I must stay with you to protect you from any unholy visitors."

I took one look at his exaggerated theatrics and said, "I'll get a corkscrew." Hell, I wasn't doing anything anyway. I walked into the kitchen to grab one off the counter and gasped. My bottle of Shiraz was corked, next to the refrigerator. What the hell was going on?

"You know," Rick called from the dining room, "Pinot Gris is the better choice with salmon. Shiraz is too heavy of a red for fish."

I may be blonde, but I am not stupid. The pieces snapped together. Rick must have somehow changed the bottles. Maybe this was one big pick-up line: *Hey baby, your house is haunted. Can I spend the night?* Of course, that was it.

I walked back into the dining room. "You haven't been completely honest with me, have you?"

"You see through me," Rick admitted. He lowered his chin. "Your father didn't ask me to check on you. That was my own idea."

He didn't say anything about the wine, but I dropped the subject. Who cared how the bottle got there? I was enjoying his company too much to let my suspicions bother me. I opened the Pinot Gris, poured him a glass, and then myself one.

"So, tell me how you became a caretaker," I said.

"I have always been interested in the dead." I must have made a face because he quickly added, "History. I was a history major."

"Oh, interesting." I decided not to share that I loathed history in college.

"This cemetery has historical significance, you know. The oldest grave is from sixteen ninety-two, an early settler of Red Grove. How familiar are you with the town?"

"Not at all. I'm a nurse at St. John's in Carlton City. I wouldn't have considered moving to Red Grove if not for my dad. He inherited the house, and I needed a place to stay." I didn't offer any more info on my embarrassing situation and thankfully he didn't ask.

"It's a small town, but it's home." He smiled. "I'll give you a tour if you like. Of the cemetery, that is. I think you can find your own way around Red Grove Grocery and Pub."

"Uh, thanks." I giggled. "Grocery and Pub. You say it like it's one building."

"It is. The first floor of Orson Thompson's place. He sells fishing bait too."

"I'll keep that in mind." The wine was starting to do its dirty work, and I could feel inhibition packing its bags. "Can I ask you a personal question, Rick?"

"Of course."

"You said your family was from Spain. How did you end up here?"

The question must have made him uncomfortable because he looked away and started tracing the edge of the table with his finger. He cleared his throat. "I guess they came for the same reasons everyone comes here. To make a new start. They used to have a farm here a long time ago. They've passed on."

"I'm so sorry." I was such a downer. Nothing like bringing up someone's dead parents to sour the mood.

"It's been years." He shrugged. The man looked desperate for a change of subject. "This is good wine."

"Yes, it is," I replied. I poured each of us another glass, emptying the last drops into mine. We'd finished the entire bottle, and I had finished my meal. "Would you like to move to the family room? Maybe watch some TV? I can grab that bottle of Shiraz."

He gave the sort of nod that starts and ends with the eyes, not just assent but anticipation. The feeling was mutual. We sojourned to the plush sofa in the family room. I discovered the television didn't have cable and settled on a *Saturday Night Live* marathon while he poured more wine.

"Hot summer we've had. Glad it's almost over," I said. *Crap*. I was such a nerd. Who talks about the weather with a could-be underwear model at her side and a glass of wine in hand?

"Very…hot," he drawled. Oh God, his lips were full. Was that a dimple in his chin?

I caught myself leaning toward him and readjusted in my seat.

"Funny thing about the heat. I'm a nurse at St. John's, and you would be surprised how many heat-related injuries come in…" My mouth was still moving, but I had no idea what was coming out. Did I just say *cooling packs*? I tried to stop, but I was having an out-of-body experience or something.

Rick placed his fingers under my still wagging chin.

"Fluids," I blurted, finishing off a sentence about something that wasn't as important as his face, so very close to mine.

"Grateful, I know you've just met me, but you are…incredible. May I kiss you?"

I'd sworn off men. I'd promised myself I'd stay in control. So why was I having so much trouble following my own rules? Of course, I'd felt attracted to Rick before he walked through the door. The effects of the wine magnified that initial attraction. He smelled good, like the outdoors. Fresh-turned earth, pine, and something else I couldn't quite place—the ocean, I think. But more than that, Rick made me feel safe. If the sensation was because he knew my father or because his job as caretaker eased my fears about the graveyard, I wasn't sure. Maybe the desire to not be alone in a strange new house was enough. Whatever the reason, I looked into those gray eyes and a wave of heat moved from my heart due south.

"Yes."

He leaned in slowly, lips brushing mine, soft, warm, and gentle at first. The kiss was closed-mouthed and conservative. I blinked lazily, enjoying the sweet gesture. He pulled back a little, like he was kissing me goodnight, restraining himself.

I can't explain what came over me. A slow burn budded between my legs. My body ached, hungry, wanting to be fed. I wasn't satisfied. This was more than attraction. I stared at him with the shaking hands, racing heart, and fevered skin of an addict. I had tasted ambrosia, and I wanted more.

Eyes locked onto his, I tangled my fingers in the dark curls at the back of his head. Coaxing his face toward mine, I returned his gentle kiss but then demanded more. I ran my tongue along the place where his lips touched.

"Open for me," I murmured in a husky version of my voice.

He gasped. It was all the invitation I needed. I couldn't resist. I slid my tongue between his teeth in a deep, wanting kiss. I thrust into his mouth, a crude imitation of what I wanted him to do to me. What my body begged for.

The heat from our lips flowed down my chest, made my stomach tighten, and moved lower. I bit his lip. Oh, he tasted good. He made a low sound like a growl and smoothed his hand over my hip. Lust rippled through me, leaving me hot and wet between my legs, my body ready for him in an instant. Lord, I wanted him. An unexpected combination of sexual attraction and possessiveness I'd never experienced took over, and the desire absolutely owned me.

"You make me burn," he whispered into my mouth.

"The feeling is mutual."

His hand circled to the small of my back, pulled me hard against his chest. A string of syllables came out of his throat in a language I didn't know but in a tone I completely understood. Rick wanted me too. My insides liquefied. My will was not my own.

I clawed the back of his head and scissored my legs to get closer to him. Why, I don't know. No room remained between us as it was. He trailed kisses down my throat and pulled the neck of my T-shirt aside to continue his mouth's exploration. Meanwhile, his other hand skimmed up my ribs, cupping and lifting my breast to bring his lips achingly close to the black lace of my bra. Electricity coursed through my body.

"Oh!"

Frantically, I worked one hand into the neck of his shirt, unbuttoning with the other. Light-headed, like when I was a kid and would run downhill so fast I thought I'd trip, I slid my fingers across his chest. That's when I felt a ridge of flesh on his left pec.

I pulled back. A crude, hooked scar marred the skin over his heart. It almost looked like he'd been branded.

Searing pain, a red-hot railroad spike, sliced through my skull. I buried my face in his opposite shoulder, hoping the headache would go away. "What happened here?" I managed, my touch lingering.

"A mark of my profession. The caretaker's scythe."

"I didn't know caretakers had a mark. Is that like how Marines get the same tattoo?"

"Not all of them." His expression changed, closing off, and he pulled his shirt back over his chest. He cleared his throat and began buttoning.

All at once, awareness that I was making out with a complete stranger hit me upside the head. I backed off, straightening my shirt in the process. This wasn't even a date, and I was practically jumping this guy. Disappointed in myself, I frowned. Had I no self-control?

"What's wrong?"

"Nothing…" My mouth hung open while I found the words. "I'm not usually like this. I got a little ahead of myself." Understatement of the year. After Gary, I should've remained three feet away from anyone who peed standing up.

"I'm not complaining, *mi cielo*." He gently wrapped his hands around my wrists and pulled me back to him. "Maybe we did get ahead of ourselves, but only because there's something here worth moving toward." He flashed brilliantly white teeth.

"What did you just call me?"

"*Mi cielo*? Literally, the phrase means 'my sky.' It's a term of endearment." He wrapped an arm around my shoulders, pulling me into his side. We snuggled like that, in front of the TV, content to be in each other's company.

Sometime after midnight, I woke as Rick gently positioned me on the couch. I'd fallen asleep in his arms. Before he left, he moved the ugly bouquet from the dining room to the coffee table near my head. The door clicked shut behind him, and I drifted back to sleep.

CHAPTER 3
Yeah, About My New House

The stench of dirty feet brought me to my senses. Where was I? I sat up and cracked my back. Memories of the night lingered like a bad case of food poisoning. What the hell happened last night? I'd sworn to stay off men until I had time to heal. After the Gary incident, I'd had to go to therapy, months of soul-wrenching therapy where I promised myself I wouldn't hand my future over to the next guy who came along. I'd given Gary control of all of my financial resources because I thought I loved him. Who does that? I'll tell you who. Pushovers. Women who need boundaries. I needed boundaries. I needed control. I needed to not straddle every cemetery caretaker who walked through my door.

I'd crossed a line into mildly slutty last night. I slapped my forehead, which was beginning to throb in protest of yesterday's alcohol ingestion. With a deep breath, I decided there was no need to berate myself. So, I'd slipped. I chalked it up to the wine and the stress of moving into the new house. Nothing too serious had happened. Last night was a test, one I'd barely passed. Obviously, Rick was my catnip. Now that I understood his effect on me, I would be more careful around him.

I cracked my back again. The family room couch did not make a good bed. Light streamed between the wood blinds. *Crap.* I glanced at my watch and then leaped to my feet. I'd have to hustle if I was going to make my shift at the hospital and, unfortunately, I hadn't unpacked my moving box. I'd have to dig out my scrubs and bathroom sundries.

Hauling my awkward cargo up to the bedroom, I retrieved all of my stuff and took the world's fastest shower. The mirror was covered in a thick layer of steam, and I struggled to get ready with a throbbing headache on top of impaired vision.

"Ow!" I yanked the mascara wand out of my eye. I was going to look like a raccoon if I wasn't careful. A raccoon with a migraine.

I dug in my purse for some ibuprofen and gulped them down with water from the sink. That's when my hangover became the least of my worries. I had the distinct impression that someone was watching me.

"Hello?" I called, sticking my head out the bathroom door.

There was no one there.

Weird. This creaky old house was messing with my head. I sighed and dressed in my scrub top, an ice-blue one with tiny penguins. As the cloth slipped over my head, I thought I saw a man's face in the foggy mirror, for a fraction of a second. Once my vision was unobstructed, nothing.

I made a second mental note to cut back on the liquor. On my way out the door, I grabbed the ugly bouquet with its dirty-foot odor and tossed it into the garbage can. The smell was definitely not helping my hangover.

As I backed out of the garage, I retrieved a frosted strawberry Pop-Tart from my glove compartment and a bottle of Frappuccino from the case behind my seat. "Breakfast of champions," I mumbled to the windshield, hoping I'd make it to work on time.

* * * * *

One of the perks of being a nurse is the twelve-hour shifts. Sure, they're long, but you only have to work three days a week. Plus, because of Michelle, I got in good with the staff during clinicals and was hired on day shift, seven a.m. to seven p.m. Cool gig for someone like me with no spouse or kids. Off early enough to enjoy a night out, plus four days of freedom a week to spend as you choose, or in my case, as I can afford. My new digs added a thirty-minute commute in each direction, twenty if you drive like I do. By the time I got home, I was mentally and physically exhausted, ready and willing to do my best impression of a slug on the couch for the rest of the night. Unfortunately, my workday wasn't over.

As part of my financial rescue strategy, I'd taken on a second job as a phone nurse. The idea was that I would do it on my days off, but that hadn't worked out this week. My coworker had some kind of personal conflict, so I was left covering the rest of her shift, eight to midnight. It wasn't exactly how I wanted to spend my night. Visions of the caretaker danced through my head, but I brushed them away with a sweep of my hand. I had work to do.

I tossed some cheese and crackers into my mouth, booted my laptop, and donned the headset that made me look like Uhura from *Star Trek*. Like a good little call center rep, I logged in at exactly eight o'clock and the calls started rolling in.

"No, Mrs. Sakston, brown urine is never normal, even if you did have asparagus for dinner. Please see your doctor."

And more calls.

"Even though the PMS is really bad, it isn't a reason to take your wife to the emergency room, Mr. Johnston. Please call her doctor in the morning for an office visit. No, I don't think she'll kill you, but maybe you should stay out of her way."

And more calls.

"How far apart are the contractions? Five minutes? Yes, you should go to the hospital now."

Until finally, around eleven thirty p.m., the calls seemed to stop and I watched the clock inch toward midnight. I was more than ready to be done with the day. The scrubs I'd thrown on that morning clung to me like a straitjacket. I longed to spend the night in a real bed after my backbreaking stint on the couch the night before.

Static in my ear at eleven fifty-nine was an unwelcome warning that a call was coming in—the sound of the switchboard routing to me. It was all that I could do not to log out and make the patient call back. But I'm not the type of person to leave my work for someone else, so I waited for the familiar beep that would signify the call's connection.

"Hello, you've reached the St. John's medi-line. How can I help you today?"

"Are you the sorter?" a grandmotherly voice asked.

"Excuse me? Ma'am? Can I help you?"

"Do you seek the book and blade?"

She sounded old. Maybe she was confused. "This is the hospital phone service. Are you in trouble? Do you need help? What's your name?"

"My name is Prudence, dear."

"Prudence, are you ill?"

"Oh no, I'm not ill."

"Can I help you with something?"

"Are you the sorter?"

"I don't know what that is, ma'am."

Click. The line disconnected. My hand reflexively shot forward and hit the button on my computer to log out.

"Freaking weird," I said. I wondered what kind of situation the lady was in. Maybe she was an Alzheimer's patient or something. She certainly wasn't making any sense.

I was in the process of removing my headset and making plans for a long, hot bath when the sound of a door swinging open on squeaky hinges made me turn toward the stairs. The sound was coming from up, way up. I rose on shaky legs and took three big steps toward the foyer.

I'm not sure what I noticed first, the woman herself or the light that surrounded her. She had the curly gray hair of a grandmother, round cheeks, and a black button front sweater over a high lace collar. Her face was a scowl and below her waist…nothing. Tendrils of mist—that was it. The glowing torso of an old lady leered at me from the top of my steps. I stopped breathing. I blinked once, then twice. She locked eyes with me.

"Are you the sorter?" she asked in a voice lined with static, as if the air between us was causing a bad connection.

I stared, eyes wide and voice mute with shock.

"Do you seek the book and blade?"

Her tendrils wormed lower, onto the next stair. I still couldn't form words, so I shook my head.

"Are you the sorter?" she asked again.

Sorter? "N-no," I stuttered.

The parchment-colored skin of her face began to glow above her high lace collar, then tightened like shrink-wrap to her skull. Her eyes became burning embers in their bony pits, and her teeth elongated.

"*Get out of my house!*" she bellowed.

What the fuck? A cold wind powered toward me, a whistling cyclone of fury that made the floor quake and the shutters bang against the walls from their place outside the windows. The pots and pans, hinged to the pot rack in the kitchen, *crash-boom-banged* in the mounting interior tornado. My laptop crashed to the hardwood floor. Papers fluttered by, my notes and work forms circling like misguided snowflakes. In the dining room, the chairs took turns pulling themselves out and then pushing themselves back in at the table.

Anyone in her right mind would have run, but I couldn't move. My muscles and vocal cords froze from fear, and my feet weighed two tons each. I couldn't even breathe.

The torso descended the stairs, weightless but menacing, piercing me with that monstrous gaze. "*Get out!*" she bellowed again.

This had to be a nightmare. I'd fallen asleep at the computer and was having a nightmare. Why weren't my muscles moving?

Closer, she drifted. I had to make a run for it. I had to move. My jaw sagged. I was still holding my breath.

A man stepped between the ghost and me. Where did *he* come from? He lifted two fingers over his shoulder, and the wind stopped, the pans clinked to a rest, the shutters halted their wicked cacophony.

"Oh thank God," I said and let the air rush out of my burning lungs.

He turned toward the ghost, held out his hand, and said, "Prudence, come on. Knock it off. You're scaring her."

"*She doesn't belong here!*" the old lady yelled.

The man turned a gentle smile and warm green eyes toward me. His sandy brown hair was unkempt, and his chin was covered in stubble that somehow seemed to add to his character. He put his hands on the hips of his jeans, flipping the sides of his sport jacket back, arms akimbo like he didn't know what to make of me.

"She's not hurting anything, Prudence. Please. Go back to the attic." He waved his arm.

The spectral crone gave an exasperated sigh and dissolved into mist.

"Th-thank you," I stuttered.

"You're welcome."

I was about to ask who he was and where he had come from when I noticed smoke. After everything else, was the house on fire? I searched for the source.

Gray tendrils curled up from his feet.

"You're on fire!" I said.

It advanced up his limbs, to his knees, to his hips, until the man was nothing but a mist with two green orbs where his eyes had been.

It was the loudest scream of my life. "*Aaaaaahhhhhhhh!*"

I don't remember opening the door, and I didn't stop for my shoes. I ran into the cool night air, arms flailing, with an unyielding, high-pitched screech that was sure to wake any soul within a five-mile radius. Across the bridge and up the walkway, I raced to the stone cottage of the only other living person I knew in Red Grove—Rick Ordenes. I don't remember knocking, only that the door opened and there was Rick.

"It was awful," I whimpered as I grabbed his shoulders. My hands slapped bare flesh. My wild eyes roved down his body: bare shoulders, bare chest, bare stomach, and *OH*! He was…*naked*.

But that wasn't the most disturbing thing. His once-gray eyes had turned black as onyx, and he didn't look happy to see me. Then I caught sight of what was behind him.

The entire inside of the stone cottage glowed like a shrine. Candles flickered. Crosses reflected the light. Skulls—*human* skulls circled the room. A painting of a skeleton woman dressed like the Virgin Mary loomed against the far wall. And that was all I saw because, at that point, my overwhelmed brain decided to turn off.

I'd never been prone to fainting, but the world tilted on its axis, threatening to toss me unfettered into the black universe. I collapsed backward, expecting to crack my head against the stone walkway.

The last thing I remember is Rick catching me in his arms as the darkness closed in around me.

CHAPTER 4
Body and Soul

B etween terror and oblivion, I lost track of time. I came to somewhere soft and warm with the sun turning the inside of my eyelids red and the stench of dirty feet curling my nose. I tentatively opened one eye and noticed a new ugly bouquet on what was undeniably the nightstand in my new house. A good sign. I opened the other eye and surveyed my surroundings.

The quilt under my chin was the one from my master bedroom. I *was* back in my house, in my own room. Had Rick carried me home and put me to bed?

I peeked under the covers. I was still wearing my scrubs. The good news? Rick had not taken advantage of me in my fragile state. The bad news? Rick had returned me to a haunted house and, by the looks of it, was some kind of hoodoo witch doctor.

If I didn't get my head around what happened last night, I was at serious risk of a mental breakdown. I sat bolt upright. Maybe this was it? Were hallucinations a symptom of a nervous breakdown? I was a nurse. Why couldn't I remember the symptoms of a nervous breakdown? I needed to call Michelle.

My phone vibrated against my cheek, not because of an incoming call but because of my shaking hands. I listened to the ringing on the other end of the line. *Pick up, pick up, pick up.* Brutal disappointment plowed into me when Michelle's voicemail answered. I left a hasty, probably incomprehensible message and hung up.

Worse, I didn't even have work to distract me. I had the whole day off. A full twenty-four hours in a house where I'd seen (or hallucinated) two ghosts.

A full-blown panic attack rocked my body. My heart started to pound. I rubbed my aching chest as my breath came in ineffective pants. I was hyperventilating. Tangled thoughts jumbled through my mind, truth and dream, reality and fantasy. I cupped my hands over my mouth and nose and tried to slow my breathing. Eventually, the panic seemed to find its way out of me in a parade of fat tears, and I bawled into my hands.

"Shhh… Please don't cry," a man's voice said low and soft, like to calm a skittish animal.

I leaped to my feet, eyes darting around the room. "Who's there?"

No answer.

I moved from t
No one by the w
highboy. I turne
cracked-open clos
anything that mov
top of my foot to ki
slammed against th
back. *Ow*. I rubb
backward as I peere

Empty, aside fron

Only one place left to look. The door to the room was left open, potentially hiding an assailant between it and the wall. I approached cautiously, knowing I could be in grave danger, slowly, silently reaching… I yanked the knob and stuck my head behind the door.

Nothing.

That was it. I'd imagined a comforting male voice in my bedroom. I was losing my mind.

"Coffee," I said to myself. "I need coffee now."

I walked to the end of the hall to the stair landing, but instead of continuing down the stairs to the kitchen, an uncontrollable impulse tipped my face in the opposite direction. I hadn't noticed before, but the stairs continued to what I presumed was the attic. That's where *she* had come from—the legless freak of nature who'd chased me out of my house. I remembered the shrill creak of the door before she'd appeared at the top of my stairs. A sudden chill goose-pimpled my flesh, and tingles radiated through my scalp.

Compulsively, I climbe
had to face this fear. N
weight step by ste
the cast-iron b
turned. Lo
but it
ki

the staircase. I had to know. I
y legs shook and moved like dead
toward the painted white door with
andle. With shaking hand, I gripped and
ked. I tugged a little harder, jostling the knob,
ouldn't budge. The keyhole was the old-fashioned
d, crafted to house one of those long, roundish keys. I'd
have to ask my dad if other keys came with the house. I
needed to know what was in there.

One thing was for certain: no ghostly old ladies were
attacking me. This was just an ordinary door to an
ordinary attic. I still wasn't sure what had happened last
night. Exhaustion? Stress? Radon poisoning? (I'd have to
ask my dad about that one.) But it wasn't ghosts. It
couldn't be, or how could I come to terms with staying
here? No, this was mental. Mind over matter.

I bounded down the stairs, feeling silly I'd ever
entertained the idea that there were actually ghosts in the
house. Yet, as I approached the foyer, a noise from the
kitchen snapped me back into jumpy mode. I crouched
down, slinking around the banister, and used the island
counter as cover. Who the hell was in my house?

When I realized the sound was the coffeemaker, I
stood, confused, and eyeballed my kitchen. The machine
percolated away, sending wafts of hazelnut in my
direction. My laptop glowed from the counter, plugged in
and powered on. The screen was cracked. *Ouch*. At least it
looked usable. All of my work forms were carefully stacked
on the counter. What had happened last night? An icy

chill ran the length of my body. I *wasn't* mental. My screen was cracked for a reason. Either my house was haunted, or someone was fucking with me.

But why the coffee? I needed to decide between three possibilities. One, I had lost my mind and actually made the coffee and cleaned up myself. Two, the same ghosts who scared the bejeezus out of me made coffee and cleaned up the mess. Or three, there was another living person in my house.

I went with three. "Rick?" I called. Maybe he'd stayed the night. That would explain the voice, as well. "Hello? Is someone here?"

Silence.

Tears of frustration burst the dam of my lower lids, and I grabbed the sides of my hair. "Who is in my house?"

"I am. But I don't want to scare you," the man said, definitely not Rick. This time I recognized his voice as the man from last night. My stomach clenched.

I was afraid, but I was more afraid of losing my mind. "Please," I said in barely a whisper, "I need to see you."

An orb of light in the middle of the living room floated toward me, the kind of thing you see every day, dust reflecting the morning glow that seeps through the slats in the blinds. This one, however, grew as it approached in a way that made the room feel like a dark tunnel, and the orb, the light at the end. The brightness made me blink, and by the time I opened my eyes again, the transparent form of the smoking man from the night before leaned against my counter.

Several questions raced through my mind at once. Things like, why was he in my house? Was his body somewhere nearby? Did he mean me any harm? But the only thing that came out of my shocked mouth was, "I can see through you."

"Ah, I'm stronger at night. It's taking an enormous degree of effort for me to hold this form right now. I should be sleeping, but I wanted to make sure you were all right. What Prudence did last night was unforgivable."

My pulse pounded in my temples. Instinct told me to run. But where would I go? I swallowed hard and rolled with the conversation. "You're a g-ghost?"

He lowered his eyes. "Yes. But don't be afraid. I'm not going to hurt you."

Well, that was a relief—said no one after seeing a ghost, ever! I took a few steps back until my ass hit one of the kitchen stools. I sat, less by will and more because my knees gave out. "How many of you are there? "

"Just the two of us."

"You and the old woman from last night. Prudence."

"Yes. I'm sorry we scared you."

Was this real? Was a ghost really apologizing to me? He seemed friendly. I tried to think of friendly ghosts, like Casper, to keep from peeing my pants—which, incidentally, were yesterday's scrubs. I seriously needed a shower.

"And you switched the wine and made me coffee?"

"You said you needed the coffee, and that wine choice was a travesty. I had to do something."

I wrinkled my brow. "Are you some kind of phantom food critic?"

"No. To be honest, I don't know what I was before I died. There are lots of things I don't remember. But Pinot Gris is definitely the better choice with salmon." The corner of his mouth curled up in an uneven smile I found oddly endearing.

Swallowing hard, I tried to calm my racing heart and focus. "What do you want? Why are you in my house?"

"Technically, you moved into our house. Prudence and I are waiting for someone. We thought you might be her."

"Waiting for someone to do what?" I asked. "Wait, Prudence asked if I was the sorter last night. What does that mean?"

"If you were the sorter, you would know."

I squirmed, uncomfortable with his non-answer. No further explanation was offered. "Are you going to hurt me?"

"No. And neither will Prudence. But for your own safety, I'm here to deliver a warning: stay away from the attic…and the caretaker."

I took a step back. "The caretaker, as in Rick?" I narrowed my eyes. The request seemed strange. To clarify, everything about this moment seemed strange, but this was especially odd. Rick had suspected the house was haunted, and now the haunter was warning me about Rick. What was the relationship? My curiosity temporarily trumped the pressing horror of the moment.

"The caretaker is dangerous for you, Grateful, as is the attic. I'm not sure why you were allowed to come here, but if you are going to stay, these are the rules."

Hmm. I tapped my fingers on my upper arm. *Allowed* to come here? Who was this guy to tell me what to do? I hadn't lived through abandonment by my last boyfriend, losing everything I owned, and swallowing my pride to move into my father's house to let a guy without a body boss me around. Still, I had no idea the kind of damage he and Prudence could do. I changed the subject.

"If you are going to be haunting me and choosing my drinks, the least you can do is tell me your name."

He frowned and looked at the floor. "I can't."

"You can't."

"I don't remember."

"You mean, you don't remember who you are—were—at all?"

"No." His green eyes hovered like two drops of rain under his lashes. "One day, I was just here. Before that…"

"But Prudence has a name."

"Yes, well, she lived here, so I think she's more attached somehow to this reality."

The story my father told me about the house came back to me all at once. "Holy crow! That's right. She's Prudence Meriwether. She's why I'm here. She left this house to my dad, Robert Knight, when she died. He hasn't been able to sell it since her death."

He blinked, not his eyes but his entire body. Gone and then back again, like what I'd said had blown through him. "You are Robert Knight's daughter?"

"Yes. Grateful, Grateful Knight. You know my dad?"

He floated closer, his eyes brightening. His presence overwhelmed me, made my skin prickle. He stared at me like he was seeing inside, sifting through my cells with his otherworldly gaze. I blinked up at him, speechless.

After a long silence, his shoulders hunched forward. "I'm tired, Grateful. Can we continue this another time?"

"Sure," I said, wondering how ghosts rested when they were tired.

"I'll come to you again tonight, midnight."

"O-Okay," I said. A thought cut through my whirling mind. "What do I call you if you don't have a name?"

"Why don't you come up with something? Just for practicality, until I remember my own." He faded to the viscosity of a watermark, nothing more than an outline.

I nodded.

"One more thing."

"Yes?"

"Can you get rid of the bouquet next to your bed? That thing stinks. It's repulsive."

"No problem. I'm not a big fan. So, I guess I'll see you tonight."

For a moment, his green eyes glowed brighter. "It's a date." He winked, and then he dissolved into thin air. Nothing remained but a wisp of mist that smelled faintly of cinnamon.

Blowing out a nervous breath, I placed both hands firmly on the counter. Did I just make a date with a ghost?

CHAPTER 5
Dates

I should move. I navigated to a real estate website and searched on Carlton City properties. A few apartments had potential. I couldn't remotely afford any of them. With the ghost gone, I took a deep breath and forced myself to think clearly. Although terrifying, were ghosts a reason to give up free rent? He'd said I was safe here, as long as I stayed away from the attic and Rick. I'd already jiggled the handle on the third floor and been alone with Rick. Nothing terrible happened. Could it be that I was worried needlessly?

"This day brought to you by the letter 'C' for caffeine," I said, filling my cup with ghost-made coffee. I sipped, then stared at the dark brown heaven in my cup. To my surprise, it was perfect. My ghost had done what no man in my life had ever accomplished. This wasn't the weak swill of a man who was trying to please me because he assumed that I, a simple female, enjoyed dark water. It wasn't the bitter sludge of a man who'd never made himself coffee before and added extra scoops because he wanted to keep me up all night. This was the brew of someone who knew how to make coffee: smooth, rich, and satisfying.

Mmmmmmm. I closed my eyes and swallowed. There was nothing better than a good cup of Joe in the morning. Maybe, if I asked nicely, my ghost would make it again tomorrow.

My ghost. Why was I calling him *my* ghost? Like he belonged to me just because he was in my house. I decided a long hot shower was in order to analyze that slip of the tongue.

Once I was under the spray, my mood lifted. For some reason, my meeting with the ghost had given me peace of mind. Prudence was terrifying and the thought of ghosts rattling around my attic, unsettling, but deep within me, I felt safe. Was this how psychics felt after their first encounter with the supernatural? Maybe I had a sixth sense about these souls. I was sure we could coexist and, oddly, their presence made me less apprehensive about the cemetery. Who knew a brush with the supernatural could actually calm my nerves?

Warm water flowed over my body, rinsing away the tension and worry of the morning. I caught myself thinking again about the ghost: those sad green eyes, sandy brown hair, the stubble that gave him an Indiana Jones sort of sexiness. I guess he didn't actually have a body, but his image was thin and muscular. As I stepped from the shower, I thought if my house had to be haunted, I was glad my ghost looked like he belonged on the cover of *GQ*.

The jeans I pulled on were the kind you wear when you want to be comfortable, broken in with little holes in the knees and the seat. I planned to spend the day unpacking and removing the layer of dust that coated everything in my new home. I thought of cleaning as a necessary evil and vowed to treat myself to a bowl of ice cream if I could finish sprucing the main floor. As I started working my hair into a ponytail, the doorbell rang. I jogged down the stairs, stretching the elastic into place before checking the side window.

It was Rick—hoodoo Rick—in a black cotton button-down shirt, blue jeans, and black boots. Sexy. And dangerous. Skulls and candles aside, my ghost had clearly stated I should stay away from him. Clearly. Hell, after Rick's first night here, I had serious misgivings about being close to him again, anyway. I couldn't trust myself. And did I mention the human skulls? So then why was I turning the deadbolt? I wished I owned a Taser…and had already done my makeup. I opened the door.

"Good morning. I came by to check on you. How are you feeling today?" Rick asked.

I stepped out onto the porch, closing the door behind me. "Better."

"What exactly happened last night? You came to my door screaming and then passed out. I carried you home."

"Bad dream," I said. I wasn't sure how much I should share with Rick after what I saw the night before. He was into some weird stuff. I'm not the judgmental type, but the human skulls were a definite red flag. I mean, where did he get them? They weren't exactly handing them out at Red Grove Grocery and Pub.

"Are you sure it wasn't something more? Has anything unusual happened since you've been here?" He tilted his head toward the house.

I narrowed my eyes. What was going on here? My intuition waved a red flag and pulled out a magnifying glass courtesy of the Nancy Drew mysteries. Fact one: my ghost wanted me to stay away from Rick. Fact two: Rick sounded like he was digging for information about my ghost and had brought up the possibility of a haunting his first time here. Fact three: Rick had produced a bouquet of herbs capable of repelling ghosts. Which led me to theory one: as a cemetery caretaker, Rick was dangerous to ghosts. Maybe he could banish them with a sprinkle of holy water or something.

"Not at all. Nothing unusual has happened," I lied. He looked at me skeptically, so I threw him a curveball. "Well, maybe seeing the weird stuff in your house last night."

"What weird stuff?"

"You know, the candles, the skulls…"

"Had you been drinking?"

"No!"

He stood up and offered me his hand, his long, graceful fingers beckoning me. "Come, come with me." His gray eyes twinkled beneath thick lashes, the bright sky glowing behind his head like a halo. Inexplicably, an avalanche of attraction rumbled down my spinal cord. I allowed him to lead me down the porch steps, stomach fluttering, and didn't immediately withdraw my hand when we reached the bottom of the steps. My fingers were as at home in his as if we'd been holding hands for decades instead of days. The suspicion I'd felt only moments before melted away, replaced with comfort, familiarity. My ghost's warning became something distant, a fading memory. What was this effect he had on me? We walked hand in hand all the way to his little stone cottage across the bridge.

The delicate tinkling of wind chimes welcomed us. Dozens of them dangled from the ceiling of the little cedar porch. Their sound reached me about the same time as the smell of wild herbs growing around his home. Strange, I hadn't noticed either last night. I must have been hysterical.

Rick opened the door to his place, and I followed him inside. The cottage was sparsely decorated. But what did I expect? The job of cemetery caretaker probably wasn't lucrative. A crocheted blanket on the couch looked like the kind grandmas everywhere made for their grandkids, and the dusty, cathode ray tube television belonged in a museum. A wood stump held up a lamp in the shape of a lantern with a fake candle inside supporting a decorative bulb. On the wall across from the door was a crucifix—one small gold crucifix. No skulls, no candles, no devilish pictures. Had I created it all in my mind?

My head hurt again. I rubbed circles over my temples. In a heartbeat, Rick's hands were on my shoulders.

"Can I get you some water?" he whispered into my ear.

"Yes, please. No. Coffee. Do you have coffee?"

"Just made a pot." He walked toward the tiny kitchen that was separated from the main room by a counter. It seemed only big enough for one, so I stayed where I was.

"I'm sorry, Rick. I don't know what happened last night."

"You were frightened. Maybe you were still half asleep."

"I was completely terrified."

"That explains it. You passed out at my door. Your nightmare must've continued when you lost consciousness."

That made sense, but something inside of me wouldn't let it go. The ghost was real, and this was too. I walked toward the only door to the rear of the house and pushed it open, sure there would be skulls and candles piled beyond the threshold. What I found was a king-sized bed, black silk sheets, and gauzy white window coverings that filtered the light into a soft glow. Was there anything about this guy that didn't scream sexy?

As if he could hear my thoughts, a mug of coffee appeared in front of me. Boy, was he smooth; I never even heard him leave the kitchen. He was close, so close his chest brushed my back. Wrapped around me holding the coffee, his inner arm created a warm tingle where it touched my shoulder.

He inhaled deeply and whispered into my ear, "Is there something you want to see in my bedroom?"

The caress of his breath on my neck made me shiver. I closed my eyes, and everything went quiet but the rhythm of my breath and the *lub-dub* of my heart. Everything in me wanted to turn, to move those last two inches and press my lips against this stranger's. With a shake of my head, I swallowed hard and took a step away.

"No." *Yes, you liar*! I turned my back to the bed and faced him.

The corners of his mouth sagged, and his head jerked backward.

I lifted the mug from his hand, brushing his fingers with mine in the process. My mouth went dry. "I mean, I hardly know you," I blurted.

"It didn't bother you the night before last, *mi cielo*."

I couldn't argue with the facts. I'd practically jumped him on my couch less than forty-eight hours ago, and now I was playing coy. "I don't usually…" I sighed. "I just think we shouldn't rush into anything. It wouldn't be right."

"So, get to know me. Have lunch with me today. I'll give you that tour of the cemetery I promised you, and then we can have a picnic lunch on Monk's Hill."

"Where's Monk's Hill?"

"Come with me this afternoon and I'll show you."

Our eyes locked. His were gray, not black. What had happened last night? What had I seen? "Deal," I said, my insides quivering at the thought.

"Meet back here at noon?"

"Looking forward to it," I said.

The corner of his mouth lifted into a lopsided grin, and something inside of me melted. I wanted to run my fingers over the cotton of his shirt and feel the contrast between the soft material and the hard muscles underneath. "It's a date."

I nodded, hyperaware that it was the second time I'd heard those words today.

"You haven't tried your coffee," he said, stepping closer.

I took a deep swig. The coffee itself was slightly bitter, but he'd added my favorite accouterments. "How did you know?" I asked.

"Know what?"

"This is exactly how I take my coffee—cream and sugar with a dash of cinnamon."

"Lucky, I guess. That's how I take mine too."

He was so close to me now, the only thing that kept us from touching was the coffee mug. It radiated a circle of heat that warmed my chest but had nothing to do with the burn working its way down my body under his intense stare. I swallowed another gulp and forced myself to blink to break the connection.

"Can I borrow this mug?" I asked. "I should probably get home. I haven't even unpacked yet."

"Of course. I'll get it back from you later."

"Great. I'll see you then." I backed toward the door.

"Oh, and Grateful," he said with a smile that made my heart skip a beat. "Wear your walking shoes."

Now, I am not the type of girl who usually dates two men at once, but since the ghost was dead, I didn't think he counted as a real date. I mean, he didn't have a body. I was sure this situation wasn't covered in *Cosmo*'s dating guide. So, I felt no guilt whatsoever as I walked out of Rick's door.

I decided I'd keep an open mind about both dates— one with the ghost and one with the graveyard.

CHAPTER 6
I Take The Tour

I finished unpacking my moving box and rummaged through my closet for something to wear. I decided to go with jeans, but I changed out of my comfy ones and into some that fell lower on the hip and were more formfitting. Then I tossed on a black lace camisole. It showcased just enough cleavage to prove I put some effort into my appearance but with enough support and coverage to be appropriate for a first date.

As I finished my makeup, the phone rang, Michelle calling me back.

"I called as soon as I got your message. What's going on? You sounded frantic."

"You wouldn't believe me if I told you."

"Grateful, I'm between classes. Spill the beans!"

"My house is haunted."

Silence. I could hear Michelle breathing but nothing more. Then she broke into laughter. "Very funny. But really, if you want to joke with me, do it when I don't have school. Okay?"

"I'm serious. But, it's all right. Turns out he's a friendly ghost."

"Yeah, okay, hon. Joke's over. Gotta go." The call ended, and Michelle was gone.

Well, what did I expect? It wasn't exactly a believable story. I tossed the phone down on the dresser in frustration. The gadget left a trail as it slid across the dusty wood. Jeez, I desperately needed to clean in here.

With my finger, I wrote myself a note in the filth. *Clean me.* Good enough. I'd get to it later. Probably. Cleaning wasn't one of my strengths. Along with cooking, it hung out in the domestic skills section in the back of my brain, a heavily cobwebbed compartment I rarely used. As I scooped the phone back up, I checked the time. Almost noon, I skipped down the stairs and snatched the borrowed mug off the counter before dashing out the door and locking it behind me.

I met Rick at his cottage, holding out the mug like the ceramic could shield me from his sexiness. He gave me the killer half-smile as he accepted it, then slipped his arm through a picnic basket waiting on the small table near the kitchen and opened the door for me.

"You made lunch?" I asked.

"Of course."

"Can you cook?"

"When you live alone as long as I have, you need skills." He smiled and held out his hand. I didn't hesitate this time. I slid my fingers into his and savored the resulting ache his touch elicited.

Rick led me across the street, the basket swinging from his elbow.

"You look like Red Riding Hood with that basket," I quipped.

He paused, turning toward me. His intense stare made my heartbeat quicken. In a deep whisper, he said, "When you look at me like that, I feel like the big, bad wolf."

Damn! I swallowed hard.

He continued to an iron gate that looked exactly like the one in my backyard. This was an entrance to the same cemetery. From the street, you couldn't see the headstones because of tall hedges and a series of maple trees framing the wide gravel path within.

It dawned on me that this was where I'd first laid eyes on him, driving into town. A heap of fresh earth told me why he'd been digging—a new signpost to the left of the gate read *Monk's Hill Cemetery: trespassers will be prosecuted.*

"Do you get a lot of trespassers?"

"You would be surprised."

"What about the people who come to visit loved ones? How do they get in?"

"There are none. The youngest grave is more than one hundred years old. No surviving relatives."

"So you maintain this place for no one?"

"It has historical significance, but to be honest, you're correct. It's been years since anyone else was here."

Weird. As we crossed the threshold of the gate, I felt both privileged and a little freaked out by the remoteness of it.

"Did you know there's a gate behind my house?" I asked.

"Yes. The only other one besides this one."

"Why?"

Releasing my hand, he retrieved a heavy key from his pocket and locked the gate behind us. "I wouldn't want you to get away, *mi cielo*," he said playfully, ignoring my question.

Mi cielo. There it was again. My sky. A warm feeling blossomed behind my breastbone at the pet name. Swoon-worthy. The smell of the outdoors rolled off him again, this time with a hint of fresh rain. My mind went blank.

"Are you wearing cologne?" I asked.

He lifted the corner of his mouth. "You like how I smell? This is a good start."

Captivated by his smile and the way his lips moved when he spoke, my head swam, maybe because all of my blood had rushed south. I stepped off the trail and almost walked into a headstone. When I realized what I'd done, I pulled up short of the faded stone marker.

"Watch your step," he said, steadying me with a hand that seemed to fill the space between my elbow and shoulder. "You're treading on Martha Whitacker."

"Oh!" I scurried back onto the path.

He laughed. "Just teasing. She's a long way from caring. This is one of the oldest graves in the cemetery. She was an early financier of Reverend Monk's."

"Reverend Monk?"

"The man Monk's Hill Cemetery is named for." He pointed up a steep hill toward a quaint chapel. "I want to take you there, to Monk's church. I'll show you where he and his wife are buried."

"All the way up there?" I rubbed my toe in the loose gravel. "I see why you warned me to wear my walking shoes."

He laughed. "I wouldn't take you for a diva. Would you rather I carried you?"

I gave him an exaggerated gasp of outrage. "Not on your life." I jogged ahead a few steps, the loose stones kicking up behind me.

Catching up, he rejoined our fingers. With my hand in his, our shoulders bumped as we walked. Whether from the sunlight, the climb, or the heat coming off him, I broke a faint sweat.

Rick knew all about the people buried around Monk's Hill. Most of them were associated in one way or another with Reverend Monk's ministry. I tried to pay attention, but it was difficult. Who could hear anything over my pounding heart? I engaged my active listening skills. I nodded at regular intervals as I watched his jaw work. Strong, sharp jaw. The mound of his shoulder muscle rolled and brushed mine when he pointed something out. Large, hard shoulder. His thumb caressed mine within the snuggle of our coupled hands. Could I wrap my fingers around his bicep? Was his stomach as hard as the muscles in his forearm?

"—and this is Monk's Hill Church," he said.

What? We'd made it to the top already? I crumpled my brow and released his hand, turning back toward the long, steep pebble trail we'd traversed. I wasn't even winded. Had I floated up here on pheromones? I smiled, back straight, fists finding my hips. I guess I was in better shape than I thought.

"What do you think of the view?" he asked from behind me.

I pivoted, taking in the panoramic view from the highest point in the cemetery. "Oh! The fence is a star." Impossible to see from ground level, the wrought iron boundary of the cemetery was a five-pointed star surrounded by a circle of trees—a pentagram. The headstones filled each of the wide pointed sections. Monk's Hill, where I stood, was at the center of the star. Double gates blunted two of the points, the one we'd entered to the south and the one that ended at my house, to the west. The part of the cemetery I'd passed driving into town was the southeastern point.

"Unbelievable," I said. "And odd. Why did they go through the trouble of making it a star? Seems overachieving for a graveyard that's hundreds of years old."

"Would you like to see inside?" Rick asked in response.

I guess he didn't know about the shape. Why were the pyramids pyramid shaped? Who knew?

"Absolutely." For a place where people were buried, Monk's Hill was surprisingly homey. As we walked toward the chapel, full-sized maple and elm trees shaded us from the late summer sun. The wide spacing resembled a park or forest preserve.

When we reached the chapel, Rick opened the painted black door for me. Two rows of wooden pews stretched toward an altar. Rick explained that the iron bins at the foot of the pews were where churchgoers would place their coals in the winter. The sconces on the walls and at the ends of the pews were for candles. Women used to sit on the left and men on the right.

"So, no one uses the church anymore?"

"No. Not regularly. There was a wedding here a few years back, but not many people want to drive all the way out here for a ceremony. Not to mention the road from the gate wasn't designed for modern automobiles."

"It's a shame, really. This place is exquisite." For a moment, I pictured the aisle lined with sprays of white flowers, candles lit and flickering in the sconces, a handsome groom waiting with a priest at the altar. This church was grossly underutilized.

The oil paintings hanging on the walls caught my interest. "Do you mind if I look at the art?"

"Go ahead. They're paintings of the parishioners."

I wandered up a row toward the closest one while Rick hung back by the altar. The portrait was labeled 1692. Stoic-faced men and women with gaunt cheeks and dark clothes were lined up in the churchyard.

"These people look like pilgrims."

"Technically, Puritans, but the terms are used interchangeably these days."

I squinted at the details in the portrait. They each had a large book in their hands, probably a Bible. I scanned the hollow faces, looking for some hint of emotion. "Why didn't people smile in old pictures?" I turned toward Rick, who was watching me, motionless and with an unreadable expression.

"Life was harder then," he said. "People here were desperate. Starving."

"Starving?"

"In sixteen eighty-nine there was a war north of here, King William's War. Refugees from Canada and upstate New York settled here in Red Grove. The people who were here first, Monk's parishioners, welcomed the refugees in because that's what Puritans did. Hospitality was part of their religion. But they were farmers, and that year there was a drought. Food was scarce, and the refugees made the situation worse."

"How awful. What did they do?"

"Some of them died. The old ones. The weak ones. Some others were able to feed themselves by hunting in the woods. All of them asked Reverend Monk for help."

"You mean, like, to pray? To ask for rain?"

"Yes. But more. Word from Salem was there had been a confession of witchcraft. Salem was starving too, but they were doing something about it. They were finding the witches who caused the problem and burning them."

"Wait, are you talking about the Salem witch trials?"

"Yes."

"But obviously there are no such things as witches. I think I read somewhere that the whole thing in Salem was caused by mass hysteria. Did Monk really believe the drought was caused by a witch?"

"Oh, yes. The hysteria had made it all the way to Red Grove, and his parishioners insisted he weed out the witch. They got more than they bargained for from Monk though, as legend has it." Rick smiled and shook his head. "I'm boring you with my stories. Let's enjoy our lunch and this beautiful afternoon."

"I'm not bored," I said. "The Salem witch trials are super creepy. I had no idea they extended all the way to New Hampshire. But I'm hungry and more than curious about what's in the picnic basket. Save the story for later?"

"Of course."

The spot we chose for lunch was under the shade of an elm tree. Rick spread out a gigantic burgundy blanket made of plush velvet. We removed our shoes and sat cross-legged in the middle. From the picnic basket, he pulled two wine glasses and a bottle of Shiraz.

"Your favorite, if I remember correctly."

I nodded. "But I don't think I should have any."

"Why not?"

"It's just...I'm coming out of a complicated relationship." I cleared my throat and twisted my fingers in front of me. So embarrassing. I had to give it to him straight, though. "Ah, I'm out, actually. Completely out of the relationship. But I've found I have a pattern of rushing into things and then suffering the consequences of losing control. And, well, I think, last time we were together, I moved too fast."

I'm not sure how it happened, but in the blink of an eye, Rick had placed the glasses down and was by my side, my hands wrapped within both of his. Logically, I knew the process was a series of movements, but he was so fast it all happened at once. I never even saw him get up. My brain tried to make sense of it, but his touch was more than distracting, and soon the thought floated away from me. How could I care how fast he'd moved when his face, his delicious smell, was so close to mine?

Remember Gary! Love at first sight is never right. Remember the blonde paradox.

He raised my fingers to his lips and kissed them gently. "You could never be too forward. Your heart is safe with me. More than you know. What happened that night was because we are kindred souls. Kindred souls that found each other."

"Kindred souls?" I laughed, temporarily breaking his spell over me. "Come on, you've known me for three days."

"But already I know you are an old soul, much older than your twenty-two years. When you say you have a pattern, I suspect it means you've experienced this more than once, probably with both men and women. As your kindred soul, I must suggest you are a wanderer, not of places but of people. And if you don't mind entertaining my opinion, relationships have been hard for you, not because you rush in, but because no one understands who you really are."

"And you're saying you do?" He was right about the relationship thing. Besides Michelle, I didn't have many close friends, and I had suffered a series of devastating romantic relationships. I wondered how Rick knew, if he could smell the failure on me like some sort of bad cologne.

"Yes. I do."

I tilted my head to the side. "Hey, how did you know how old I was?"

He laughed and looked away. "You told me. You don't remember?"

I didn't remember telling him my age, but then I'd had a lot of wine. "Well, I never thought of myself as an old soul, but the rest of what you say is true. I'm not sure that makes us kindred souls, though."

"Oh, we are, *mi cielo*. Ask me anything. I bet I know more about you than you think."

"Okay. I'll play. What's my favorite color?"

He grinned and rubbed his chin. Then he raked his eyes over me from head to toe, his gaze a palpable thing that made my skin tingle. "You tell people red because you think it's what they want to hear, but your favorite color is actually silver. You love it as you love the winter—cold, calm, and magical."

"What the hell? How did you guess that?"

"Kindred souls." His fingers motioned back and forth between us.

"What's my favorite food?"

"Lamb."

I shivered. This was getting creepy. Lamb *was* my favorite. How could he possibly know that? "My favorite music?"

"Metal."

"Finally you get one wrong."

"You don't like metal?"

"It's not that I don't like it, but it's just not my favorite. I mean, as older music goes, definitely, but lately I really like—"

"Rap," he interrupted.

Oh. My. God. "How did you know?"

"You like your music to energize you. It has to be bold, loud, and hard. I can tell."

Heat crawled up my cheeks as I thought about how I'd attacked him on the couch. I knew how he could tell.

Rick was closer now, leaning over me so that I could feel his breath on my cheek. "I know one more thing about you, *mi cielo*."

"What?"

"You are compassionate to a fault. Someone who cares deeply about others."

I turned toward him and touched my forehead to his. "I do care about people. It's why I became a nurse. Even though I struggle with relationships, I care."

My heart picked up its pace, and the scent of the outdoors washed over me again, even more complex, with a hint of honeysuckle. I closed my eyes and inhaled deeply until my insides twisted, begging me to kiss him. My head felt light again. His face, his body were so close. He wanted to kiss me and maybe more, I could feel it. But it was like he was waiting for something—maybe a sign of consent on my part? I knew I shouldn't rush into things, but all the blood had rushed from my brain again to someplace lower on my body.

I leaned forward and feathered my lips up his cheek to his ear. "What do you know about kindred souls, Rick?"

"They usually think alike. And right now, I'm thinking about kissing you."

I nodded, a dimwitted gesture necessary because my mouth had grown useless with desire. Whatever promises I'd made to myself about going slow melted in the heat of the arm that wrapped around my shoulders and lowered me to the velvet. Balanced above me on his elbows and cradling my head in his hands, he brought his lips down on mine. I opened my mouth, accepting his probing tongue. I could sense his need for me in the kiss, and it was more than sexual. It was like he was drinking me in, trying to climb inside my skin.

I grabbed the back of his head and pulled his full weight on top of me on the blanket. I could feel his erection through our jeans, and I thrust my hips up to rub against him. Electric ribbons ran the length of my body from the sweet spot of pressure between my legs.

He moaned into my mouth. I'd rested my palm on his spine, beneath his shirt, and a ripple cascaded under my touch.

"*Mi cielo*, you make it difficult to preserve your honor when you tempt me so."

I giggled. The way he said it was so old-fashioned. After the story he'd just told me about Monk's parishioners and the stoic faces in the painting, I wondered if his historical knowledge had bled into his present life. Maybe being in the cemetery made him feel like what we were doing was inappropriate. But my body ached for him, absolutely pouted for his touch. I couldn't get close enough.

"It's a good thing it's not sixteen ninety-two then, because last I checked, preserving a woman's honor isn't a requirement." I reached for his lips with mine, picking up where we left off.

He explored every corner of my mouth, then kissed his way down my neck, running his tongue in wet trails over my pulse. My nipples strained against my cami. Rick pulled the lace down, exposing my breasts to the soft afternoon breeze. Bolstered by the fabric, they perked to attention. He flicked his thumb across one before lowering his mouth to tease the other with his able tongue. I reached for the buttons of his shirt like they were the bow to a birthday present I desperately wanted.

"No, *mi cielo*. I want this time to be for you, just you." Straddling me, he pressed my wrists to the velvet above my head. His fingertips brushed featherlight down my wrist, along the inside of my arm, the side of my breast, and lower, to my navel. Working his fingers under the bottom of my cami, he pushed it up under my exposed breasts. He buried his mouth in my stomach, nuzzling, kissing, licking his way to the top of my jeans. My button released between his teeth.

Waves of desire washed over me, every cell of my body ready, yearning for his touch, aching for more, leaving me wet. I could feel myself opening, blossoming under his heat, a flower in the sun. He worked my jeans down past my ankles, leaving me exposed to the blue sky, stretched long across the blanket with my arms above my head. Returning to hover above me, his upper thigh rubbed my core as his elbows came down on either side of my chest. His contained erection throbbed at my hip.

I reached for his face.

He stopped, grabbed my wrists. "No moving these," he said insistently, planting both wrists above my head in the velvet again. He kissed me, long and deep, before reaching down to slide his hand from my knee to my inner thigh and then teasingly to my bikini briefs.

I thanked my lucky stars I'd worn the cute black ones with the pink piping instead of the comfortable beige ones.

He worked his fingers under the waistband and rubbed me with tantalizing pressure. "You are so wet."

Responding to his breathy words, I arched my back, pressing myself into his hand. When his fingers entered me, it was like he had a map. No man, no boyfriend had ever known just where to touch me without being told.

I moaned, working my hips into his hand. The pleasure built, rising like the tide, lapping my body with a million tiny tongues. Slowly at first, he stroked inside me, increasing the rhythm at just the right time as if he could feel what I was feeling. He was going to bring me to climax with his fingers. I gasped at the intensity and moved my hands to his hair. But just as I neared that golden edge, he slowed his pace.

"Oh no, not yet," he said into my lips. He pressed my wrists into the velvet above my head once more. "Don't move these or I'll stop."

I squeezed my eyes shut, swearing silently that I might never move my hands again. His head moved down my body. Teeth grazed my nipple. Hot, wet tongue trailed down my stomach. The stubble of his cheek brushed my inner thigh.

I heard a ripping sound and realized my panties weren't on any more. Then his lips moved down my thigh to the place where his fingers kept working in and out slowly, coaxing the ache between my legs. His tongue flicked across me, soft as butterfly wings and right up the center, igniting a trail of fire that burned up my spine and out to my fingertips. The next lick was harder, pressure and languid heat. He picked up the pace. He sucked and lapped while his fingers rubbed. I couldn't see him from my position with my hands above my head, but I could hear him, the sound as erotic as the way his tongue felt between my legs. His black hair was just visible over the mound of my breasts.

Everything was wet-hot. In a rhythm of intense bliss, his mouth did sinful things: tongue licking, teeth nibbling, and sucking me again and again, coaxing, teasing, until every neuron in my body fired at once. The orgasm poured out of me in a ray of energy that made me call out his name.

"Rick! Oh...God...Rick." I forgot about the rule and moved my hands. I grabbed his head, running my fingers through his dark waves and pulling him up on top of me as the last echoes of the orgasm rang through my body. When I stopped writhing, he stretched out next to me, drawing me into the curl of his chest. Wrapped in his muscular arms, he held me until my breath evened out and my heart rate was almost normal.

"That's what kindred souls do," he said into my ear. "And then they eat."

"I think I might like being kindred souls," I whimpered.

He sat up and poured some wine, handing me the glass. I sipped it appreciatively. From the basket, he retrieved a baguette and spread some cheese on a corner. Then, he shifted me into the harbor of his arms and fed me. Leaning against him in the late summer sunshine, I watched as he bit into the bread right over the section I'd eaten. I can't explain why, but it was intimate, almost sacred.

When I was done eating, I moved to get dressed. I found my panties in the grass and held what was left of them between my fingers. Wadding them into a ball, I ended up going commando. I carried them home, bewildered as to how he'd managed to do the damage that he did.

They weren't just torn. They were shredded.

CHAPTER 7
I Give My Ghost A Name

Back at the homestead, I flopped onto the floral sofa, muscles sandbagging over the overstuffed cushions and still sans panties, which was becoming increasingly uncomfortable. As I chewed my thumbnail while examining my new ceiling, I decided I had no regrets. I was a single, independent woman. Couldn't a girl enjoy oral sex for the sake of pleasure without rushing into a relationship with her partner? We hadn't had intercourse, after all. Nothing life changing going on here. *I did not have sex with that man.* If that logic was good enough for President Clinton, it was good enough for me.

I moved on to my next fingernail. Why had I fallen so effortlessly into his arms? Every meeting with Rick was like being swept out to sea, like I couldn't control myself around him. Things were going too far, too fast. No matter how "kindred" our souls were, guys like that always had secrets. Oh God, what if he was married? Or in the witness protection program? That would explain why he lived out here in the boonies.

After rolling my aching limbs off the sofa, I poured myself another cup of coffee and decided choosing a name for my ghost would be a welcome distraction. *Shit*, I was meeting with an honest-to-God spectral presence in like four hours. My palms began to sweat. I poured my coffee down the sink and ran for the cellar. I needed a drink and not the caffeinated kind.

Moments later, I stood before the bookshelves in the family room, Shiraz in hand, inspecting Prudence Meriwether's sizable collection of classic literature. Seemed like as good a place as any to find a name. I perused the spines, yanked a leather volume from the shelf and read a random page. Somehow, Romeo seemed completely inappropriate. I moved on to the next volume. Heathcliff? Definitely not. Edward, Fitzwilliam, and Darcy? Too stuffy. He didn't look like a renaissance man. I needed something modern but not metrosexual, smart but not stuffy.

Hours later, from the center ring of a circle of open texts, the name popped out of my brain like candy from a Pez dispenser. Logan. I'd always liked the name Logan. But beyond that, something inside me thought Logan might be his real name. My scalp prickled slightly when I tested it on my tongue and warmth swelled behind my ribcage.

With a self-satisfied smile, I returned the books, two by two to the shelf. As I stacked the last one, a cold wind scuttled across the base of my neck. I spun around thinking my ghost had come down early.

"Ahhh!" I jumped backward pressing myself into the bookshelf.

Prudence's torso glowed at me above her smoky tendrils. "Find the key," the ghost demanded, waving me forward. "Find the key and bring the vessel. Claim your inheritance."

"I don't have any key. I'm not who you're looking for!"

Prudence's old lady face produced an animal like growl and her skin peeled back into a fang-filled mask of horror. Her ghoulish form raced toward me. I tucked into a ball circa 1980's elementary school tornado drill. Icy wind coursed through my body. I hugged my head between my knees and held my breath as not to breathe in any old lady molecules. When I couldn't hold it any longer, I gasped and popped my head up. She was gone.

"*Fuck me!*" I patted my chest and arms to make sure I wasn't injured, then grabbed my bottom to check if I'd wet myself. Still wasn't wearing any underwear. I reached for my wine glass. Empty. Storming to the counter, I pulled the cork from the bottle and chugged. I took it with me as I climbed the stairs to my room for a hot shower. The thought of running out the door and never coming back did cross my mind. Why didn't I? Logan. I wanted to give him his name. I wanted to hear what he had to say. I wanted to know more about this house and the promised "sorter." You could say I had warring emotions and at that moment curiosity was winning...or else killing the cat.

After a long shower and a cold dinner that consisted of a slice of cheese, a scoop of peanut butter, and a handful of radishes from the back of the fridge, I waited for midnight. I drummed my fingers on the kitchen counter, leaned against the dining room table, posed in the foyer as if I was casually leaning against the wall instead of panicking from the inside out.

My ghost arrived exactly at midnight, when I was leaning my butt against the island stool. The attic door creaked open above me, and then a green orb glowed at the top of the stairs. It expanded as it floated toward me, branching out like a star, burning brighter until my ghost stood in front of me. He looked as solid as I did.

"Wow. You are different at night," I said, feeling stupid for saying so when his expression soured. "I just mean, I can't see through you like I could this afternoon."

"Yeah, midnight is when I have the most control over my form. It takes some mental effort for me to hold myself together like this, but not nearly as much as during the day."

"I don't even know if I should ask you to sit down. Do ghosts sit?"

"I don't need to. Strictly speaking, I don't have a body, so I don't need to physically rest. But I think in this case it would be better if I did—more comfortable for the both of us."

I nodded and moved toward the dining room table. The weird thing about being followed by a ghost is the lack of sound. I watched him walk across the wood floor, looking as human as anyone I'd ever met, but there wasn't even a hint of a footstep. I sat down at the table, and he walked behind the chair next to me and stopped. I waited for him to sit, but he just looked at the back of the chair mournfully. I pushed it back with my foot. He floated into it, his body bending unnaturally before coming to rest on the wood. The action made it impossible for me to forget he was a ghost, no matter how alive he looked.

"You're scared of me," he said.

"A little." Did it show?

"I'm sorry, Grateful, for everything. I know I keep scaring you. I don't intend to. This is what I am now, and it's all I can be."

Even I, the relationship-impaired, know that when you meet a man who can admit his insecurities, you need to appreciate it while it lasts. I put on my big-girl panties and stopped thinking so much. "No, *I'm* sorry. You've been nothing but kind to me. Thank you for helping with Prudence and for making me coffee."

"It's the least I could do."

"Hey, wait a minute," I said. "If you can't pull out your own chair, how did you make the coffee this morning?"

"I *can* move things with my energy. But when I made the coffee I was in my other form. Right now, I'm concentrating on looking like my human self. There's nothing left over for moving the chair." Half of his mouth lifted, wrinkling the corners of his eyes and making the stubble on his chin remind me of a lover who'd spent the night and forgot a razor. I had to keep reminding myself that he was dead, that he didn't have a body.

"My turn to have my question answered," he said. "What is my name, Grateful?"

"Well, I don't know what your real name is, but would you mind if I called you Logan?"

"Yes. Logan. I am Logan." He said the words with relief. What must it be like to float around in someone's attic not knowing your own name?

I allowed myself to look at him, really look at him. The spiky blondish hair, the green eyes, sport coat, jeans, and loafers. Handsome would be an apt description but not in an obvious way. Not handsome in the way that Rick was handsome, for example. When you saw Rick, it was like watching a male model walk off the pages of a magazine. He was all heat and swagger. Sex oozed from his pores. Logan was attractive but in the way a neighbor might be or a best friend's brother. There was a realness about him. His smile made me feel warm, like coming home after a long day.

"What exactly did you do when you were alive?" I asked, pondering if what he was wearing was what he'd died in, or some universal version of himself.

"I told you, I don't remember," he said. "None of us ever knows."

"Us?"

"The ghosts who pass through your attic. Prudence says we know we're waiting for something, but we don't know what."

Huh? "There've been others? How long have you been here?"

"Prudence told me about the others. Time is hard for me, but I know I came after Prudence died because I'm still here."

"I...I don't understand. What do you mean, Prudence died and that's why you're still here?"

The question made him go all staticky for a minute. He cleared his throat—a pointless gesture, considering he didn't have one—and I knew he was stalling.

I scowled in his direction. "You said before that you are waiting for a sorter. Prudence asked me if I was the sorter. That must be someone who helps you move on. Was Prudence the last sorter?"

"You catch on quick."

"And now, because she died, you have to wait for a new sorter to help you cross over."

He nodded. "She remembers you, you know."

"What do you mean, she remembers me?"

"Once she realized who you were, she was relieved you'd finally come. She told me some things about you. Things I hadn't expected."

"She doesn't even know me."

"She says she does, from when you were a baby."

"Wow, my father and I lived in Red Grove when I was born, but I don't remember living here. We moved before I was two."

"You made an impression."

The way he said it made me squirm in my seat. Why was I so memorable to Prudence? "You never answered my question about why you ended up in my attic in the first place."

The sigh he emitted was also unnecessary for any purpose other than letting me know he didn't want to answer my question. "There are some things in life that happen when they're supposed to happen. I'm not supposed to talk to you about this now. Prudence says I can't. It wouldn't be right."

"But Logan, now I know you and Prudence have a secret. Can't you give me a hint?"

Rubbing his chin, he considered me in silence for some time. "I warned you to stay away from the caretaker. You didn't."

I sighed. "Why does it matter? Rick seems like a perfectly nice guy."

"Do you know what a caretaker is, Grateful?"

"I think so. He's someone who maintains the cemetery."

My ghost looked disappointed. "I think you have a lot to learn about Red Grove." He frowned. "Don't get involved with the caretaker until you figure it out."

"What does my involvement with Rick have to do with anything? Are you afraid I'll tell him about you?"

"It's not what *you* tell *him*."

"Aargh!" I slapped my forehead in frustration. "You're not making any sense."

"Maybe not." His face turned serious. "I'm sorry. This was supposed to be fun. A date." He smiled. "Let's start again. Tell me why you've moved to Red Grove."

"Ugh. It's a long, sad story. Believe me, we'd be better off talking about Prudence."

"Hey, all I've got is time…I think. And since I have few memories of my own, I'd enjoy hearing yours. Unless, of course, you'd like a play-by-play of my dusting."

I pressed a finger into my lips, eyes darting around the room. I craned my neck to eyeball the living room. "You cleaned today."

"Yes."

"The whole house?"

"Yes," he said, smiling sheepishly. "I saw your note in the dust on the dresser upstairs. 'Clean me.'"

I leaned forward pressing my hand into my chest. "That note was a reminder for me! I thought you slept during the day."

"I did for a little while, but I knew you would appreciate the help."

"I do. I really, really do," I said emphatically.

"So, pay me back. Tell me how you ended up here." Elbow on the table, he leaned his head into his hand.

I gave him the condensed version. "I'm broke. My dad is letting me stay here for free. Sure, it's a commute, but I don't really have a choice."

"The first night I met you, you were wearing scrubs and answered the phone for St. John's Hospital. You're a nurse, right?"

I nodded.

"If you have a job, why are you broke?"

"My ex-boyfriend took all of my money."

Logan crossed his arms, his outline rippling as he concentrated. The way he held himself seemed almost lawyer-ish. I felt like he was interrogating me. "A man stole your money. Did you go to the police?"

"It's a long story."

"I have all night. Hell, I might have eternity." The ghost's molecules shifted to his smile as if the energy from his feelings was driving his physical form. For a moment, his mouth and teeth glowed, flashing at me in the dim light of the dining room. Then the expression faded to the same opaque as the rest of his body. The Cheshire cat act made the hair on my arms stand up.

"He screwed me, okay? Totally screwed me. Broke my heart, stole all of my money, and abandoned me without so much as a note. I loved him, and he screwed me."

Logan frowned and folded his hands across the table, an all-too-human gesture that made it hard to remember he wasn't alive. "You can't blame yourself for loving someone, Grateful. I may not know who I was in life, but I do remember that there are some things that just happen to you. That's why they call it *falling in love*. You fall. It's an uncontrollable act of gravity that has nothing to do with choice and everything to do with fate."

"You're pretty smart for someone without a brain."

"Ha, ha. I have a brain. It's just decomposing wherever my body happens to be."

I giggled, but the thought made me gag a little. "But see, I caused him to steal my money. It was the blonde paradox."

"What the hell is the blonde paradox?"

"I'm blonde, right? And sort of look like Barbie. Well, that attracts men because their caveman brain thinks I'm more fertile. But then they assume I'm stupid due to societal stereotypes about blondes, and they ironically become less intelligent in my presence. It's like my looks are toxic to a healthy relationship."

"Let me get this straight. You think that because of the way you look, men are drawn to you primarily for sex and then treat you like crap due to the same good looks."

"It's science."

"I think it's bullshit."

"Really."

The level of concentration necessary for whatever he was thinking about must have been steep because he flickered at the edges. Silence stretched out between us. By his expression, he was turning something over in his mind, trying to think of something to say. I crossed my arms over my chest and braced myself for a judgmental commentary.

Finally, he said, "You know what your problem is?"

"My house is haunted and I'm broke?"

"No. Your problem is you're still angry at your ex, but you're punishing yourself."

"I'm not punishing myself."

"You are! You're blaming yourself for something he did. What was his name?"

"Gary."

"You need to take all of that anger and guilt you're holding, wrap it up in a great big karmic ball, and throw that sucker right at *Gary*."

I rolled that around in my brain. "Gary's gone. What are you proposing?"

He grinned and waggled his eyebrows. "I think I have a better idea. Do you have a picture of Gary?"

I waved my hand in front of my face as if the notion stunk. "Of course not. I shredded every last one."

Logan raised an eyebrow. "All of them?"

God, his eyes bore into me. Was this some kind of ghostly water torture? He was practically wringing out my soul for information with his stare.

"Okay! I might have one."

"Where is it?"

My eyes darted to the black purse I'd dumped in the corner of the counter when I'd come home from work yesterday.

"You still keep his picture in your wallet?"

"Hey, it's not like I remembered it was in there or anything until just now. I just think there might be one in the secret compartment."

Logan bobbed his head and made a gimme gesture with his hand. "Well?"

With a sigh, I strode to the purse and with my back to Logan pulled Gary's picture out of the clear plastic photo holder it was still in. My God I was a loser. Reluctantly, I handed it over.

Concentrating his energy on his fingertips, Logan inspected the photo. After a moment or two he raised his eyes to me. A shiver started in his hair and descended, shaking his entire ghostly form until he was nothing but a blur. When he formed again, my ghost had transformed his sandy blonde hair to Gary's saddle brown coif. His green eyes were now blue. And although I could tell that the shape of his head was slightly off, Logan could've been Gary's twin.

"Grab the kitchen knives," he said.

* * * * *

I poured myself a glass of wine and tried to come to terms with what I was about to do. We'd moved downstairs, and I'd balanced a piece of plywood against the brick wall across from the wine cellar. With his arms extended to the sides, back pressed to the plywood, Logan goaded me on.

"Come on, Grateful. I promise it won't hurt me."

"For the five hundredth time, this just seems wrong."

"Get over it. It will help."

To my side was the block of knives from the kitchen. This was Logan's idea. Why not play along? I gulped down half my glass of Shiraz. After testing the weight of each of the wooden handles, I selected the largest one. I think it's called a chef's knife. I removed it from its slot.

"That's what I'm talking about, Grateful. Hit me! Say to me what you want to say to Gary."

I raised the knife over my shoulder. "You used me!" I yelled and tossed the blade as hard as I could. It tumbled through the air, stabbing through Logan's abdomen and reverberating in the plywood behind him. My eyebrows shot up in surprise at the accuracy of my throw.

"Yes!" I said, pumping my arm. I had a hidden talent.

"Gah!" Logan clutched the section of his stomach the knife had passed through as if in pain.

My hands shot to my mouth. "Did I hurt you?"

He chuckled. "No. I was just acting to make it more realistic."

"Good, because I'm starting to enjoy this." I raised another knife. "Gary, you stole my money. All of my money. How could you do that to me? I thought you loved me." I hurled the knife. It passed through Logan's crotch.

"Wow, Grateful, let it all out—"

"Because of you, I lost my home and my self-respect!" I heaved three at his head, one after the other. "Because of you, Gary, I lost my ability to trust. You asshole. I hope you rot in hell." The knife rotated from my fingers and sliced through Gary's image, right where his heart should have been.

Logan didn't move. There were so many knives through his ghostly form, it reminded me of a *Looney Tunes* episode when you know the Coyote should be dead from the anvil but he's not. I couldn't help it. I started laughing.

"I think I want you to be you again, Logan."

He stepped away from the wall, shaking off Gary's image like a dog shakes off after a swim. I leaned my hip against the pool table.

"Better?" he asked.

"Yeah. Thank you."

Our eyes met, and there was a connection. A heaviness formed at the center of my chest and my scalp prickled again, the same as when I thought of his name. The closest I could call it was déjà vu, like we'd met before or something. He must have felt it too because he leaned toward me, eyes hooded.

When he was close enough to tickle my skin with whatever he was made of, I came to my senses and took a step back. What the hell was that all about? He'd practically been close enough to kiss me. It was like we were both caught in some strange tractor beam.

Logan dematerialized in a flash of light.

"Sorry," his voice echoed around me. "I–I'm not sure what happened there. I think I should go."

A mist hovered above my head. I tilted my face up. "Uh, me neither. Weird though. It's way past my bedtime anyway. See you tomorrow?"

"Well, *I'm* not going anywhere...I think." The mist filtered up through the vent.

I approached the plywood board and started prying the knives from the wood.

CHAPTER 8
Good Morning

Alone in my bed that night, I slept better than I had in a long time. I didn't even dream until the early morning hours. In that space between sleep and awake, I was running through the cemetery—naked. Logan was up ahead, calling my name. He needed help. He needed me. But something was behind me, at my heels with panting breath and heavy footsteps. Just before I reached Logan, a hand gripped my shoulder. I twisted my head around. Rick was behind me, naked and panting. His eyes were black as coal. I fell into his arms. Under the elm tree where we'd had lunch, between rows of headstones, he took me from behind, sliding into me and driving his hips home.

It might have been a scary dream, but it wasn't. I had the overwhelming feeling that I'd wanted Rick to catch me all along. Like he was saving me from something or someone. We were two pieces of a puzzle, fitting together in a way that was right.

When I woke up, I was on the floor next to my bed. What the hell? Had I humped my way off the mattress in my sleep? My obsession with the caretaker and his dark and dangerous persona had officially made it into my subconscious. What did this say about my mental state? Maybe it was biological. It had been months since I'd had sex. A girl has needs.

Cheek to the carpet, I pressed my hands to the floor to push myself up. When I turned my head to crack my neck, I saw a wink of raspberry beyond the dust ruffle and lowered myself back down. Prudence had left something under the bed. I reached out a hand and fished the object toward me, then crisscrossed my legs under me.

The old-fashioned hatbox had stripes down the sides and a gorgeous floral lid that gave it a Victorian quality. I rubbed my hands together, anxious to see what Prudence left behind, maybe an antique hat or, I don't know, a box full of money might be nice. With both hands, I attempted to lift the lid. "Ow!" Blood bubbled from a pinprick-sized hole in my finger. I stuck it in my mouth rather than wipe it on my shirt. With my good hand, I turned the box and found the offending staple. It looked like the box had originally had a handle of some sort. Carefully, I reached for the lid again, avoiding the sharp barb.

What I found when I lifted the lid was a leather scrapbook. I cracked the cover. On the first page was a clipped newspaper column: MOTHER DIES GIVING BIRTH. I scanned the article. This was about my mother! Why did Prudence have an article about my mother's death under her bed? I flipped a page, and then in confusion, I flipped another. Pictures of me as a baby, riding my first bike, my first dance, singing in the church choir, my graduation from nursing school. All of them taken from far away, like paparazzi pictures taken with a telephoto lens. What. The. Fuck. I closed the scrapbook and tipped the box toward me. The only other thing in there was a blue velvet bag, the kind large jewelry might be stored in, but the bag was empty.

Two theories formed behind my fluttering lids. One, Prudence was a stalker who targeted me as a child. Two, this was my father's album left in Prudence's house. Neither theory made sense.

I tucked the scrapbook under my arm and jogged downstairs. Logan had again made me coffee and also an omelet fit for a five-star restaurant. It was steaming hot when I reached the kitchen. Either he had amazing timing or, more likely, had been watching me.

I flopped the scrapbook onto the counter. "What is this Logan?"

"I have no idea." He materialized as he spoke.

Flipping open to a spread that included six photos of six-year-old me with my first dog, Nigel, I held it up in the direction of his glowing orb.

He sighed. "I can't talk about it. I literally cannot. Prudence has forbidden me to, and since she's the senior ghost, I must obey her."

I slapped the counter. "Why can't you tell me anything? You still haven't explained how you ended up in my attic."

"I told you, I'm not supposed to talk about that, either."

"Why not? What possible reason could Prudence have for not telling me why you're living in *my* attic? Or why she kept pictures of me under her bed."

"It's for your protection, to keep you safe. The secret must be revealed in a certain way."

I groaned, exasperated. "Can't you give me a clue? Anything?"

He placed his hands on his hips and hung his head.

"Logan, come on," I said.

"How did you get the name Grateful, anyway?"

Way to change the subject. I hated talking about my name, but people were naturally curious about it. I decided I'd try to use it as leverage. "I'll tell you, but in exchange you need to tell me what I want to know." I crossed my arms and tapped my foot.

"I told you—"

"I know you can't say it straight out, but you can give me a clue. That's all I'm asking for."

"Deal."

"My dad named me Grateful because my mother died in childbirth and he was grateful to have me."

"That must have made for a difficult childhood."

The comment caught me off guard. "Not really. My dad has always been there for me. I mean, there were times I missed having a mom, but it's not the same as missing a person you actually knew. I'd never met her."

"Has your father ever told you the full story of how it happened?"

I considered his question. "I guess not really. I mean, I know now that she bled out. There's a medical term— disseminated intravascular coagulation, or DIC. No one was to blame. I work in the hospital where she died. Every year on my birthday, my dad used to send a card to the nurse who helped with my delivery."

"What was the nurse's name?"

"You know, I don't remember. I just know my dad thought the world of her."

"Ask your father. Ask him for the nurse's name."

"Why?" I asked.

"Because that's the clue I promised you."

"Oh, you can't be serious! What possible connection could there be? You made this up."

"That was our deal. Take it or leave it."

I sighed. "Take it."

He blinked out of sight and the omelet he made me slid across the table in my direction. "Eat."

I tucked the scrapbook in the cabinet under the island and took a seat on the barstool. "Thanks, Logan," I said, forking eggs into my mouth. I was usually a Pop-Tartsfor-breakfast kind of girl. I wondered what my body would do with these newfound vitamins and minerals.

"I did a load of laundry too," his disembodied voice said. I couldn't make him out at all.

"Logan, you don't have to do my cooking or my cleaning." A pang of guilt cut through me for treating him like a spectral slave.

"It gives me something to do."

I smiled in the direction I thought he was in. "I appreciate it. I can't cook, and I'm a shitty housekeeper."

"There's a way you can pay me back."

"How?"

"Stay away from the caretaker."

Shaking my head, I said, "You never quit."

"The caretaker is dangerous for you, Grateful."

"So you keep telling me." I dropped my fork and checked the time. "Shit, I've gotta get ready for work." I lifted the plate to clear the table.

"Leave that for me. Go ahead. Get outta here."

"Thanks, Logan." I grabbed my keys and took him up on his offer to clean up.

* * * * *

The hospital where I work is thirty minutes from Red Grove. I hopped into my Jeep and peeled out of the driveway, hoping I could still make my shift on time. The sight of Rick painting the cemetery fence shirtless had me slamming on the brakes before I could say "gonna be late."

"I hoped I would catch you this morning," Rick called, dropping the paintbrush into the pan at his feet and walking toward me. "Would you have dinner with me tonight?"

I was having trouble concentrating. The memory of my dream from that morning was fresh in my mind. My body responded just thinking about it.

Rick stopped a few feet from me and closed his eyes. He took a deep breath. Fast as the flutter of hummingbird wings, he was leaning in my window.

"How did you do that?" I asked.

"Do what?"

"Move so quickly just now?"

"If I was quick, it was for good reason. A man should never keep a beautiful woman waiting."

My cheeks blazed.

"Dinner tonight?" he asked again. He licked his full lips.

My mouth began to form the word *yes,* but I caught myself. Warnings buzzed in my head. Rick was dangerous. I needed to slow things down. "I think I need to catch up on some sleep."

His eyes narrowed. "You're having trouble sleeping? I have some herbs—"

"No," I said too quickly. I shook my head and smiled. "I'm fine, really. I've just been distracted with the move and everything. Haven't got to bed at a decent hour." And hell if I was going to invite another foot-stink bouquet into my residence.

He nodded, but the twist of his mouth told me he didn't quite believe my excuse.

I couldn't tell him about Logan. Not only would it potentially mark me as a lunatic, but I had a strong gut feeling that I shouldn't. "How about Friday night?" I countered.

"When can I expect you?"

"I get off at seven," I said. "I can be there around eight."

"Then eight it is." The corner of his mouth lifted, and for just a moment, I sensed something. Call it premonition. I'd known this man. I would know him again. The feeling passed as quickly as it had come, and I realized I'd unconsciously leaned through the window and kissed him.

I removed my lips from his and smoothed my scrubs. "Sorry," I said. "I don't know what came over me."

"Never apologize, *mi cielo*. Not for that."

I nodded, but I wasn't at all sure I agreed. I had a nasty habit of losing control with Rick. Visions of calling in sick so that I could show him exactly what I'd dreamed about played out in my head. My heart picked up its pace. All of my girl parts petitioned for amnesty from my brain as I silently repeated: *I need my job, I need my job.*

As if he could hear my thoughts, he raised an eyebrow and smiled wickedly. He stepped back from my Jeep. "See you Friday, Grateful," he said.

I regained my composure and waved goodbye, then accelerated for work, hoping I'd make it on time.

CHAPTER 9
Gary

St. John's is a modern hospital with windows that take up the entire wall and big, airy spaces that defy the claustrophobic feel of older buildings. But the fact that you could see the parking lot from the hallway to the ICU did not bode well for concealing my lateness, the result of my late-night knife-throwing session with Logan and subsequent hangover. Luckily, Michelle raced to meet me at the doublewide, automatic doors to my unit.

"I've been covering for you. You're ten minutes late." She grabbed my purse from me and tossed it without regard for the contents into the break room where our lockers were. "You have three-oh-three and three-oh-four, cardiac arrest and pneumonia. Vitals are normal. You've been at the blood bank for three-oh-three."

The last word was barely out of her mouth when my boss, Kathleen, rounded the corner and met my eyes.

"Where've you been, Grateful?" she asked. Her lips pulled into a stern line.

"At the blood bank for three-oh-three. I forgot the type and match and had to come back up."

"I must have missed you when you came in," she said. Her voice held a hint of skepticism.

"I got report from, uh…" I cleared my throat. I had no idea who had my rooms before me.

"Megan. Wasn't it Megan I saw you with this morning?" Michelle filled in.

"Yes, Megan," I followed. "Had to get started right away. Sorry I missed you."

Kathleen nodded curtly and rushed off to her next victim.

"I owe you one, Michelle."

We walked side by side toward our rooms.

"You can pay me back after work today by coming with me to check out a patient on Neuro. Maureen asked me to stop over."

"Sorry, hon. Can't today. I have plans."

"With who?"

I stopped myself. I didn't actually have plans. But I hoped to corner Logan and try to find out more about the scrapbook. Not only would Michelle not believe me if I told her the truth, but she might go all mental-health nurse on me. If I didn't want to end up on Haldol, I figured Logan needed to stay my little secret. "With me."

"What?"

"Listen, I've been totally stressed lately. I just want to paint my toes and go to bed early, you know?"

"Totally. Totally get it. Tomorrow's euchre night with Manny." She sighed. "You wanna go to Valentine's for drinks Friday?"

I adjusted a box of latex gloves on the counter, unable to look Michelle in the eye. "I have a date."

"Another date with your toes?"

"No, a real date."

"With who?"

"My new neighbor, Rick." I rubbed behind my ear. "I kinda had a date with him yesterday. I think we hit it off." Boy, was that the understatement of the year, but telling Michelle he'd gotten me off on the first date was an equally bad idea as telling her about Logan. I wasn't proud to be hiding things from my best friend, but my life was a little weird right now. I'd be straight with her once I got a grip on things.

"What's wrong with him?"

I gasped and gave her an appalled stare. "There's nothing wrong with him."

"Are you forgetting the blonde paradox? Fast to come is fast to go."

"I'm not forgetting, but he's perfectly normal. I have a good feeling about this relationship. We seem destined somehow."

"You've known him for like three days."

"I know. Well, four if you count today."

Michelle did not look impressed. She rolled her eyes and made a raspberry sound with her lips. "Call me when you need ice cream therapy," she said.

"Thanks for the vote of confidence."

She gave me a firm hug. "I'm confident in you, but not so much in the opposite sex. But I know you, Grateful; you tend to rush into things. You hand over your heart—no, not just your heart, your life—too quickly."

"Besides Gary, name one relationship I rushed into."

Michelle didn't even pause for breath. "Paul: he sang in the choir with you. You lost your virginity to him after three dates and were sure he would marry you. He didn't. Todd: picked him up at a bar, remember? Lasted fifteen dates. He was so controlling you almost failed chemistry because he'd never let you out of the apartment to go to class. Brian. Remember the Brian semester in college? He almost had you convinced you should drop nursing and become an accountant. An accountant, Grateful!"

"Okay, okay. Stop!" I slapped a hand over my eyes. "You're right. You are always right. I do rush into things. This time I've got to keep the reins firmly in hand."

"Exactly." She rubbed my shoulder. "You can do it. Gotta get back to work. See you later." She walked off toward her patient.

The intensive care unit was busy that day, and I was swept away in a routine of assessments and medication administration. Nursing is a blessing in that way. It's impossible to think about your own problems when you're wrapped up in someone else's. The day flew by. Before I knew it, I was relieved by the night nurse and passing through the fishbowl hallway to get to the elevator. I paused and looked over the parking lot, enjoying the late summer twilight. Lightning bugs danced over the cars, flirting with the floodlights. The scene was stunning. I stepped toward the glass, allowing myself a moment to unwind. I scanned the rows of cars, reflexively trying to pick mine out of the pack.

I found my Jeep—and something else I wasn't expecting. There was a man standing next to my car—a man who looked a whole lot like Gary.

I beat feet to the end of the hallway, then down the stairwell, not waiting for the elevator. Exploding out the side exit into the parking lot, I raced toward my Jeep, having no idea what I would do if it really was Gary. What would I say? I didn't have a block of knives to back me up.

My Jeep waited for me in the third row where I left it. No one was there. I even squatted to look underneath. Shaking my head, I pulled my keys out of my pocket and reached for the door. The stench of Gary's cologne wafted over me and I whipped around. Nothing.

I climbed behind the wheel and turned the key in the ignition. The engine rumbled to life. Stupid Gary. Stealing my money wasn't enough; now he wanted the car too? If it *was* him, he'd better hope I never caught him near my stuff again, or there was a very real possibility I'd make him disappear again. Permanently.

CHAPTER 10
My Past Haunts Me

Logan didn't come out that night, probably avoiding another confrontation about Prudence and the scrapbook. In fact, my house was pleasantly devoid of ghosts. I went to bed early thinking about our last conversation. Logan's words kept repeating in my head. *"Ask your father. Ask him for the nurse's name. That's your clue."*

The next day, I decided to follow up on Logan's clue and call my dad over my lunch break. Across the street from the hospital is a restaurant called Valentine's. St. John's employees love it, because if you're wearing scrubs they serve you first. It's nice when people recognize a long lunch could mean someone's life. Plus, the food is better than the cafeteria, and they serve a yummy cappuccino. After seven p.m., they open a bar in the back with a small dance floor surrounded by dartboards and pool tables. It's a great place to hang out.

I found a quiet booth and ordered a sandwich from an annoyingly perky waitress. Then I dialed Dad on my cell. It was a hard conversation to start. How do you ask a man about the day his wife bled to death? The topic was generally avoided in our family.

But when I thought about backing down, I thought about my ghost. Logan had hinted that this story would help me understand why he was in my attic and what I needed to know about Rick. I wanted to solve the mystery of my haunted house, but I also wanted to help him find peace. Not everyone would take a knife in the gut to help a friend, ghost or not. Logan was a good person, dead or alive.

"Hello," my dad said in his real estate agent voice, like he pooped sunshine and rainbows. It was why he was so good at what he did.

"Dad, it's me."

"Hi, sweetie. Everything okay with the new place?"

"Sure, yeah. It's great."

"What's up then?"

"I need to talk to you about when I was a baby. It's just something I've been thinking about, and I have to know. I want you to tell me the whole story. Everything you remember about when I was born."

Silence. I checked to make sure the call was still connected.

"What brought this on?" he finally asked.

"Well, now that I'm a nurse myself, and I'm working at the same hospital where I was born, I just feel the need to know. I'm only twenty-two, and some of the staff here has been around for thirty or forty years. What if I run into someone who was involved with my birth?"

"There's no chance of that." My father's voice sounded grim.

I was sorry for ruining his day by digging up ancient memories, but I needed to know. "Why?"

"Listen, I'll come over tonight. We'll talk about this in person. This isn't a conversation for the phone."

"Okay." The word came out of my throat like a cough.

"I'll see you tonight."

"I get off at seven."

We ended the call, but words that needed to be aired pressed themselves against the phone. I wasn't sure how my ghost knew, but my dad had something to tell me. I both welcomed and dreaded his visit.

* * * * *

Robert Knight, real estate agent, walked up to my house minutes after I arrived home. He wore a tailored gray suit with a black leather satchel strung across the shoulders and only became Dad when I opened the door and my hug broke his professional demeanor.

"Hi, Dad. Thanks for coming."

He kissed the top of my head. With a full coif of short black hair and only a slight pattern of gray above his ears, people often mistook him for ten years younger than he was. His movie star good looks and athletic physique added to the illusion of youth. Growing up, neighborhood women and house-hunting clients were always making excuses to flirt with him, but he never seemed interested. I never really thought about why. As a kid, my innocent mind just assumed he was happy with our family and didn't need another wife.

"Can I get you something to drink?"

He followed me into the kitchen and took a seat on a stool at the island. "Yeah. Scotch, straight up."

I laughed. "Scotch? Sorry, I don't drink the stuff."

"There's some in the cabinet above the fridge."

I stretched to open the little door he motioned toward. I never used that cabinet. Too hard to reach. Sure enough, there was half a bottle of scotch there. I poured him a glass. "Did you store this up there before I moved in?"

"Actually, it was here since before Prudence died. I used to come visit her occasionally. She kept it for me."

Uh-oh. "Dad, please tell me you weren't having an affair with her." Prudence was almost twenty years older than my father. I shuddered to think they were somehow involved.

"No. No, affair. We were just friends."

I squinted in his direction. "Close enough friends that she left you her house when she died, kept your favorite liquor, and had this under her bed." I retrieved the scrapbook from where I'd left it in the island cabinet and flopped it down in front of him.

"What's this?"

"You tell me."

He scrubbed his face with his hands, flashing his Rolex in the process. "Maybe it would be better if I started at the beginning."

"Yeah, I think that would be best."

The way he ran his thumb across his eyebrow and took a swig of scotch before he started told me I needed to sit down for this. I pulled up a stool.

"Your mother and I had tried for years to have a baby. She had some female problem I never really understood. We'd given up entirely by the time you came along. You were a miracle. Such an incredible surprise." He took another drink.

"Go on." I wasn't sure what this had to do with Prudence, but I'd asked him here to tell me about mom's death. I guess he was starting there.

"We were so happy. When you've wanted something for so long and think you'll never have it, and then someone tells you fate has changed her mind, and you're getting it after all…well, I don't know if I can explain how that feels. Anyway, when Elena went into labor, we were ready. The nursery was done. We couldn't wait to bring you home."

I placed my hand on his and nodded.

"At first, everything proceeded as expected. The birth itself was rough, but the doctor said it was normal. But then she started to bleed. They pressed on her stomach and gave her medicine, but they couldn't stop it. She died.

But you knew that, didn't you?" The scotch was gone. He stood and poured himself another.

I held my tongue. So far, he hadn't shared anything I hadn't figured out on my own. But I could feel it coming. There was something else. Something big.

"I never told you this before, Grateful, and I'm so sorry to admit it. I couldn't even look at you when you were born. I didn't hold you. I didn't name you." My father's voice came out shaky, and his eyes welled with tears. "I left. I abandoned you in that hospital the moment I found out she was dead."

It took me a while to process what he was saying. "Do you mean you left me at the hospital with no intention of coming back…ever?"

"Exactly. I never even asked about you for two full weeks. I just ran."

Holy shit. I felt like someone had slugged me in the stomach.

"Finally, I came to my senses. I returned to the hospital and found the nurse who'd delivered you. I begged her to tell me where you were. I figured you'd be in foster care somewhere with the state. The nurse pulled me aside and explained she'd taken pity on me. She'd forged my name on a few documents to make it look like I was a normal, caring father, and she'd taken you home herself. Then she returned you to me. She…"

Fuck. My dad was losing it, crying openly into his glass. I'd never seen my father cry. I circumnavigated the counter and snaked my arm around his neck.

"That's when and why I named you Grateful. There was no one more grateful than I was to have you and for the nurse who saved our family."

Eyes wide, I wondered how different things must have been back then for a nurse to take a chance like that. She could've gone to prison and lost her license. The story was almost unbelievable, but then so was the sight of my father sobbing in my arms. "So that's why you sent the nurse a card every year on my birthday."

"You remember that?"

I nodded. "Who was the nurse, Dad? Can I meet her?"

"No. I'm sorry. I'd intended to introduce you someday, but she passed away so suddenly." He slid the scrapbook in front of him and started flipping through the pages. "I guess this was her way of remembering you. She didn't have any children of her own."

The room began to spin. "What?"

"The nurse who kept you in my absence was Prudence Meriwether. You're living in her house."

I plopped down on the stool next to Dad, snatched his scotch, and tossed it to the back of my throat. I coughed at the harsh burn of the liquor.

"Prudence and I always had a close relationship after what happened with you. She didn't have any other family, so she left the house to me. She would've been so happy to know you were using it. God, I wish I'd had the guts to introduce you while she was still alive. I just couldn't bring myself to do it. I knew if I did, I'd have to explain, and it kills me to admit the truth. It kills me." His shoulders bobbed with the rhythm of his sobbing.

Now, I considered blabbing to my dad that Prudence had never left this house. I really did. I opened my mouth several times to broach the subject. But I didn't. I told myself it was because he'd never believe me, but it was bigger than that. I didn't tell because my ghosts were my secret. As crazy as it sounds, some deep-set instinct kept me from sharing Prudence's ghostly presence.

Instead, I patted him on the back. "Dad, I can't say I'm not totally floored right now. But I'm a nurse, okay? I see what the death of a loved one does to people. I can't really say I understand, not personally, because I've never been through it. I guess what I'm trying to say is…the important thing is… You came back for me. I mean, you were a good dad to me when it counted. I don't even remember those first weeks."

He buried his face in his hands. I noticed his glass was empty again.

"I forgive you, Dad. Okay? I forgive you."

The hug he gave me made me cry. It was so desperate. My chest hurt to think he'd been carrying this secret and the resulting guilt around for so many years.

"You're a good kid, Grateful. A really good kid." Dad pulled himself together, smoothing his suit coat down and wiping under his eyes. "I should go." Standing, his realtor self snapped back on his frame like a Lego part. He ran a hand through his hair and gave me one last hug.

His hand was on the doorknob when I remembered there was more I needed to ask him. "Hey, do you know if more keys came with this place? I can't get the attic door open."

His mouth tightened and his eyebrows knitted together. "I know for certain there are no other keys. I'm careful about labeling everything. Who knows where Prudence kept it? Go ahead and call a locksmith if you want. I'll pay for it. Going to need it if I sell the place someday, anyway."

"Okay."

He left, looking as fresh as when he'd come, like he'd never had a major heart-to-heart with his only daughter. That was my dad.

I watched him pull out of my drive, thinking about what Logan had said. After he'd told Prudence I was Robert Knight's daughter, the baby she'd cared for twenty-two years ago, he'd said she remembered me. The ghost in my attic knew me. She'd helped deliver me.

Unfortunately, I still didn't understand what any of this had to do with Rick, or why Logan was being so secretive about why he was in my attic. In fact, I was more confused than ever.

* * * * *

"Prudence was the nurse who delivered me. What does it mean, Logan?"

Logan sat across from me at the dining room table, watching me eat a late dinner he'd prepared. It was some sort of chicken dish that melted in my mouth and tasted of butter and fresh herbs. He'd insisted, and I couldn't refuse.

"I told you I can't say," he muttered.

"Can you ask Prudence to talk to me?"

He hesitated, looked away. "Sure. I'll ask."

I rolled another delicious bite around in my mouth, amazed a ghost had prepared it. "Don't you remember anything about your life at all?" I asked.

"I see bits and pieces sometimes. I know things about eating. Like how to cook and what wine goes with what dessert. I think I liked motorcycles. Everything…all my memories are loose inside my head. I can't connect them logically."

Part of me could relate. Some days I didn't know who I was either. The arc of my life just seemed to happen with no driving force behind it, as if I were going along with a script rather than meeting it head-on. Part of it I could blame on being in my early twenties, but the rest was all me.

"In an odd way, I can empathize," I said. "I may know my name, but sometimes I wonder if I will ever understand who I really am." The words surprised me as they poured out of my mouth. What was it about Logan that made me share the most intimate details of my life with him?

"I have a vague sense that I was lonely when I was alive. There's a hollowness at the center of me. I don't remember what my life was like, but something about me seems disconnected. It's hard to explain."

I rubbed a circle over my sternum with my palm. I could relate to that too. "Gary did that to me. Maybe you had a similar situation before you, um, died."

Logan's despondent eyes fixated on his interlaced fingers. "I wish I remembered."

"I wish I could forget."

Glowing green eyes met mine. Logan and I had a moment of connection, a communion of thoughts that conveyed a mutual desire to comfort, although no words were said. I reached forward to place my hand over his, and my flesh sank through him. A tingling pressure eased over my skin until my palm hit the table.

"Oh. Sorry." I retracted my fingers.

He shrugged awkwardly. The room fell silent. I ate the last bite off my plate.

"Would you like to play a game?" I asked.

"Sure," he said, brightening in his chair. "What did you have in mind?"

"There's a pool table downstairs. Eight ball?"

Logan nodded. "I remember. I remember how to play."

He followed me downstairs, and I racked the balls. In order to manipulate the pool cue, Logan had to disappear. I knew from the break I was in trouble. Whoever Logan had been in his life, he was damned good at pool.

"Do you have another date with the caretaker?" he asked out of the blue.

"Uh, yes. Tomorrow night."

He lined up another shot. "I've warned you, Grateful—"

"I'm a big girl, Logan. I can make my own decisions."

"Did anything, um, happen on your first date?"

My face was on fire. I placed my hand on my cheek. "That is none of your business."

"Why are you turning red? Oh...fuck..."

Embarrassed, I felt obligated to defend my honor. "We fooled around, but you know, nothing more."

A relieved sigh came from his side of the table.

What? Who did he think he was prying into my private life? If he wanted me to stay away from Rick, he needed to give a better explanation. "Why do you care so much, Logan?" I snapped.

He formed next to me, his aura burning brighter than I'd ever seen it. As if on impulse, he leaned in and kissed me. The cool vibration of his lips sent tingles over my scalp and down my spine.

When he pulled away, he broke apart and sifted into the air vent.

So much for my theory that Logan's intentions were solely platonic. Body or no body, his kiss was more than friendly.

CHAPTER 11
I Don't Even Get Dinner First?

Friday was usually my day off, but I'd picked up an extra shift. I was glad I did. Logan had made me breakfast again, but I avoided him. Confused about the kiss and not wanting to broach the subject of my date with Rick, I tossed a quick "thank you" over my shoulder as I took the scone and coffee he'd made to go, never giving him an opening for conversation.

Similarly, I worked late so that I would be rushed getting ready. I showered and primped, slipping into my favorite little black dress as quickly as possible. The material was the perfect balance of stretch and drape, capable of hiding an array of imperfections while simultaneously enhancing my body's best assets. In other words, it was the perfect dress for another hot date with

Rick. I zipped on my favorite knee-high black boots and checked myself out in the mirror.

"You look amazing." Logan's voice startled me, and I turned toward the door to see him leaning against the frame. The botanical print from the hall was barely visible through his cloudy form. *Shit.* I felt like a teenager caught sneaking out.

"Thanks," I said. "Hey, you're out early."

"I wanted to see you before you left."

"It's good to see you, too."

"Can I ask you something?" He stepped into the room, but in his current form, it was more like he floated.

"I'm kind of in a hurry—"

"If I were human," he blurted, "could you see us, you know, dating?"

I thought about that for a minute. I didn't want to lie. If Logan's ghost looked anything like he did when he was alive, then he was undeniably attractive. I'm sure if I'd met him in the flesh, physical attraction would've been a real possibility. Logan was a kind soul, with or without a body. "I think when you kissed me last night that it was more than a friendly kiss. I think you meant it. Like when a man kisses a woman."

"Yes. I did."

I tucked my hair behind my ear and bit my lip. "I was afraid you might say that. It doesn't feel right to pursue something with you. I'm sorry."

"Is it because I don't have a body?"

"No," I said. "It's not just because you're a ghost. You're a good man, Logan, and I do find you attractive. I'm just not…available."

The expression that rippled through him made his aura glow brighter and the lights blink. "Because of the caretaker." He said "caretaker" like it was a curse.

"I need to go." I grabbed my purse off the dresser and passed him to get to the door.

"This can't wait. There's something else I need to tell you."

I stopped in the hallway. "What is it?"

"You asked me to talk to Prudence."

"Yes! Will she speak with me?"

He frowned. "Only in the attic. Unfortunately, you'll need a key. The door that opens for me is a metaphysical one. It won't work for you."

"She's come out before. Why can't she talk to me down here?"

"Prudence has different rules. The key is like an, um, pass to speak with her."

"Huh. That's why she was like '*find the key*' blah-blah-blah."

"Uh-huh."

"Crap. I haven't been able to find it. I'll have to look later. I'm really late." I strode toward the staircase.

Logan rippled next to me. His ghostly hands balled into fists. "You need to ask the caretaker to tell you the truth."

I paused in the foyer. "What would Rick know about any of this?"

"Listen, I can't say any more than I have. But there's something I want you to know."

"What?"

"The caretaker has a story about how things are and how things will be. I just want you to know that as far as I'm concerned, you have a choice about how this story ends. You should choose what's best for you."

"What? What choice? What is Rick going to tell me?"

Logan shook his head, looked at the floor, and dissolved without uttering another word.

"That was childish," I yelled at the ceiling. "If you have something to say, just say it. Enough with these cryptic messages." Arms crossed, I stomped my foot. "See you later, Logan. Much later. Maybe then you'll give me a clue what you're talking about."

I tucked my purse under my arm and headed out the door toward Rick's place. Of all the houses in the world, I had to move into the one with some wicked ghostly mystery. If I didn't get some answers soon, I was going to wig out. I mean, I think I'd been more than patient with the supernatural in my life. What was this big secret? Logan said that Rick would tell me, but as far as I knew, Rick didn't even know about Logan. And how did Prudence play into all of this?

Beyond the bridge, I could hear the wind chimes singing in the evening breeze. I stopped in front of the door to Rick's stone cottage but was distracted by a faint glow moving behind the cemetery gates across the street. It looked like someone walking with a candle in the distance.

"Rick?" I called toward the cemetery.

"I'm here," Rick said from behind me.

I turned around to face a work of art in the frame of the doorway. His white shirt stretched across his chest as if the fabric itself enjoyed the feel of him. The denim of his jeans hugged his narrow hips and hung to his bare feet. The material looked silky, maybe something designed in Europe that you'd see a movie star wear. For someone who worked with his hands, Rick was oddly fashionable.

"I thought I saw someone in the cemetery. I thought it was you."

Rick looked over my shoulder toward the gate. His face hardened; his gray eyes turning black and as cold as ice. I blinked twice, thinking it must be a trick of the light.

As quickly as his expression had changed, he warmed again and escorted me into his home. "I am sure it's nothing. Come in and make yourself at home."

As he swept his hand toward his living room, for the first time I noticed how graceful he was. Rick didn't move like a man who planted trees and repositioned headstones for a living. He moved like a ballet dancer, muscles long and lean. I tried not to stare, but the word *sexy* was an understatement and his cologne, the smell of a walk through the forest, had wrapped itself around me. My reaction was an instant and illogical lust.

"Sorry I'm late. I would have called you, but I didn't have your number," I said, moving into the room.

"I don't have one," he said.

"Huh? You don't have a phone at all? Not even a cell phone?"

"No." He shook his head.

"Isn't that inconvenient?"

He took a deep breath and blew it out slowly. "I've always found that handling things in person is more effective."

I frowned. No phone. Rick was a mystery.

"May I get you something to drink?" he asked.

"Maybe a glass of wine?"

"Of course."

He disappeared into the kitchen and returned with two glasses of red. I recognized mine as my favorite Shiraz, but his must have been different. It was darker, thicker, maybe a merlot. I took a sip from my glass and sat at a small table he'd set near the kitchen. Candles dripped wax over silver candlesticks at the center. The long edges of the tablecloth draped across my knee.

"What's that wonderful smell?"

"Roast lamb. You said it was your favorite. It will be ready in a moment. I hope you have an appetite."

"Yes. I do." I meant them to be innocent words, but even I could hear the sexual promise in them as they hit the air between us. I was baffled by myself, this uncontrollable desire I had for this man. With deep breaths, I tried to slow my racing heart.

Rick lifted my hand from the table. "Would you like to dance?"

"There's no music."

With graceful strides, he crossed the room and hit the button on a silver box on the bookshelf. The stereo began to play Latin music. I wasn't familiar with the tune, and I didn't speak Spanish, so the meaning was a mystery, but it was the type you would expect to hear in a dance club, perfectly at home with pressed bodies, heat, and sweat.

"Is this to your liking?"

"Sure, but I can't dance. I tried once and almost hurt someone." I was just being honest. If you mapped relative coordination on a graph, I would be way behind the bell curve.

"You won't hurt me." He laughed and offered me his long, graceful fingers. "I'll teach you."

My hand slid into his in a natural way as if we'd held hands for years rather than days. With a short jerk, he pulled me flush against his chest and placed his free hand in the small of my back. His hips pressed against mine, guiding my movements.

Left, together, right, hip, step back, hip, step forward. I had no idea what I was doing. My feet fell clumsily on either side of his right knee, and I tried my best to keep up without tripping. Suddenly, the five-inch heels on my boots seemed like a bad idea. The music pounded in my ears, his heart beat against my chest, and I ineptly followed him, even though I had no idea how to do the dance.

Then the oddest thing happened. One minute I was tripping over his feet, the only thing keeping me upright was his hand on my back, and the next minute he was inside my head. Pictures of what he was about to do, how he would move next, slid across my mind and somehow I knew just how I was supposed to react as if he were whispering my part into my ear. I fell into pace with him, my hips gyrating against his in a way I would have never thought possible. We circled his living room, dancing and spinning until the song came to conclusion with two crashing beats and me bent backward in a low dip, panting into Rick's neck.

I tilted my chin up and met his gaze. Whatever connection we'd had while we were dancing was still there, and I knew he would kiss me. He did, long and deep until heat flowed straight to my core. But then I saw what he wanted, a play by play of his fantasy.

Just like the dance, my body responded. My lips crashed into his as I raked my nails over his shirt. Soft fabric over hard muscle teased my fingertips. Without him saying a word, I knew he didn't want me to take it off. I skimmed past the buttons, my hands traveling around his sides and down his back to give the luscious mound of his ass a squeeze. My head felt light, like that day in the cemetery, as if I was a little drunk, but better. Instead of everything seeming fuzzy, each moment was brilliantly clear, every smell and sound more alive.

His fingers twisted into my hair. "*Mi cielo.*"

I unbuttoned his pants and dropped to my knees. His jeans slid to the floor with me. Kneeling in front of him, I had a moment of anxiety. He was erect and gigantic. His shaft was as thick as my wrist and stretched almost to his navel where the darker swell mushroomed at the tip. But my brain was promising ecstasy, and the fantasy played in my head like a favorite tune. Slowly, I slid my lips around him. Intense pleasure bloomed between my legs as if he were feeding his enjoyment directly into my head. I sucked hard, taking him deep inside my throat and moaned.

Pure bliss. I went to work. Anything I did to him echoed through me, spurring me on. I hollowed my cheeks and found a rhythm, sucking and licking, swirling my tongue around the tip. I stroked a finger up his inner thigh, teasing between his legs with one hand and wrapping my other around the part of him that wouldn't fit into my mouth. Harder, faster, around and around.

A guttural whimper escaped Rick's throat, elation crafted into a command that only made me work harder to please him. He cradled my neck as the orgasm rippled through *me*. I tossed my head back into his hands and felt his release echo my own. Through half-closed eyes, I watched him shiver, then collapse to his knees in front of me.

CHAPTER 12
More Than I Wanted To Know

When he'd recovered, Rick retrieved a towel from his bedroom and cleaned me up. The connection faded gradually, and my logical mind brought me back to the reality of what just happened.

"I...I've never done anything like that before," I said. Heat crawled up my neck and settled in my cheeks.

His eyes widened and he blew a puff of air out his nose, tipping his head to the side. "You are very good at it, *mi cielo*."

"That was, I mean, it wasn't... You were in my head! What was that?"

"I think dinner is ready. Let me make you a plate."

He walked into the kitchen, but the more time I had to think about it, the louder every alarm in my head blared. "Rick, did you drug me?"

"No! I would never do such a thing," he snapped.

"Then tell me what that was!" I yelled. Something in me knew this wasn't normal. I had wanted it to happen. I'd enjoyed it. I didn't regret it. But something had lowered my inhibitions. What happened was almost beyond my control.

"I was hoping this conversation could wait a little longer," he said.

"So, you do have something to tell me! A secret."

"You know?"

"Logan told me."

"Who is Logan?"

"Never mind. Say it. What is it that you are supposed to tell me?"

"It is about you, Grateful. About who you are and where you come from."

"What?" I narrowed my eyes, feeling my entire face tense.

"Please, sit down." He waved his hand toward a chair at the table.

"I'm listening," I said, taking a seat. I was fully dressed. He was naked from the waist down.

Rick reached for his glass, draining the thick red liquid in two swallows. "Remember when I told you about Reverend Monk and the people of Red Grove? About how they were starving to death?"

"I remember." What did this have to do with the fact that he just mind-fucked me?

"Things were miserable. Children were dying. The congregation had prayed and prayed. No help came. Reverend Monk decided the drought was the work of a witch, and it so happened that there *was* a witch in Red Grove."

I rested my chin in my palm. "You mean a person who practices Wicca, right? There are a few nurses on my floor who are Wiccan."

"No. I mean a queen of the damned. A natural sorceress so strong that no practice could define her."

"Oh, come on." I rolled my eyes.

"I'm telling you the truth."

"You're saying there was a real spell-casting witch in Red Grove? Don't insult my intelligence."

I tried to stand, but he stretched across the table and pressed me back into my seat. "Calling her a witch is an understatement. Her name was Isabella Lockhart, and she was more powerful than any to walk this earth. She was a sorceress of the dead and, although Monk didn't know it, she had been protecting the town of Red Grove for years from the supernatural beings passing through these woods."

I pursed my lips. "So, did Monk burn her at the stake or what?"

Rick grimaced. "Monk had a secret. One night he took a long walk in the forest behind the chapel, on the land that is now Monk's Hill cemetery. He was praying for a way to keep his parishioners alive, some source of food to help them through the winter. Reverend Monk would later tell his people that he met an angel in those woods. But the creature Monk met was no angel. Monk came face to face with a demon in disguise. The demon gave Monk a book, *The Book of Flesh and Bone*. Inside the book, dark spells were written, spells to bind death to life, spells to raise the dead.

"He brought the book back to his church believing it was a book of prayers. As Monk read the book, an idea came to him, a way to end his people's suffering. On October thirty-first, sixteen ninety-two, the townspeople, at the direction of Monk, marched with their torches to the home of Isabella Lockhart, chanting prayers from *The Book of Flesh and Bone*—prayers that were actually spells. They bound her to her human form, preventing her escape, making her vulnerable to the angry crowd."

Rick folded his hands across the table, eyes red around the edges. I knew he loved history, but the passion he infused into the legend seemed a little cray-cray. I squirmed in my seat under the intensity he was putting off and wished he'd just get to the point.

"They burned her alive, Grateful, at the center of what is now the cemetery, right in front of the church."

My hand went to my throat. I heard my breath rush into my lungs on a gasp. I didn't know why I was getting so wrapped up in the obviously made-up story, but the thought of someone being burned alive yards from where I was sitting left me riveted.

"A sorceress as strong as Isabella could not be killed by natural means. But with the book's words repeated on the lips of the parishioners, the assault was supernatural. She was burned in demon fire."

"So the witch was killed. Let me guess, it didn't fix the drought."

A dark chuckle crossed his lips. "No. But it was not the drought that killed them all."

"Huh?"

"*The Book of Flesh and Bone* demands a high price. All who chanted the spell died—and by their blood leaching into the ground and the death of the witch, the magic opened a gateway to hell. The earth shook and cracked open. All of the supernatural creatures Isabella had protected the townsfolk from for so many years emerged from the cracked ground and returned to the dark forest."

"Supernatural? What, like vampires?" I laughed. I wasn't sure where Rick was going with this. I suspected he was messing with me, trying to distract me from what was happening between us.

"Vampires, zombies, ghouls—all types of unholy beasts. Monk never told his people about the true source of the book and never warned them of the consequences. His people never asked. They didn't want to know. Innocent blood was spilled with an evil spell that robbed the town of the one person who could control the supernatural element here, cursing this land forever."

"Cursed? Is this the big secret? I'm living on cursed land?"

"Before she died, Isabella cast one last spell. Long before the day she burned, she had planted the seed, the foundation to execute the magic. There was a man, a lover. She was betrothed to be married." Rick stood and started unbuttoning his shirt. He turned his back to me. "He knew she was different but didn't suspect how different."

He tossed his shirt aside. The beautiful muscles of his back peaked and grooved under perfect tanned skin, a work of art. I was suddenly very aware that he was naked.

I shook my head. He still hadn't explained what had happened tonight. "What does this story have to do with me?"

Rick began again, but his voice sounded heavy, and he spoke toward the kitchen as if he didn't want to meet my eyes. "The night they burned her, the lover tried to stop them, but he was outnumbered. They made him watch while she burned. He would have gladly taken her place." He swallowed hard.

I stiffened. The way he told it sounded like he was there. It was creepy.

"The flames ate her body. All was lost. She was dead. But then her charred hand lifted from her side and pointed at him. With her last breath she uttered the words, 'Akmut ghut rae mud ed tyn.' A ray of light burst from her hand and cut into the man's chest, directly over his heart."

I swallowed and tucked my hair behind my ears. "What did it mean?"

"'Akmut ghut rae mud ed tyn' means roughly 'caretaker of the light, always.'" Slowly, he pivoted to face me and traced a finger over the scythe-shaped scar on his chest.

Pain sliced through my head, and I rubbed my temple. Goosebumps marched up my arms.

Rick continued in a rush. "At first, the man didn't understand what had happened to him, but he learned. Isabella had stored a piece of her soul inside his body, along with her magic. He used that magic to seal the cemetery and imprison the supernatural within its gates. And today he keeps the balance, policing the supernatural with her and in her absence."

"This is stupid. We were up there yesterday, and the cemetery was completely normal. Not a ghoulie in sight."

He ignored my comment and continued. "Whoever sent the demon to give Monk *The Book of Flesh and Bone* wanted Isabella dead. But what they didn't know was that by killing Isabella the way Monk did, he bound her eternally to this place. The Monk's Hill witch, as she came to call herself, oversees this hellmouth. No soul goes in or out without her knowledge. She is judge, jury, and executioner, but she is not immortal. So when she dies, her caretaker holds a piece of her soul until she returns. And she always returns to me. All I have to do is wait."

"To you? What are you talking about?"

His gray eyes settled on my face. "I am the caretaker, Grateful." His finger tapped the scar on his chest. "And you are the Monk's Hill witch. Your soul has returned to me again as it does each time you die. Your work awaits you. All you have to do is accept your role, and it will be done."

"This isn't funny."

"I assure you, I'm not trying to amuse."

The room spun. The walls pressed in around me. My head pounded like it might split open. I stood up and backed toward the door. "You're insane."

"Think about it. Have you any other explanation for our connection? The physical and mental link we have is because we've already spent lifetimes together. We've been married. We could be married again."

"Married? I've barely known you a week!" I held the sides of my pounding head. "Besides, you took me to Monk's Hill. There were no vampires. We had lunch in front of the chapel."

"They come at night. The sun seals the hellmouth, but after sunset, it opens again."

"I won't listen to this." I backed toward the door and placed my hand on the knob.

"Grateful, please—"

I couldn't take any more. I had to get out of there. Out the door and into the night I ran, but I did not go home. I ran straight across the street to the source of the lie, the cemetery. I was surprised to find the gate open. During our date, Rick had made a point of keeping it locked. Maybe he'd wanted me to enter. I cast the notion aside.

He was behind me the instant I crossed the threshold, closing and locking the gate from the inside. Great, now I was trapped inside the graveyard with a lunatic. This

might not have been my wisest decision. I sprinted away
from him the best I could in my high-heeled boots, up the
steep gravel path toward Monk's Chapel. Somehow, with
blister-inducing effort, I made it to the top without
breaking a heel.

I glanced back but didn't see Rick. Considering he
could easily catch me with these patent leather torture
devices zipped to my feet, I hoped he'd given up and gone
home. Breath coming in huffs, my legs burned from the
effort of the climb and I pitched forward, resting my
hands on my knees while I caught my breath. The night
was quiet except for the stones under my shifting feet and
the persistent song of crickets.

Under the light of the full moon, the white walls of the
chapel seemed to glow. Straightening, I moved toward it,
thinking I'd have a rest inside. The door was locked. *Crap.*
I pressed my back against the wood and looked out over
the graveyard. All was quiet. Nothing. After this, Rick
would have to drop his ludicrous story and tell me the
truth, if I even cared to hear it. At the moment, I was
leaning toward cutting the crazy man out of my life for
good, although the thought made my chest feel heavy.

The hedges to my right rustled and two large yellow
eyes blinked in my direction. A raccoon? The animal
turned, and the moon reflected off silver skin. An
opossum. A very large opossum. A loud snap to my left
attracted my attention away from whatever slithered from
the bushes. The looming silhouette of a man moved
toward me, too far away for me to make out his face.

"Rick, is that you?" I called, but if it was Rick, he didn't answer.

"Excuse me, is there something I can help you with?" said a smooth voice from beside me. I whirled. A pale man with slicked-back red hair and luminescent blue eyes smiled at me.

"What are you doing in here?" I asked him.

"Waiting."

"For what?" He was in the middle of a cemetery at night. What could he be waiting for? I hugged my chest.

"Something to eat."

"There's a soup kitchen downtown," I blurted, but even as the words came out I had the awful feeling there was something very wrong with this man. I was a nurse. I assessed people for a living. His skin was too pale, his eyes too large in his head, and his chest wasn't moving. Whatever was in front of me was not breathing.

"I won't be needing a soup kitchen," he said and peeled his lips back from razor-sharp incisors. He held out his hand. "Why don't you join me?"

Did he assume I couldn't see his fangs, or did he just believe I'd be too frightened to run? I shuffled away from his hand and turned to bolt. My face smacked into someone.

"Oh, excuse me," I said automatically, then looked at what I'd hit.

Rotting flesh, swimming milky eyeballs, decomposing clothes, and a smell that I only recognized from my time working in the morgue. I was face to face with the walking dead.

I screamed, dodging left. The zombie's sluggish grasp brushed the top of my hair. Laughing, the vampire stepped toward me, slowly, deliberately. The silver animal rushed from the bushes, pursuing me with flashing claws and teeth. At the competition for my flesh, the vamp hissed and swiped the creature aside. I used the distraction to scurry down the pebble pathway, but the gate was too far off. I'd never outrun them. Worse, dark figures rose from the tombstones ahead, turning dead eyes in my direction. My heart fluttered in panic. Ice water filled my veins.

"Rick!" I screamed. "Riiiiick! I believe you. I believe you!"

Above me, an eerie wind blew my hair forward. *Wump-wump-wump*. The sound of beating wings closed in. I wrestled my hair back from my eyes, while my feet continued their forward pursuit, and turned my face to the sky. A monstrous, leathery wing passed over me.

Shit! Things in here could fly? I waved my hands above my head as if I could shoo the flying beast away and wailed loud enough to wake any dead who weren't already chasing me.

Crack. My right heel snapped off my boot, sending me flying. Ass over teacup, I somersaulted down the pebble path. I landed on my back with a clear view of the source of the flapping. Like nothing I'd ever seen before, the thing had fur *and* scales, with a barbed tail. The beast descended from above and landed on the path. Dragon-like, the huge creature flapped its leathery wings between Monk's Chapel and me.

The giant silver opossum thing pounced, ducking around the dragon-beast in pursuit of my fallen body. I covered my head with my arms. The strike never came. Instead, an eerie shriek filled the night as the dragon scooped the silver beast into its reptilian jaws and swallowed it whole. Sobbing, I crab-walked toward the gate. A dead hand landed on my shoulder. Zombie! Before I could scream, the dragon's jaws clamped around the zombie's body. Black blood sprayed across my torso.

I scrambled to my feet, desperate not to be the dragon's next victim. I wasn't fast enough.

Talons closed around my torso. I pounded on the paws and yanked on the fur to no avail. The monster took to the sky, me screaming beneath it. Where was it taking me? Would I become a meal for some baby dragon creature?

Ugg. I wished more than anything that I could just pass out, that the fear would kill me before this creature or its offspring ripped me apart. But before I could process what was happening, it dropped me on the grass in front of Rick's cottage and landed on the road a few feet away.

When I realized sharp teeth weren't impaling me, I stopped screaming and pushed myself up in the grass. Dots of black blood speckled my arms and the front of my dress, but I was otherwise unharmed.

The monster sniffed me from the road. Close up, the face was more like a dog's than a dragon's, with glossy black eyes, a leathery snout, and tufts of black hair sprouting from the tops of its ears. More hair grew between its scales, which ran from the jowls all the way back to the tip of the beast's barbed tail. It plopped down on the pavement. I scrambled backward toward Rick's porch.

With a flap of its leather wings, the beast's skin started to bubble, its blood boiling under the surface. The thing folded in on itself, the head tucking into the middle and the tail wrapping around the body. Under the skin, bones cracked and organs rearranged. To my amazement, when this process was done, what was left looked exactly like a naked man bent at the waist.

When the man stood up, everything I knew about the world crumbled to dust. From his black wavy hair to the sickle-shaped scar on his chest, there was no denying who it was.

"Rick, oh my God! *Oh my God*," I yelled. "What the hell are you?" I struggled to my feet, limping on my broken heel.

"I told you, Grateful. I am your caretaker. If you would step inside, I will explain further. I realize this may come as somewhat of a shock." He positioned himself between my house and me.

"You kissed me. You touched me. We did...things together! You're not human, are you?" I was near panic again. My heart was threatening to explode out of my chest.

"No. I am immortal and you, *mi cielo*, are eternal."

Rick tried to take a step toward me. I jumped in the opposite direction. "Don't touch me. Don't ever touch me."

He halted his pursuit, but I could see the hurt in his eyes, the absolute pain. I didn't care. He'd led me to believe he was *human*. Why hadn't he told me this on day one? Why the long talk at my place? The picnic? I thought about his hands on me, his lips, the feel of him in my mouth. I'd done those things with a shape-shifter, a monster.

I limped across the bridge toward my house, moving around him in a wide arc. I wished I could wake up from all of this, to open my eyes and know that I lived in a world without ghosts or zombies. My head hurt. My brain couldn't process everything I'd just learned. One thought kept irking me above all the others—Michelle was right.

Like every other man in my life, Rick had turned out to be a total nightmare.

CHAPTER 13
My Ghost Comforts Me

I stumbled through the front door of my house and locked it behind me. Not that a deadbolt could stop anything I'd seen tonight. Or could it? I didn't know the rules of the game I was playing. Obviously, the unholy couldn't get through the gate, but was that because of the lock or because of Rick's magic?

"They can't come in uninvited," Logan said from the stairs.

I turned toward him, shaking so forcefully it was hard to form words. "Wha-What?"

"Prudence says in your last life you put a spell around this place. Nothing preternatural can come in without an invitation."

I hugged myself. "But what about you?"

"I'm natural, a human spirit. Still, I came through the portal in the attic. I'm not sure even *I* could walk through the front door."

He abruptly disappeared. Before I had a chance to ask where he'd gone, a plush blanket floated toward me from the family room and wrapped itself around my shoulders.

"Sit down, Grateful. Let me make you a cup of hot chocolate." Logan's disembodied voice came from the kitchen.

I pulled the blanket tighter around me and took a seat on a stool behind the island. "Is it true? All of it?"

"I'm not sure how to answer that. Without knowing what the caretaker told you, I can hardly say which parts are true. Plus, I've only been here a few months and the sole source of my knowledge is Prudence."

A pot on the stove filled itself with milk, cocoa, vanilla, and sugar. From the drawer on the left, a spoon floated to the pot and began stirring the mixture. There was no one holding the spoon. The animated utensil didn't scare me. I'd grown accustomed to Logan the way you do a hot bath, immersing yourself gradually. Now his presence comforted me.

"Did Reverend Monk unleash the unholy on Red Grove?"

"Yes, I'm afraid so. He wanted to save his followers, but when you give the devil an inch, he takes a mile. Monk unknowingly opened a portal to the underworld. Every vile creature—vampires, zombies, ghouls, demons— all of them have access to our world at sunset. Only the caretaker and, of course, you when you've been here, keep the world safe from their menace."

"So you think I'm the Monk's Hill witch?"

"Oh, I'm certain of it."

"But I can't be. Prudence lived here before me. She must have been the witch."

"Prudence was never the witch, Grateful. It's always been you. You planned for your own reincarnation. You gave Prudence the power to maintain and protect this house because it is your seat of magic. The only trouble was, you couldn't foresee that Prudence would die two years before your time to come back."

"That doesn't make any sense. I knew Prudence when I was a baby. I couldn't have passed her any magic."

"No, I think she worked with the old you. You were both nurses at St. John's in your last life. That's how you met each other before you were born."

I tried to wrap my head around the idea of being alive before, of having a relationship with Prudence when she was a young woman. "What does the witch even do? I saw that thing Rick turns into. I hardly think he needs my help."

A mug floated down from the cupboard and the cocoa poured itself, releasing tendrils of steam that curled oddly against the force that was Logan. Once the pan was back on the stove, his body formed and hardened into a solid-looking version of himself.

He leaned his elbows on the counter. "Think of the cemetery as a prison for the unholy. The caretaker is law enforcement. The witch is the law. When a supernatural being steps out of line, she judges if they are guilty or innocent. If they're innocent, they walk. If they're guilty, she sentences them to the hellmouth. She decides. The caretaker enforces her decision."

I took a long, deep drink. I wasn't the judgmental type. Could I send someone's soul, vampire or not, to hell if I had to? I didn't think so.

"Rick said that when I was Isabella Lockhart I saved myself by storing a piece of my soul inside of him."

"Isabella made Rick the vessel to contain the immortal part of her outside of her human body."

I swallowed hard. "And Prudence has another part?"

"Not a part of your soul but of your magic. Think of Rick as the key and you as the lock and the house as the box that holds the magic. Prudence took care of the box."

I wasn't sure I followed his correlation, but I had a deeper question to ask. "But if a piece of my soul is in Rick and another part of who I was is in this house, what's left inside of me?" My voice gave out with the last words, but Logan seemed to understand anyway. Was I some kind of half-person? Was I living my life with less of a soul than everyone else?

He cupped my face with his hand, a warm tingle registering on my cheek. "Oh, Grateful, some part of you may be Isabella Lockhart but another is Grateful Knight, a new person with a new body, living in a new time. If you don't take up this burden, life will go on. The caretaker will make do, and the part of you that is the witch will transfer to another host. You have a choice. You don't have to accept the power back. You don't have to do this."

"I don't have to be the witch?"

"No."

I exhaled. The tension in my shoulders eased slightly, but a rogue thought niggled at the back of my brain. I was forgetting something. I sipped my cocoa and pretended my insides weren't writhing with unrest. It came to me with the rich chocolate aftertaste.

"What about you? Why are you in the witch's attic?"

He folded his arms across his chest. "The witch is the sorter."

I covered my mouth with my hand. "Get. Out. *I* am the sorter. Prudence was trying to tell me from the very beginning!"

"Sometimes people die unexpectedly, and their souls don't know where to go. The witch helps them. As the ruler of the hellmouth, she has the power to usher the supernatural between heaven and hell. She can do that for us ghosts too. She's the only one who can do it for us."

The implications of what Logan said weaseled into my brain. "So, I'm supposed to sort you."

He nodded with the woeful expression of someone breaking bad news.

"Do you want to be sorted?"

He shifted his hip against the counter. "It depends. I'd rather not end up in hell."

I scowled at the possibility. "But I could decide that. How do I sort you?"

"First, you'd accept your power back from Rick and Prudence. Then you'd give me a name and command my soul in one direction or the other."

"I've already given you a name."

"It has to be my full name, and you have to accept the power first."

"Then how do I accept the power? How do I become the witch?" I asked.

My ghost looked at the floor. His body flickered between levels of transparency. He didn't answer me.

"What are you keeping from me, Logan?"

"I just don't think you should be forced into something you might not want to do."

I slapped my hand on the counter and asked again. "When you say I need to accept the power back from Rick and Prudence, what does that mean?"

Logan looked me in the eye. The thing about knowing a ghost is that you see straight through to their soul. Logan seemed to want nothing but the best for me.

"Please, Logan. Let it be my decision. Tell me."

"You have to have sex with the caretaker."

It took a moment for that to sink in. So that's why Logan had been so interested in my physical relationship with Rick. If I'd had sex with him, I might already be the witch. The thought of sex with the man who turned into that thing, that monster, made me nauseous. It must have shown on my face because Logan wrapped his hands around mine, a gesture that sent a soft vibration through my skin.

"You don't have to do it," he said again.

"Sex? That's the only way?"

"It's not just sex, Grateful. It's what the sex means. Because of what he is, he will take your blood. He will give you his. It's a lifetime commitment to this role, to this state of being."

I grimaced. "Blood? Why does he need my blood?"

"The caretaker is an immortal. He drinks blood, and drinking his blood will give you power."

"What, like a vampire?"

"No, vampires are from the underworld. They live on blood like leeches and are not nearly as powerful as a caretaker. Rick can feed on blood, or the undead, or sex. He will drink your blood to bind you to him, not for nourishment."

My body stiffened. I was chilled from the bones out. More than anything, I just wanted to go home, to my first, real home with my dad, where everything was safe and taken care of. I didn't want to be the Monk's Hill witch. I certainly didn't want to "do it" with a blood-sucking immortal who turned into a zombie-eating beast after dark. It was disgusting enough that I'd had oral sex with him.

I stared into my finished hot chocolate, but there were no answers at the bottom of the mug. "Is it true that I was married to Rick? In another life?"

"Yes. That is true. But you don't have to make the same commitment in this one. You don't have to make the same choices."

Logan's face was close enough to mine that his energy created a static charge that pulled me toward him. His expression was pure concern. Ghost or not, Logan was an honorable man.

I understood what he was saying. I even agreed to a certain extent. But I was a product of my upbringing, and I'd been taught not to shirk responsibility. I was in this mess because I'd decided not to file bankruptcy, to take full accountability for what happened with Gary. It wasn't in my nature to take the easy way out.

"Logan, what happens to you if you don't get sorted?"

He flickered in front of me but did not answer. The mug became much more interesting to him, and he refused to meet my eyes.

"Tell me."

"If I'm not sorted, I stay here forever. The longer I stay in this state, the more attached I become to this life. By the time a new witch comes, it may be too late."

"I'm so sorry, Logan. How horrible for you to be at the mercy of my choice."

"No, don't think that. I've enjoyed this time with you. It doesn't scare me anymore to think of spending more time here, especially if you are here."

"You'd sacrifice your soul, your eternal rest, for my happiness?"

"Yes, I would."

Sometimes in life there are easy decisions, where the right thing to do pops out at you. I had to decide between sex with a monster that would result in a lifetime of moonlighting as a witch, and living with the guilt of condemning the nicest soul I'd ever met to an eternity in my attic. As decisions went, this was one hell of a ding-dong.

"I've got to think. Logan, I need to talk to Prudence. She said to find the key and bring the vessel. Rick is the vessel. Do you know where the key is?"

"Are you sure? A good night's rest might make everything clear."

"I'm sure. Where is it?"

Logan walked over to the cabinet and opened the door. A silver canister engraved with the word *coffee* rested in front of the Tupperware. He waited. I pulled down the canister and opened the lid. The top of a key stuck out from the grounds.

"This is why you made my coffee every morning. You haven't wanted me to go up there. You've been trying to keep me from the truth!"

He hung his head.

"Why? Why would you do this?"

"For the same reason I told you to stay away from the caretaker. But you're right. It should be your decision, either way."

"Damn right it should. We are not finished with this conversation." I pointed at his ghostly form, grabbed the key, and headed for the stairs.

CHAPTER 14

Prudence Meriwether

Old-fashioned and weighty, I rolled the antique key in my hand. The wide end looped around twice like butterfly wings before twisting and melding into the blade of the key. Was it forged by hand? Hundreds of years old? If this house was built for Isabella, it was ancient. A house of secrets.

I climbed the stairs one apprehensive step at a time, glancing back at Logan until I took the bend at the second-floor landing. At the attic door, I paused. What I was about to do would change me forever, no matter what I decided.

The key slid into the lock, and the mechanism began to glow. The door transformed, the chipped paint gleaming white, the wrought iron knob turning to pearl. I opened the door and stepped into pure light and warmth, an open space with soft edges and stained glass. Beyond the windows, I could see it was night outside, but the light came from within, from the floor and the walls. I took a step inside. The door closed behind me.

"I wondered when you would come, Grateful."

A dark-haired woman, about my age, stood near the closest window. Her heart-shaped face turned toward me. She was wearing a nursing uniform from the 1960s: white skirt, white blouse, complete with one of those white square hats that nobody wears anymore.

"Prudence?" The ghost was a far cry from the glowing torso I'd seen on my stairs and in the family room, but really, who else would be in here?

"Yes, it's me." She smiled all the way to her eyes, a peaceful, authentic smile. "I can't believe how much you've grown, my dear."

"But you look so young. Weren't you, like, seventy when you died?"

"Seventy-two, but who's counting? That's the beauty of death. You can take any form from your life. Today, I'm my twenty-six-year-old self. That was the year I first met you."

"I'm only twenty-two. You would have been fifty when I was born."

"I mean, the *last* you. Your name was Samantha Graves. I was twenty-six, and you looked to be about the same age, but of course you were much older."

"I don't understand. You mean I looked younger than I was?"

"Quite. The witch is not immortal in the sense that she can be killed, as you were, but she does not age, so long as she takes her caretaker's blood."

"Yes, the blood thing. I wanted to talk to you about that. Can you explain what exactly becoming the witch entails? Does there have to be sex and blood, or is there another way?"

"Oh, dear. Have you seen the caretaker?" She giggled to herself, then frowned when I didn't join in. "In my day, women would have clawed each other's eyes out for a night with Rick. Have tastes changed so much?"

"Ah, no. He's gorgeous by anyone's standards. I'm just not sure I want to rush into a relationship."

She knitted her brow. "Rush? You do know you spent more than a lifetime together? That you were married more than once?"

"Yes, he told me. But that wasn't this body. I don't have those memories."

"Oh, I see. Are you a virgin then? Unwilling or afraid to complete the act itself? Morally against premarital sex?"

"Um, no. I lost my virginity when I was eighteen to a guy in the singles group at my church."

"Then you are with someone? Are you still seeing the church boy, is that it?"

This was getting embarrassing. "No."

"Then what is it, dear? What is keeping you from accepting your responsibility back from me? Is one act of sex with a gorgeous immortal for the sake of maintaining the balance of good and evil so appalling to you?"

Okay, she was getting angry. That was the voice nurses used with uncooperative patients. "It's not just the sex. It's what the sex means. It's a lifetime commitment. I get freaked out when I think that I might be in the same *career* for the rest of my life. That's why I chose nursing—because you can move around and do different things. But this feels permanent."

"And what exactly is wrong with committing to your life's purpose?"

"I…" I couldn't answer that question.

"If you don't take up this responsibility, Grateful, the repercussions will be horrific."

"What? What will happen?"

"Rick will weaken. It's what the vampires wanted when they killed you."

"I thought Reverend Monk killed me."

"Reverend Monk killed the first you, Isabella Lockhart. I'm talking about the last you, Samantha; the one I knew and loved. And I've always speculated that Reverend Monk was a pawn for whomever gave him *The Book of Flesh and Bone*."

I paced, rubbing my palms together. "In my last life, I was killed by vampires, and my death weakened Rick? I thought he was immortal."

"Immortal he is, but Rick feeds on sex, on blood, and on love. Those were things you provided him when you were alive. Without them, he weakens. Without you, he has to control the population of the unholy himself. More work with less strength. The last twenty-two years have been hard on him."

"So, that's all I am? His food?"

"Stupid girl! Haven't you been listening at all?" She was definitely angry now. "He is yours. He is your caretaker. You strengthen him so that he can protect you. You love him, and he loves you. You are the witch, and he is the caretaker. You balance each other. There are things that you can do that Rick can't. You were very powerful once. You could be again."

"If Rick was supposed to protect me, if I was so powerful, then how did I die?"

"Why don't you see for yourself?" Prudence moved toward an altar at the back of the room. I didn't remember seeing it when I first came in. On top was an enormous book. When I say enormous, I mean *Guinness World Records* sized. Once when I was a kid, my father and I visited the Library of Congress where I saw the Gutenberg Bible. This book dwarfed that one.

"This is your spell book," Prudence said. "It is called *The Book of Light*. Everything you need to know about controlling evil is in its pages. You also stored your memories in it. If you want to know how you died, open it and ask."

I stepped up to the leather-bound volume. It took both hands working together to open the thing, and as I did, I said in a loud, clear voice, "How did I die?"

Light poured out of the book, blinding me. The attic melted away. When I could see again, I was standing in the graveyard, only the hedges in front of the fence were missing, so I had a clear view of Rick's cottage across the street. The maple trees were mere saplings. Somehow I knew it was Halloween, and it didn't take long for me to figure out I was reliving my own memory.

Three teenagers paced outside the cemetery gate, two boys and a girl. Great. Hormone-fueled idiocy. I couldn't get a break tonight. I slipped behind a granite monolith because I didn't want to give the teens any excuse to hop the fence. With any luck, they'd get bored and move on.

Rick's wings beat in the distance near the chapel on Monk's Hill. He'd gone to break up a group of vampires congregating there. Vamps could look human when they wanted and were highly intelligent. Usually, they were selfish and territorial, but lately, they'd been organizing, designating leaders and, we suspected, planning an escape. Hopefully, Rick would be able to nip the problem in the budding fang, but that meant I needed to handle these kids on my own.

My reflection in the shiny surface of the monolith temporarily distracted me. The blurred image had red hair and was wearing head-to-toe black. I lifted an arm. Leather. Wow, I was a badass in my past life.

"Come on, I'll boost you over," one of the boys said. He was dressed as Michael Jackson, complete with sparkly glove.

"I don't know. It looks creepy. Let's go back to my place and hang out," the girl said. Smart girl.

"It'll be cool," the other boy said. The antennas of his alien costume bobbed around his head as he spoke. He kneeled down and cupped his hands.

Maybe I gave the girl too much credit by calling her smart. She placed her foot in his palm and launched herself to the top of the fence. Once she was over, Michael Jackson helped the alien, and then, in a rare display of upper body strength, scaled the fence on his own.

"Stupid kids," I heard myself say, only it wasn't my voice. "You guys have to get out of here," I whispered.

"Hey, did you hear something?" the alien said.

I closed my eyes and concentrated on sending them feelings of fear and anxiety. Pushing thoughts into people's heads was an ability Rick was teaching me. I hadn't mastered it yet, but it was worth a shot.

The girl backed toward the gate. "I don't like it here. Take me home," she said to Michael Jackson.

The brain thing worked, but I'd have to hold off on my victory lap. Mist rolled in behind the teens, and two vampires materialized, way too close for comfort.

"Cool!" the girl said to the vamps. "How'd you guys do that?"

The vamp closest to her held out his hand and shook his shaggy blond head. "Come here, and I will whisper the secret into your ear, Amanda."

I cringed. He'd read her mind. I could see the girl was instantly intrigued.

"How did you know my name?" she asked.

Another vampire with a tight red buzz cut moved in. "No cheating. If you want to know the secret, you must take his hand."

To the girl's credit, she backed between her friends.

A third vamp emerged from shadow, a male with a long black ponytail and muscles like a linebacker. The vamps formed a triangle around the teens. Trouble.

"What are you guys doing in here?" the alien asked the vamps.

"Waiting for you," the black-haired vamp said.

"Marcus, we were here first," the redhead hissed and took a step toward Amanda.

"Don't get greedy. There's enough to go around." Marcus appeared in front of the alien boy.

"Hey, back off, buddy," the boy said.

The vamps had forced the teens into a tight clump and were closing in, licking their lips. So much for any hope the teens would scale the fence and get out of there. I braced myself for a good old-fashioned vampire slaying.

I stepped out from behind the tombstone, my right hand instinctively reaching for the sword I kept in the sheath down my back. "Hold it right there, bloodsuckers," I said in that strange voice. My boots hit the stones with running steps.

The vamps glanced my way but moved toward the teens.

Screams rang out as the three teens either noticed the vampires' fangs or my sword. They ran for the fence, but they were too late. The vamps pounced. Shaggy Blond sank fang into Michael Jackson. I launched myself off a tombstone, pivoting in the air and delivering a tornado kick to his head before sinking my blade into the vamp's chest. The undead exploded into a shower of sparks.

Bleeding, Michael Jackson ran for the fence and strong-armed his way over. Marcus had Amanda pressed against his body, and he was ready to strike. She didn't stand a chance. But to get to her I needed to go through the growling and snapping ginger-headed vamp doing his best to make a meal of the alien boy. I flipped over Alien's head and drove my blade into the vamp's shoulder. He melted like wax. Alien ran screaming like someone was pulling his toenails out, but unlike Michael Jackson, he wasn't strong enough to pull himself over the wrought iron. I'd have to help him when I finished off the last one.

I whirled around to face Marcus, who had succeeded in exposing Amanda's neck. With a warrior's howl, I leaped toward him, my sword above my head.

"Sorry, witch," Marcus hissed. "Not this time."

Claws ripped me from the air and tossed me backward to the stones. *What the fuck?* I landed on my back. Four more vamps appeared out of nowhere and wrestled me to the ground. This was an ambush. This was meant for me!

I watched Marcus sink teeth into the girl. Her scream sounded wet, like a gurgle. Blood was flowing down her trachea. She'd be dead in seconds. I tried with everything I had to help, but there was something on the vamps' hands restraining me. My magic wouldn't work.

Marcus drained the girl, wiping the last of her blood from his mouth with the back of his hand. "Don't bother, witch. Helleborine root." He licked his lips. "A little birdie told me it would temporarily render you powerless. Enjoy the show."

He easily overcame Alien Boy who wailed pitifully until he died. His squeals brought droves of the undead. There would be nothing left of either body by morning. The vamps would drink the blood, the zombies were partial to the internal organs, and the ghouls would eat the rest.

Pain coursed through my body as the vamps tightened their hold on my struggling limbs. "*Rick!*" I screamed with everything I had, but it was too late. They'd staged the gathering at the chapel to distract him, and the teens were an all-too-convenient and unexpected way to lure me out. Their real goal was to kill me, and now they would.

With human blood in his veins, Marcus was three hundred times stronger than normal, stronger than me and maybe even stronger than Rick. He strode toward me. In one graceful move, he straddled my chest and lowered himself to his knees. His razor-sharp fangs elongated near my chin.

"Stop, Marcus. If you kill me, Rick will have your head."

"I think not. With your blood strengthening me, I'll have his. And you know the beauty of caretaker flesh is that it goes on forever."

With that, he bit the place where my neck met my right shoulder, and I heard the rush of my blood flowing down his throat before my flesh tore from my neck. As I died, I had one piece of magic left the helleborine couldn't restrain; it wasn't tied to *this* body. I released my soul, allowing my light to escape through my open mouth. It blew west on the fall wind. The spell took me into town, inside the open window of the nearest woman of appropriate age. I fluttered to her abdomen, and then sank beneath her skin before the blackness swallowed me.

My last thoughts were of Rick. I prayed for his safety.

As I died in my memory, the book spat me out and I was back in the attic, gasping for breath and holding my neck. I collapsed to the floor.

"Oh my," Prudence said. "I suppose reliving one's death would be a disturbing experience." She took my pulse and propped my head in her lap.

I met her eyes. "It was my mother. I saw the light enter my mother."

"I told you, you were very powerful."

I sat up to see Prudence more clearly and crisscrossed my legs in front of me. I had so many questions. I didn't know where to start. "What happened to Marcus after I died?"

"Rick tried to kill him. They fought until dawn when Marcus was forced to retreat into the underworld. With your blood and that of the two humans giving him power, he's become the leader of the vampire coven inside the hellmouth. The vampires haven't found a way out of the cemetery yet, but Rick's been working overtime to keep it that way."

"Marcus said someone had told him to use helleborine on me."

"Yes. Helleborine does not grow within the graveyard. Marcus had help from the outside. Maybe from the same entity that provided Monk with *The Book of Flesh and Bone*. Rick's spent years trying to track down your true killer."

"And without me, Rick is weaker?"

"Yes. Not only has the world missed your talents for the last twenty-two years, every day that Rick goes without you as his partner becomes more difficult for him."

"But there could be another, right? If I say no, the part of me that is the witch will move to someone else."

She sighed. "Yes. When you die, the piece of you that is the witch will be freed from your body and find another host. There has to be balance. But that would take a lifetime. And what about us? Do you know what will happen to Logan and me?"

"Logan said that the next witch might be able to sort you, but the longer it took, the harder it would be."

"Death is the great forgetting. You as the Monk's Hill witch sort the souls who are caught between life and death. You do so by remembering for us. You give us a name. You call us out and send us on. Every day that a soul isn't sorted, that soul loses more memories of his or her life. Eventually, there aren't enough clues left for you or any witch to name the dead. Logan has already forgotten. If you accepted your responsibility tomorrow, it might not be soon enough for him. And now that the magic you've given me is wearing off, I will forget too. I've been here two full years waiting for you. Logan's only been here a few months. Think how fast I will forget now that my purpose has been fulfilled."

All anger had bled from Prudence's expression, and she patted my hand, the nurse in her coming out over all else.

"I'm too young for this kind of responsibility, Prudence. I'm sorry."

"Do you know why I kept the scrapbook of your life?" Prudence asked.

"Uh, no. Stalker comes to mind though, to be very honest."

"Every stage of your life proved your worth. At six years old, you never forgot to feed the dog. By eleven, you were cooking meals for your dad. Do you remember?"

I nodded reluctantly.

"You are here because you are responsible. A lesser person might declare bankruptcy and move on. Not you, Grateful. You are working off every dime of Gary's debt."

"It's the right thing to do."

"And at twenty-two, you are choosing to do the right thing. Seems you are more responsible than you give yourself credit."

She had a point, but I wasn't ready to pull the Band-Aid off. It was all happening too fast. I needed more time.

"Let me think about it," I said.

CHAPTER 15
Grave Matters

Someone had injected me with liquid concrete. I dragged my limbs to bed, unable to form a coherent thought and fully aware that the best night's sleep of my life wasn't going to solve this dilemma. The summer heat had left the room stuffy, so I dressed in a cool silk camisole and shorts. But I didn't dare open a window. Every sound terrified me. The wind blowing a branch into the glass filled me with dread. After tonight, I pictured the things I'd seen in the graveyard and in my past-life memory fighting to get in, to hurt me. As tired as I was, sleep was impossible. I tossed and turned, drifting off only to startle awake and see the clock had advanced a mere five or ten minutes.

Fate's arrow had hit my ultimate weak spot; I had no control. Tonight, Rick and Prudence had taken away my world of safety and security and replaced it with horror and uncertainty. My body ached with tension. My mind raced. I rolled on my back and stared at the ceiling.

All at once, I sensed a familiar presence that registered as a heaviness in the pit of my chest. "Logan?"

"I'm here." His voice came from the corner of the room, and his body formed there.

"How long have you been watching me?"

"Since you went to bed. I was worried about you."

"I'm not doing much sleeping. But it helps to know you're here."

"I'm here, Grateful."

"Will you stay with me?"

He was suddenly standing next to the bed. "Yes."

"All night?" I asked.

"All night," he answered.

I scooted to one side of the bed. As he slid in next to me, I knew he didn't need to lie down but was doing it for my sake. I tried to close my eyes again, restless. Logan touched my face. Whatever he was made of brushed over me, an electrically charged feather, somewhere between a tickle and a purr. I reached for his hand. The density changed as my fingers passed through him, like plunging my hand into warm water.

Before Logan, I would have assumed a ghost would feel cold, and his kiss had. But on the inside, it was different. My hand slid through his, and he moved inside my skin, like warm fur caressing toward my shoulder.

"Mmm," I said, closing my eyes. Amazing.

He pressed closer, sinking his other hand into my side. Something low inside my body tightened. I arched into his hand and closed my eyes.

"This is... I've never done this before. Am I hurting you?" Logan asked.

"No. It feels good. Warm and tingly."

"Do you want me to keep going? I'm not sure what'll happen, but I like it. It feels right."

Several things went through my mind at that moment. I told myself that having Logan inside of me was not "sex"—he didn't have a body. And I needed comfort. I was a raw nerve, a frayed rope. Twelve hours ago I'd thought Rick might be "the one." Now, he was a monster. My whole world had gone topsy-turvy, and I was holding on to a ghost as if he were the most solid object in my universe.

"Don't stop, Logan," I said.

He leaned into me, quite literally. His entire form slid into my body. The plush electric buzz ran just under my skin from my scalp to my toes. For a second, the pleasure was so intense that I couldn't breathe. Inevitably, my body responded by growing wet, my nipples stretching my silk camisole.

I took a long, deep breath. I had to get naked, to see if I could touch the purr that ran right under my skin. Lifting the camisole over my head, I writhed against the mattress and Logan rolled in response. Just pulling my silk shorts down sent a warm rush through me.

I ran my hands over my breasts, tugging gently on my nipples, but the sensation happened from the inside out. Caressing lower, over my stomach, his hands followed mine on the other side of my skin. My fingers found the space between my legs, and so did Logan. He filled me with his power. I guessed he could be any shape or size he wanted to be, and right now he was exactly the right size to make every cell in my body call out for more.

Allowing my knees to drift apart, I rubbed myself faster as the power surged in and out of me. A thousand fingers massaged up my back. His power explored my mouth and reached places I'd never found erotic before, the arches of my feet, the back of my knees, my inner arms. I arched my back, throwing my head into the pillow.

"More. Please. Don't stop," I cried. I spread my arms wide on the mattress and let his power drive into me. Hot thrusts pounded, throbbing, stroking in just the right places. I neared the great shimmering cliff. He coaxed me over the edge, and I came apart. The power of it pushed Logan out of my body. I writhed on the bed and watched him flicker next to me, pure wonder in his eyes.

"I wasn't expecting that," I breathed.

"I wasn't either." His voice sounded weak, distant.

"Are you all right?"

"I think being inside of you has drained my energy. I'm sorry, I can't stay. I need to rest."

And with that, he broke apart in a flash of light. The mist he was made of soaked into the ceiling, probably returning to the attic. I rolled onto my side feeling sated, but racked with guilt. I hadn't meant for that to happen. On top of everything else, I now had the added complexity of having led my ghost on. My gut told me what happened meant more to Logan than it did to me.

And despite what I'd just done, my last thoughts before falling asleep were of Rick. Rick the monster. Rick, who'd used our connection to take advantage of me. Rick, who I wanted even now.

Rick, who in a past life I was married to.

* * * * *

There's something addictive about having a cup of coffee and a hot breakfast prepared for you each morning. As I savored the berry crepes Logan left for me, I was racked with guilt. I couldn't objectively make the decision to become or not become the witch on my own. After the orgasm Logan had given me the night before, and the perfect cup of coffee he'd made, I could almost forget it was his eternal soul I was dealing with. Not to mention his feelings.

I didn't want to be the witch, and frankly I could get used to having Logan around forever. He'd never leave me. I could fall into a relationship with Logan so easily. It would be as simple as doing nothing. But easy and right were two different things. As hurt as I'd been over the last several years, and as much as I needed control to feel safe, I still had a conscience.

I needed help. Someone who wasn't afraid to give me a firm kick in the pants if it was warranted.

I needed Michelle.

For the sake of our friendship, I decided not to tell her the entire truth. She would never believe me. But more than that, her specialty was mental health, and I didn't want to end up in the state mental ward. I had to figure out a way to ask her without really asking her.

I jumped in the shower. Usually the hot water was soothing, like I could wash away all of my worries, but today my insides crawled with unrest. Flashes of the last couple of days overwhelmed me. I closed my eyes and leaned my forehead against the shower wall. The pit of my chest felt heavy with...guilt? Fear?

"Are you okay?" Logan's voice came from behind the shower door.

I jolted at the sound. "Yeah. I was just thinking."

"Oh."

"How long have you been watching me shower?"

My answer came in the silence.

"*Logan!*"

He gave a charming, boy-next-door laugh. "It's one of the few advantages of being a ghost."

I turned off the water and reached for my towel. "I should have kept the bouquet of herbs from Rick. This whole time I felt you watching me, but I thought it was all in my head. "

"I'm sorry," he said, contrite. "Now that I know it bothers you, I won't do it again."

"Do you promise?"

"Yes. In fact, I'll leave you now. It's time for me to rest, anyway. Have a good day."

"You too."

During the whole conversation, I'd never actually seen Logan. His voice had come from the empty corner of the bathroom. But I could tell when he wasn't there anymore. Some part of me had sensed him even before he'd spoken. The weight I'd noticed in the middle of my chest, as if I'd forgotten something important, came and went with his presence. This was new. While I hadn't recognized the feeling until it vanished, I was sure I would in the future.

Was I changing? Becoming more sensitive to the otherworldly? It made sense that I might be. I'd heard it took professional wine tasters years to perfect their ability to separate complex flavors and aromas. Maybe I was developing a taste for the supernatural.

I tossed on a pair of ruby red scrubs and tied my hair back into the tightest ponytail I could, not a hair out of place. In my head, I thought through the events of the night before with painful clarity. I needed to fix this. I needed a plan.

Rain pelted the Jeep as I backed out of the garage and onto the street. I crossed the stone bridge. My heart sank when I neared Rick's place, the wind chimes creating a cacophony in the building storm. Emotions flooded me— a confusing concoction of anger, unrequited passion, fear, and an odd and unexpected longing. Between the rain and the mist welling up in my eyes, I didn't notice Rick standing in the middle of the road until it was too late.

I slammed on the brakes. The Jeep skidded sideways on the wet asphalt, knocking me against the door. I screamed with horror as I plowed into Rick. Only, there was no collision. At the moment of impact, he dissolved into a smoky mist and re-formed behind the revolving metal of my vehicle.

Wearing nothing but black jeans and a trench coat, he reached forward and, in the blink of an eye, grabbed my rear bumper, stopping the Jeep's momentum. He saved me from an almost certain roll in the ditch. My heart pounded. He approached. His dark silhouette sliced through the storm.

Before I had a chance to say a word, he was sitting beside me in the passenger's seat. He'd never opened the door.

I gasped, pressing myself against my window and clutching at my chest as if the personal CPR could coax my heart into beating again. "I didn't know you could do that," I said.

He raised an eyebrow. "I can do anything they can do. I am the balance."

Over his shoulder, the entrance to the cemetery seemed to taunt me with its daytime innocence. "You mean, because the demons can become a mist, you can become a mist."

He nodded. "I can dematerialize like a vampire, I'm fast like a ghoul, strong as a zombie, and there are other things."

I refrained from asking about the other things. I wasn't ready to know. "So, if the vampires developed the ability to travel through time, you would suddenly be able to travel through time?"

"Yes. Although I sincerely hope that particular skill evades them." He leaned forward, crossing the center console and entering my personal space. "I am the caretaker, and in order to do my job, my power has to balance the evil. Balance is a natural law that applies to the supernatural. The only power uniquely mine is the beast."

"Oh." He was so very close. The intensity of his stare left me uneasy.

He frowned. "You smell of the dead."

I sniffed my scrubs, then grasped that he must mean Logan. I knew what a dead body smelled like, and I wasn't wearing that particular scent.

"What do you want?" I asked, suddenly defensive.

He looked at me with black eyes. Beads of rain dripped from his hair and ran in trails down his chest. The attraction was instantaneous. I crossed my legs and had to look away to keep from touching him.

"Have you thought about what happened last night?" he asked.

"Yes," I said toward the floorboard.

"Then, will you be with me tonight?" He reached across the seat and placed his hand on my thigh, his voice was thick with longing.

"No." I pushed his hand away. "You lied to me."

"I never lied to you."

"Well then, you omitted the truth. Same difference. Why didn't you tell me right away? Why didn't you tell me before—" I stopped myself. I'd almost said, *before I fell in love with you*. Why had I almost said that? Was I in love with him? How could I be in love with a monster?

"Before what?"

"Before now," I said.

"I wanted to get to know you like we were human."

"I am human," I said through my teeth.

"I did not want to scare you away. I knew this would be hard for you."

"You got that right." I fidgeted in my seat. "I have a choice, Rick. I don't have to do this."

Before I knew what was happening, he was across the seat and in my face. With his hand on the dash and his knee on the seat next to me, there was no place for me to go. I was trapped.

"What do you mean?" he growled.

My breath came out shaky. I swallowed hard. The first time I'd met Rick I thought he reminded me of a matador. At the time, I'd been referring to his Spanish good looks. But now I realized the comparison went further. A matador's job was to sever the bull's spine with his sword. The red cape is to distract the bull so that the matador can have his way with it. Rick was beautiful, but he was deadly. I was the bull. All of this—his seduction of me—had been the cape, a distraction to get what he really wanted. My soul.

"I mean," I said, my voice cracking with fear, "that this is my life. No matter what or who I was in the past, I don't have to be that now, or ever."

He jerked backward as if I'd punched him in the gut. The expression on his face was tortured, a pure agony that almost made me regret my words. "Who is he?" he gasped.

"Who is who?"

"The ghost whose smell lies under your skin?"

"His name is Logan. He lives in my attic."

His fist came down on the dash and the resulting boom startled me. The back of my head hit the window when I jumped. "Of course he does. Grateful, he's there to be sorted!"

"So? He says it doesn't matter to him. He says I have a choice." I rubbed the lump already forming on the back of my head.

"Do you not see that your attraction to him is an echo of who you were? Something in you seeks the power, even as you deny it. You could be a queen of souls, yet you waste yourself on one of them."

"Logan wasn't a waste, but I'm beginning to think this conversation is." Anger drowned out my fear, and I moved forward in my seat. "You can't bully me into this, Rick."

It was his turn to shake. A tear gathered in the corner of his eye. He shook his head, and it was gone. "I am not trying to bully you into anything. You must remember that when I look at you, I see my wife. I see my long-lost love. I forget that you are young. I forget that you are a new person. Forgive me."

He didn't wait for my reply. Before I could pull my next breath, he was gone.

CHAPTER 16
I Seek Wise Counsel

It wasn't even seven o'clock in the morning by the time I reached St. John's Hospital, but my body told me I'd packed a week of living into the first hours of the day. My shoulders sagged, and there was an ache deep inside my chest. I didn't have a name for all of my emotions. In nursing school, they teach you to help people in crisis— illness, death, disfigurement, that type of thing. No book ever covered what to do when you find out you are the reincarnated soul of a witch, your neighbor is a blood-drinking immortal, and you have ghosts in your attic. I was in new territory here.

I stepped out of the break room with my stethoscope slung around my neck, knowing that no amount of medicine could cheat death. I've always known this. I've seen dozens of people die during my career. Only, today, a revelation—death was not the end. Death meant change. Death meant forgetting. Death meant moving on.

On the way to see my first patient, I passed room three twelve. The door was open. A teenaged girl sobbed into her hands, her brown hair tangled around her face. I knocked on the open door.

"Everything okay in here?" I asked softly.

She stroked her hair back from her red-rimmed eyes. "My grandmother…" She pointed toward the bed. "She just died. The nurse went to call my mother and make arrangements."

I shifted my focus from the girl to the body. Grandma may have died, but she was still in the room. My jaw dropped. Her soul looked down on me as I stepped, trancelike, to her granddaughter's side.

"Her soul is so bright!" Had I said that out loud?

"What?"

With my hand on the girl's shoulder, I struggled to regain my composure. The ascending light filled the room. Desperately, I wanted to tell this girl that her grandma's soul radiated pure good, warmth, and love. I was struck dumb. Her soul smiled at me, broke apart into a thousand pinpoints of light and circled up through the ceiling. I gripped my chest as a weight, one I'd come to associate with Logan, was lifted from me.

"Miss, are you all right?" the girl asked.

I faced her with tears in my eyes, my jaw working as my brain struggled to find the right words. "Your grandma was a wonderful person. If it gives you any comfort, for as long as I've been nursing, I've never seen a more peaceful death. You can tell...by her body. She was ready, and obviously loved." My voice gave out on the last word.

Eyes wide, she patted my hand. "Thank you."

I suddenly felt small and inconsequential in the face of the great and mysterious world around me. For the first time, the part of me that was the witch awakened, stretched her arms toward the sun, and beckoned me forward. *Come. Accept my gifts. Know the unknown. Seize your power.*

As I retreated from the room and the girl, I really wished the witch would shut the fuck up.

* * * * *

My two patients kept me more than busy. They were both sedated, hooked up to machines that helped them breathe. One was in a diabetic coma, the other recovering from a heart attack. Like any other day, I did my assessments and administered my medications. But unlike yesterday, I knew they wouldn't die. *Crap.* Whether it was because of Logan, Rick, or my past life, I could sense death like a cold room. Although my diabetic coma patient gave off a chilly breeze, she wasn't there yet. On one hand, this new spidey-sense came in handy as a nurse. On the other, it was creepier than a hillbilly with a chainsaw.

"Are you ready for lunch?" Michelle caught me outside the medication room, a lopsided grin on her face. "I thought we could go check on that Neuro patient."

"What Neuro patient?"

"You know, the transfer from St. Augustus. Maureen on Neuro wants our professional opinion."

"Can it wait for another day? I really need to talk to you about something."

"Sure." Her expression turned serious. "What's going on?"

"It's a long story. Let me tell Kathleen I'm leaving, and we can go to Valentine's."

She nodded. A few moments later, we headed across the street to our favorite restaurant. I slid into a secluded booth at the back, and Michelle got comfortable across from me. I dove right into the conversation. Hell, I'd burst if I didn't vent to someone.

"Michelle, I need your advice."

"Shoot."

"Let's say you knew two men."

"I like this scenario already." She smiled and opened her menu.

"The first man is sexy beyond belief. Every time you see him your body begs you to throw yourself at him," I said.

"Sounds good to me. What's the catch?"

"He's a monster."

Her eyes popped over the top of her menu, and she laughed like I was being ridiculous. "What do you mean, like a murderer?"

I rolled that around in my brain. Rick was not the equivalent of a murderer, but I wasn't sure what to compare him to. "Not a murderer. Someone who lives two lives, like a mob boss. By day, he's a normal businessman. Behind closed doors, he's unscrupulous."

Michelle raised an eyebrow and frowned. "But not like the Sopranos—no killing."

"Well, if there is killing it's only the bad guys. He's got a conscience, but he doesn't live a traditional life."

"Like a pimp, a good pimp. Like he takes really good care of his prostitutes but still he's into something horrible, like prostitution."

"No, that's not it either. It's not just what he does. It's who he is. Like, let's say he has herpes or leprosy." I cringed. The words were out. No getting them back.

"Oh my God. He's contagious?"

I rubbed my forehead. "Yes, let's pretend he's contagious with something that is disfiguring, not deadly."

"But that's not really it."

"No. Stop. You're missing the point. The guy is gorgeous, but he isn't your traditional take-home-to-mom husband material. His life is complicated and would complicate mine. Just leave it at that."

Michelle sighed. "Okay. What about the other guy?"

"The other guy treats you like a queen. He's someone you can talk to all night long and knows you better than almost anyone else. But your feelings are more…comfortable than intense."

She raised an eyebrow. "Comfortable. Hmm. Is he ugly?"

"No, he's very attractive. However, he doesn't have a body. I mean, he doesn't have full use of his body. He's a quadriplegic." Was my nose growing? I was rambling, making it up as I went along.

"Wow." She let that sink in. "So, how independent is he? Is he someone who has his own life without you?"

I had to think about that one too. The leprosy analogy was somewhat of a stretch, but the quadriplegic was a bit too close for comfort. Even though Logan was independent and was in many ways taking care of me, he wasn't able to leave the house. He had Prudence and me—that was it.

"He's very independent but socially isolated due to his condition."

A brunette waitress bopped over to our table and took our drink order. As soon as she turned her back, Michelle set down her menu and leaned across the table.

"So, the dilemma you're facing is whether to choose body or soul. You're wondering whether you should feel guilty for wanting the body of the first man when the second may be the more ethical choice because he deserves your love more."

"Yes, I think that's it."

"Grateful," Michelle started, "how certain are you that each of these men is what they seem? You haven't known them for long. Do you know for sure that bad-boy dangerous guy is as shallow as you make him out to be? And the deep soul, will he always have the emotional connection to you that he does now? A lot can change once the newness wears off."

This is why I like talking to Michelle. She has a way of simplifying everything, even when it isn't what I want to hear. "I guess you're right. I haven't known either of them long enough to know for sure. But Mr. Dangerous did lie to me."

"About what?"

"Well, he omitted the truth about what he did for a living."

"But you described what he did as monstrous."

"Yeah, so?"

"Can you blame him for omitting the truth? He's probably embarrassed about what he is. Maybe he wishes he could change."

I hated to admit that she might be right. I didn't know Rick, not really. I wasn't sure of his intentions. Maybe my former self had been married to him, had lived a whole life with him, but that wasn't me. That was someone else.

"And the other one, the perfect soul, it's easy to do the right thing when you don't have any other option. If he's isolated, you might grow tired of him. No one can be the center of someone's universe forever. It isn't healthy. I'm sure the disability you could live with, but the dependence? You couldn't take more than a week of it. You'll feel suffocated."

She was right. I couldn't use Logan for coffee and breakfast indefinitely. He wasn't my housekeeper. Besides Prudence, I was all he had. What would happen to him when I moved out? I didn't know for sure. Logan said that the next witch might not be able to send him on, but what did that mean? What would happen to him here?

"Grateful?"

"What?"

Michelle spread her hands. "Did you hear what I just said?"

"No, um, sorry. I phased out just then. What were you saying?"

"Why can't you choose bachelor number three? I mean, why is this such a pressing issue? It's a free country. Don't underestimate your ability to not commit."

I blinked in her direction. "Like, don't commit to either of them?"

"Yes. Remember the blonde paradox? Remember Gary? You tend to rush into things, only to find out that the guy isn't who you thought he was. Why don't you just wait, take it slow this time, and see where it goes?"

"Uh, I've already not taken it slow…with both of them."

The server returned with our drinks. I ordered a Valentine burger with cheese. Michelle opted for the garden salad, definitely the healthier choice. She was always making the healthier choice. She glared at me until the waitress stepped out of earshot.

"You're right. You're right," I admitted. "I'm not good at going slow. I have needs."

"Wait. When you say you haven't taken it slow, you mean, um…" Michelle leaned across the table, looking around her to make sure no one was listening, "You mean sex, right?"

"Well, yes." I bobbed my head back and forth on my shoulders. "Not sex exactly, but enough."

"Come on, Grateful. You're twenty-two years old. You can have sex responsibly without opening your whole life to a person. Keep sex where sex belongs, in the bedroom. Keep your heart where your heart belongs—in your chest, tightly guarded by your brain. You know, if you were a man we wouldn't be having this conversation."

Uh-oh. I'd tapped on Michelle's passionate feelings about gender equality. Better change the subject, or this could take a while. "I thought you were supposed to tell me to follow my heart."

"No! That's terrible advice. Hearts make knee-jerk emotional decisions. Your heart picked Gary, and look how that turned out. This time, you need to use your head."

I knew she was right. Michelle was always right. But could I do it her way? Could I just wait and not make a decision about Rick or Logan or becoming the witch?

CHAPTER 17
Strange Cup of Joe

I did not make a decision. Weeks passed. Nothing happened. The ground didn't open up. I wasn't struck by lightning. As far as I was concerned, I could do non-committal for as long as it took. To fill my days and keep my mind busy, I picked up extra shifts at the hospital and fell into an exhausting routine.

Logan proved amicable with my non-decision, although disappointed I wasn't choosing him romantically. No matter how many times I tried to explain our joining was a mistake, like literally an unexpected accident, I could sense that his feelings for me ran strong. He continued to cook and clean. He was an excellent listener. It was flattering…and completely wrong.

I passed Rick's stone cottage an average of twice a day, sometimes catching him on the porch or working near the cemetery, but I did not stop. With sad eyes, he'd watch me go, but he didn't come for me. Although he was fast enough and strong enough to press the issue, he never did.

Summer, in pursuit of greener pastures, packed its bags and left New Hampshire, ushering autumn to Red Grove. Overnight, the trees grew bolder personalities, dressing in garnet and persimmon and welcoming my Jeep home with an increasing number of free-spirited leaves.

"You can't put us off forever," Prudence said one night from the edge of my bed. Tonight she was her young, nursey self, soft spoken and vulnerable. "It's not fair to Rick or to Logan."

"Or to you. Don't forget yourself, Prudence," I snapped.

She sighed heavily.

I circled my hand in the air. "You know who this entire situation isn't fair to? Me. This isn't fair to me."

Prudence rippled and blinked out of sight. "Perhaps," her disembodied voice said, and then she was gone.

The next morning, I worked a full day and an hour of overtime. I plodded to my car, exhausted from thirteen hours of beeping machines, blood, and drugs. The extra shifts were catching up with me, along with the stress of avoiding the supernatural entities in my life. On the way home, I called my dad. I'd neglected our relationship since what I'd come to refer to as "the big reveal." The call went straight to voicemail.

"Dad, I just wanted to tell you I love you. I'm so glad you told me the truth about Mom. Maybe we can have dinner Sunday night. Call me when you get a chance."

I ended the call and pulled into a Java Jane's for a cup of coffee. I wasn't sure I'd stay awake on the country roads to Red Grove without it. A line had formed for the drive-thru, so I parked and drifted to the counter half asleep.

"I'll have a Fall Spice Latte," I said to the barista.

She nodded and requested an exorbitant amount of money in exchange, which I promptly handed over. All part of the Java Jane's experience. I folded into a wooden chair at one of the bistro-style tables while I waited for my grande. Even though I was exhausted, I couldn't help but notice an old man in the corner of the café staring at me. He was giving me the hairy eyeball, as if he'd just seen me on *America's Most Wanted*. Beady eyes peeked out from a deeply wrinkled face of a yellow color that only comes from a lifetime of heavy smoking and abuse of alcohol.

Every self-defense class I've ever taken emphasized that eye contact simply encourages the aggressor, so I looked away, hoping he'd lose interest. I heard him scoot his chair back on the tile and out of the corner of my eye, saw him scratch his potbelly through his stained T-shirt. Besides the barista, he and I were the only ones inside. I silently prayed he'd leave. No luck. I didn't hear him approach until he was right next to me, close enough for me to smell his foul breath—a smell I could only compare to the stench of gangrene.

"I see you," he said in a raspy drawl that made the hair on the back of my neck stand up.

My protective instincts told me to run. Instead, I turned my head and looked him square in the face, my most professional demeanor sliding into place like a mask. "If you need a doctor, the hospital is a mile north of here. You can get treatment in the emergency room."

The wrinkles of his face swallowed his eyes as he considered what I said. He tilted his head to the side, contemplating me with such intensity I stood up and stepped toward the counter just to get away from him.

"I'll be right with you," the barista said, busy finishing my latte.

The old man showed a mouthful of yellow teeth. Was that supposed to be a smile? "For now, heh-cah-tee," he rasped. "But I see you. I see you." And then, to my relief, he left, laughing all the way out the door.

"Here's your latte," the barista said, handing me the cup.

"Thanks. Jeez, that guy was creepy, huh?"

"What guy?" she asked.

"The old man who was just here talking to me. The one with wrinkles like a Shar-Pei."

She looked at me blankly. "I didn't see anyone. Gosh, I hope he doesn't complain to the manager. I'm supposed to greet everyone who comes in."

Annoyed, I grabbed my coffee and headed for the parking lot. I looked both ways, seriously freaked out by the old man's vibe, and then strode toward my car as quickly as possible. The girl must have been half deaf and blind to miss that guy. Not to mention the smell. Ew.

I'm not sure what set me off. I didn't hear him come up behind me, and his body was out of sight. But I knew when he lunged for me. I expected it.

One of his hands shot around my waist, the other clutched at my mouth. I grabbed both and lurched forward, sending my backside into his fat belly and using his forward momentum to launch him over my shoulder. He landed flat on his back on the pavement. Thank you, hapkido. I slipped inside my Jeep and used my key fob to lock the doors. Cell phone, STAT! Receipts and tissues flew as I dug through the Bermuda Triangle of handbags.

I ditched that plan when movement out my window caught my eye. The wrinkled old man rose unnaturally from the pavement, tipping up onto his feet like gravity forgot about him. *Fuck!* I slammed the keys into the ignition. Who the hell was this guy? The impact from that fall should've broken something, and it wasn't like he was in tip-top physical condition.

He lunged for my car. I shifted into reverse and slammed on the gas. The man pursued me. Like a high school track star, he sprinted after my Jeep. Tires squealing, I stopped, shifted, accelerated forward in a car-on-man game of chicken. He didn't flinch. I swerved before impact, narrowly missing him and gunned it toward Red Grove. I only slowed when I'd put miles between his wrinkled face and my bumper.

With shaking hands, I dialed 911 and relayed what had happened. Identifying myself as a nurse, I suggested the man was mentally ill and probably on PCP or something. The dispatcher promised to send a squad car.

Describing the scenario forced me to analyze it with a clinical eye. Nurses are assaulted more than any other helping profession. Sick people aren't in their right minds, and drug users often have what seems like superhuman strength. I'd taken self-defense classes for years and used my skills on more than one occasion. The fact the man attacked me outside the hospital was irrelevant. He'd seen my scrubs and wanted something from me. What had he said? Hecate? Probably a new name for heroin. Maybe he thought I could get him some.

Halfway home, I remembered the coffee in my cup holder. I didn't need it anymore. The scare woke me right up. I drank it anyway, for comfort more than caffeine. Why did my life have to be so bizarre? I came to Red Grove to get over Gary and move on, but all I'd found was one crisis after another. I wanted a normal life. I didn't want to be a witch, and I didn't want a supernatural relationship.

I contemplated leaving Red Grove and all of my problems behind. My mind raced while my subconscious drove. It wasn't the safest way to travel. But before I knew it, the garage door was opening, welcoming me home.

Entering the kitchen from the garage, the smell that wafted around me made my mouth water. On the stove, a bubbling pot stirred itself. The oven opened, and a roast slid out, basted itself, and retreated.

"Logan?"

He formed in front of the kitchen island. "Grateful, welcome home. How was your day?"

"Fucked up. An old man with drug-induced strength tried to kill me at the coffee shop." I gave him a blow by blow of the incident.

Logan frowned. "He called you Hecate? You're sure?"

"Ah, yeah! A girl wouldn't forget something like that."

"Hecate is another name for what you are."

My breath caught in my throat. "Are you saying that the man knew I had part of the witch inside of me?"

"I'm saying he probably wasn't a man. Prudence says now that you know what you are, you'll start to change. It's part of the transition until you take your power back or reject it. The magic inside of you is visible by certain…creatures."

I threw my keys on the counter so hard they skidded into the wall. "Isn't that just the theme of the fucking year? Everyone knows about how this works but me."

"I'm sorry—"

Prudence formed then, crossing her arms over her chest. "Probably a demon. I'm not sure a vampire could tell who you are. Not yet. But a demon might be able to smell it on you."

"But what does Hecate mean?

"Hecate is an ancient name for the goddess of the dead. It's fitting. They say Isabella was a daughter to the goddess herself."

I huffed. "Goddess? I have a big enough problem with the title *witch*!"

"A sorceress by any other name would be as powerful." She laughed. "You called yourself the Monk's Hill witch in your last life because you thought it had a ring to it, but truly Hecate would be more accurate."

I rolled my eyes. "Save it. I don't need this right now." I was pissed. I wanted my life back. "What is this, Logan?" I waved a hand over the bubbling mess that was my kitchen.

"Dinner. I thought we could have a date."

"It's not even ten. You're hardly opaque. It's too early for you."

"I knew you'd be tired, and I wanted to spend some time with you before you fell asleep. You've worked every night this week."

"I…" What could I say? It was a thoughtful gesture, so why did it feel so suffocating? Even as I asked myself that question, I knew the answer. After what happened at Java Jane's, I wanted to be alone, to pretend for one night that my house wasn't haunted.

Plus, this was exactly what Michelle had warned me about. He was too dependent on me. I wasn't ready to be in a relationship, especially one that felt forced. Logan lived here, and I lived here. What did that mean for my desire not to choose? I needed time and space.

"I need a bath," I said, marching toward the stairs.

"You don't have to decide, Grateful."

I turned back toward him. "No? How about if I decide I want my life back? No ghosts. No demons. No caretakers. That's not going to happen, is it?"

"You're considering being with Rick, aren't you?"

"I'm not having this conversation with you. You're the one who told me I had a choice. It goes both ways, and the only one who can make it is me."

Logan flickered. Whatever was on the stove began bubbling over. I hurried to turn off the burner. Clarity came to me in Michelle's words: *How do you know they are what they seem?*

I focused my attention on what I could see of Logan's head. "Be honest. What's the real reason you don't want me to become the witch? What would make you want to be a ghost forever?"

By the length of time it took Logan to answer, I knew I was onto something. He blended into the wall, his desire to dodge the inquiry bleeding the energy out of him. But I wasn't going to let him off that easily.

I dug in my heels. "I'll be here all night. Oh, and the next day, and the next day. You're kind of stuck with me. Out with it. Why are you afraid to be sorted?"

"I don't know who I am," he blurted.

"So? Isn't that what the witch is supposed to figure out?"

"I don't know what type of life I've lived. I don't know who I was. Was I a doctor, a mobster, a priest, a criminal?

I have no idea. Don't you get it? I don't know which way I'll be sorted."

"Oh." It had never occurred to me that Logan could be anything but a good soul. Kindness just seemed like an integral part of his character. But he was right. I had no idea what went into sorting or how much control I'd have if I did it. What if I had to sort him to the underworld? What if Rick ended up eating his soul for supper? The thought was horrifying.

"The worst part is, if I wasn't a good person, you'll know. It'll be you who makes the call. Despite what you think, I do care for you. It's the major reason I'm not afraid to stay. Being with you, it makes this existence worth it."

"I can't be your whole existence." There, I'd said it. "I don't want to share my life with someone for eternity." Silence settled between us until we were interrupted by the timer on the oven.

"The roast is done," he murmured.

"How did you get all of this food? I'm sure I didn't leave a roast in the refrigerator."

"Um, yeah, you may owe around fifty dollars to Red Grove Grocery and Pub. I had it delivered."

"They delivered this on credit?"

He rubbed the back of his neck. "I may have taken the package while the delivery boy was distracted. Like, maybe the door opened by itself and the package fell from his hands before the door closed again."

"I see. I'll make sure the grocery bill gets paid, but please, in the future, give me a heads-up first. I won't allow you to steal anything from anyone, and I can't afford to eat like this every night. Plus, I can't have the residents of Red Grove suspecting this place is haunted."

"Understood." I could have been mistaken, but for a moment, Logan appeared to be blushing. I'd never known a ghost could blush, but then Logan was my first.

"Listen, Logan, dinner smells awesome. I'm sorry I'm not more appreciative, but I need to be alone right now."

He lowered his head, and I made for the bathtub by way of the wine cellar.

CHAPTER 18

My Personal Crisis Intervention

Hot soapy water cures a multitude of ailments. Wine, the rest of them. I soaked in the bathtub, sipping Pinot Noir since I'd polished off all the Shiraz, and tried to clear my mind. An image cut through the darkness. A thought. A dream. Maybe a memory.

Rick, in a bar, upside down. Wait, no, I was upside down, my red hair dragging on the floor below me. A grunge band rocked out in the background, and I was having trouble keeping my hockey jersey tucked into my pants in my inverted position.

The human pyramid suspending me chanted my name. *Sam, Sam, Sam.* I raised a shot of tequila to my lips, tossed it back and swallowed. The hot liquor coursed up to my stomach, the heat radiating to my toes.

"Whoa-oh-oooh," a man's voice said from behind me. I felt myself begin to tip, but it was hard to tell if it was gravity or the alcohol making my head swim. It was gravity. My human suspension system toppled like a deck of cards, arms and legs and bar stools flying. I reached out, prepared to handspring off the sticky mess of a bar floor to safety. I didn't have to. I landed in the cradle of Rick's arms. A cheer rose up from the bar behind us as the patrons realized they wouldn't need to call an ambulance after all.

"Upside-down shots?" Rick asked, eyebrow raised.

"It's the newest thing. You should try it."

He flashed his quirky half-smile. "I think I'll pass. Looks dangerous."

"So do you." His eyes had bled to black, and he was staring at me like he was hungry. "Will you always be waiting to catch me when I fall?" I raised my hand to run my nails through the sides of his hair.

His eyes searched mine. "Always." Slowly, his lips lowered. I'd take care of that hunger.

"Take me home," I whispered into his kiss.

I startled awake in the tub, the vision passing like a thick fog. One word rattled like an echo through my brain. "Always."

* * * * *

Sufficiently pruney, I dressed and descended to the kitchen. I hadn't eaten since an early lunch and prayed that Logan hadn't trashed dinner, even though I deserved as much.

Logan waited exactly where I'd left him, the roast covered on the stove. "I kept it warm for you," he said.

My heart melted, and I let it show in my smile. No sense letting it go to waste. I'd think more clearly on a full stomach. I needed all of the clarity I could get. "Thank you." I fixed myself a plate. "This looks too good to eat in here. Dining room?"

Logan agreed and followed me to the table.

"I'm sorry I was so hard on you earlier. This is great, Logan. Of all the ghosts I know, you are the best cook."

"I'm the only ghost you know."

"Not true. I know Prudence. But regardless, of all the people I know, you are the best cook. Whoever you were in life, you could cook."

"I wish I knew if that were true," Logan said.

The comment made me wonder. If I decided against being the witch, would Logan eventually forget how to cook? Just thinking about it made me eat slower and savor every bite.

"I'm sensing a change in you. Have you decided?"

"No, not yet."

"But you're considering it. You're considering being with him." A dark wave of smoke swirled through Logan, the jealousy rolling off him and filling the room with the scent of burnt toast.

"I don't like the idea of being with Rick. He lied to me and manipulated my memories to take advantage of me physically."

"Did he hurt you?" Logan fumed.

"No. But he did enough, and although I consented, I did so without understanding how our connection was influencing me. I don't know if I would have made the same choices without it."

"That bastard. I wouldn't do that to you, Grateful." Logan's green eyes smoldered.

"I know. You've always been completely honorable."

"So then, don't be with him."

"I'm beginning to see there's no other way. The witch is in me, like it or not. When that demon attacked me tonight, it made me realize I can choose not to accept my power, but I can't choose not to be the witch. She's part of who I am."

"It doesn't have to be."

"Yes. It does. I can see people's *souls*, Logan. Not to mention, I can't let you stay in limbo forever."

"If you sort me, we'll never see each other again."

Just thinking about Logan gone for good was a red-hot poker directly through the chest. My heart was skewered, roasting over the thought. I rubbed the ache and was happy for my nurse's brain. It allowed me to see beyond the emotional pain to the logical argument. "If I remain human, I'll eventually die, but you could be here for eternity."

"I don't care. I'm willing."

"Until I die, another witch can't replace me. Red Grove will become a very dangerous place, for all of us."

He had no answer for that. His eyes closed against the words, squeezing them shut as if he could hide from the truth behind his nonexistent eyelids.

"And, there's something else. I'm not sure how I feel about you, Logan. I haven't known you long enough to know. Frankly, I think your feelings for me have more to do with who I was in my past life than you will admit. You can sense I'm the sorter. Your soul is drawn to my latent power. It may feel like more, but…it's not."

"But I *am* sure."

"How can you be when you don't even know who *you* are?"

He flashed against the wall, broke apart, and then came back together. "That was a low blow."

"I'm sorry. It needed to be said."

Time drifted by us as I finished my meal, gulping down the glass of cabernet he'd poured for me and thinking it was perfectly paired with the beef. I ate every bite to show I appreciated the effort Logan put into it. The meal was perfect, but I hardly tasted it. I was too concerned about the feelings of the ghost who watched me eat it. Something in Logan was dying tonight—some hope of clinging to what remained of this life.

I crossed my fork and knife on my plate. "Everything was perfect. The food was the most delicious I've ever had."

Logan disappeared. A moment later, a romantic ballad crooned from the speakers in the family room. "Unforgettable" by Natalie Cole. The choice wasn't lost on me. He reappeared next to my chair, so solid I would have guessed he was human if I hadn't known better. I didn't have to look at the clock to know it must be midnight.

"Will you dance with me?" he asked, extending his arm. "For one dance, let's pretend we met when we had choices. When I was human, and you were carefree, and the world turned. Let's dance like there is no magic, just two human beings and the music."

I remembered how I'd danced with Rick and the…results. The music was different, and so was the man. I would give Logan this. We would dance, and we would always have this memory. I took his arm and stood, smiling as if I lived in the pretend world he wanted for us. I placed one arm on his hip, the cool tingle letting me know where his molecules began, and held his hand with my other. It was more difficult than I expected. I couldn't lean into him like I might with a human dancer. But we swayed to the music, my arms growing sore from holding the position. I smiled, and he pretended, and then the song ended.

I dropped my hands to my sides. Logan ran his fingers up my outer arms, making the tiny hairs stand on end. He leaned forward and the focused current of air that was his kiss brushed my lips. When I opened my eyes, the look he gave me was soul crushing. Pure unrequited love.

"I should get some sleep," I said.

He nodded.

"Good night, Logan."

Halfway up the stairs I heard him say, "I love you." I pretended not to hear him and continued up the stairs. I never made it to the top.

Just then the door to the garage burst open. Michelle entered the kitchen, her arms full of Ben and Jerry's ice cream. "Grateful? Your garage door was open. I hope you don't mind, I let myself—" Michelle stopped at the entrance to the dining room. She stared at Logan, and her jaw dropped.

Logan was doing his best to appear normal. He focused his energy to look as solid as possible. I wasn't sure how long the illusion would last.

I jogged back down the stairs and placed myself between them. "Of course it's okay," I said, hugging her in such a way as to block her view of Logan. I spun her around toward the kitchen. "Come on. Let's get some bowls for the ice cream."

"Wait. Aren't you going to introduce me to your friend?" She pivoted toward Logan.

Had she turned inward, toward me, I would have been able to stop her with my body. I would have made some excuse as to why the man I was with was suddenly gone. But Michelle rotated outward, away from me, making it almost impossible to maneuver in front of her. Logan dissolved at the precise moment she turned. If I had to guess, I'd say he took the opportunity of her facing the kitchen to make his escape and then couldn't stop the process halfway. But it was also entirely possible that he ran out of energy. After all, he'd spent the entire evening making me dinner and holding his molecules together. This whole situation was more than stressful to the poor guy—I mean, ghost.

Whatever the reason, Logan went up in smoke right in front of Michelle.

"Michelle, I—" My attempted explanation fell on deaf ears.

Her mouth opened and a head-splitting scream sliced through the room. The ice cream toppled from her fingers. She scrambled for the door.

"Michelle, stop!" I called, but she'd totally freaked. She spilled into the street before I could stop her. There was only one place to go from my house if you were following the road—across the bridge and straight to Rick's.

Unfortunately, it was after midnight, and Rick was working. At the top of the bridge, I could see what Michelle had already seen. Rick was standing in front of his house, completely naked. She stopped in the middle of the road like a deer in headlights.

"Stop. Please," he said. He held out a hand toward her.

She shook her head and backed away from him. Unfortunately, that meant she was backing toward the graveyard.

"Michelle, stop. I can explain," I called. I jogged toward her with my hands out.

It was no use. She was in full-blown panic mode. I wasn't even sure she could hear me.

"What's going on?" she said in a shaky voice.

I started to answer her, but was distracted by the fog rolling in behind the gate. Fingers of thick black mist filtered through the hedges, licking at the bars of the fence. If Michelle got any closer, the darkness would reach her.

"Michelle, move away from the gate," I said, voice trembling. I gestured with my hand for her to come to me.

Rick took a step forward.

She didn't move. "No. Tell me what's going on." She stepped backward.

The fog stretched for her.

"Please, trust me. Take a step toward me," I said. I wasn't sure what the fog was exactly, only that it was making Rick's skin bubble under the surface. His beast knew it was evil. Plus, nothing good came out of the hellmouth at night.

She did not move.

Rick glanced at me, and his thoughts were as clear as if he'd whispered in my ear. He wanted permission to take her by force.

I nodded. It had to be done.

Michelle's screams broke our connection. She was too close. Tendrils of fog wrapped themselves around her waist and slid her up the wrought iron spindles to the top of the gate. Rick was there in an instant but not fast enough. Michelle's legs followed her body over the top.

I started forward. Rick's hand shot out. "No, Grateful. You're not equipped for this. It will be of no use if they have you too. I will get her."

"Please, Rick. Hurry. She's my best friend."

His skin bubbled, violently. The smell that always clung to Rick—pine, holy water, and earth—grew stronger, surrounding me, filling me. I realized now what the scent was. It was the smell of a fresh grave. I watched his bones grow, bend, and reshape his body. His chin extended as he folded to the earth, his ears growing to a point on each side of his head. Claws sprouted from his knuckles. Scales and fur budded from his skin and over his backbone, which extended into a tail. Rick transformed into a monster, both reptilian and wolf-like. Two iridescent stretches of leathery flesh unfolded from his back. Wings.

The beast ran a few steps and took to the air.

Through the bars of the gate, I watched the fog channel itself into three forms. The redheaded vamp I'd seen my first night in the cemetery fleshed out and grinned at me, licking his lips. A vamp I'd never seen before, huge and bald like the strong man at the circus, formed next. But when the fog that held Michelle formed into muscled flesh with a black ponytail, my stomach twisted. Marcus.

In my head, I heard his voice. *Come, girl. Come over the fence and we'll play a game. It'll be fun.* He didn't recognize me. I guess that was the benefit of having a brand-new body.

I backed away from the gate.

Marcus frowned and narrowed his eyes. Rick swooped into the cemetery. The vamps scattered. Red Hair wasn't fast enough, and Rick's beast flipped him into his mouth, sinking teeth through his abdomen. The sound of bones crunching made me gag, and blood sprayed across the pebble pathway. I swallowed rapidly, trying to keep my dinner down.

Michelle released a head-splitting screech as more blood sprayed across her face. Marcus clamped a hand over her mouth, cutting off the scream. She collapsed in his arms, eyes rolling back and limbs going limp. "Michelle!" I screamed. Had he hurt her? Was she dead? Her chest rose and fell. No—she'd passed out. At least she wasn't panicking anymore. Now the only one panicking was me.

Marcus ducked behind a monolith, dragging Michelle with him. I looked back toward the strongman and watched him break off a piece of a marble headstone. He hurled the sharp shard of stone at Rick.

"Rick, watch out!" I yelled.

The beast lunged to the side, but the granite sliced through his outer shoulder. The yelp Rick's beast emitted was somewhere between the howl of an oncoming tornado and the growl of a wolf. The sound was so loud it hurt. I covered my ears with my palms. Apparently, it had a similar effect on the vamps because the strongman was distracted long enough for Rick to swallow him whole. Then Rick turned toward Marcus.

"Watch your step, caretaker. One wrong move and the girl dies," Marcus hissed. "In fact, I think it might be safer for me on the inside." Marcus thrust his arm into Michelle's chest; her eyes popped open in terror.

"Stop! Get out of her," I screamed, racing to the gate and gripping the bars. The vamp slid into her body like he was putting on a coat.

Rick's beast howled and scratched the earth.

Michelle craned her neck and laughed. "Kill me and you kill the girl."

The beast charged but stopped short. He paced in front of Michelle, who had taken on an evil expression that didn't belong on my friend's face. I wanted in there. I wanted to bust Marcus' ass for what he'd done to her. Instead, I watched Michelle pass her hand in front of a grave, never taking her eyes off Rick. The ground broke open, revealing a stone stairway. My hands went to my heart. He was taking her to the underworld.

"No. No!" I picked up a stone and hurled it uselessly through the gate at Marcus.

Michelle's head snapped toward me, giving Rick enough time to shoot forward and snatch her from the top step. He clutched her in his talons. I covered my mouth and looked away. I couldn't watch. Oh God, Michelle. Tears clouded my eyes. The sound of moving earth signaled the door to the underworld had closed. And then the smell of the grave indicated Rick was changing. I braved a glance back. The talons around Michelle transformed into a human arm.

"Let me go," Marcus/Michelle said. Her head shook, and her grin said it all. Marcus was sure Rick would never hurt Michelle to get to him.

"How do we get him out?" I yelled.

"There is a spell."

"Then do it!" I paced helplessly.

"I'm not strong enough," he rasped.

Marcus laughed.

This was exactly what Prudence had warned me about. Rick was weakening, and it could have dire consequences. I closed my eyes and took a deep breath. "If the Monk's Hill witch came back, could she do this?"

"Yes," he said. The tiny word was loaded with emotion.

"She's dead," Marcus said. "The Monk's Hill witch is dead, and you will never find another."

I balled my hands into fists and shot Marcus my sharpest stare. "Then let's go awaken the witch, Rick."

His eyes snapped to mine in surprise. "Are you sure?"

"Oh, absolutely. There is nothing I'd like better than to have the power to kick this vampire's ass."

"No," Marcus barked. "It's impossible!" He struggled against Rick's arm without success.

The good thing about having a mental connection with someone is that you feel the person smile before their expression actually changes. Rick smiled from the inside out and filled my brain with memories. I saw our first kiss and our second first kiss, along with the day we got married the first time. It was overwhelming and heartwarming all at once.

Even though I couldn't say for sure that I loved Rick in this life, I wanted to love him. I wanted to know if this supernova erupting in my chest was the product of the memories fed into my brain or my actual feelings. But more than anything, I wanted to become who I was supposed to be. Ready or not, becoming the witch was the only way to save Michelle and end Marcus.

CHAPTER 19
The Proposal

I didn't know as much as I thought I did about vampires. For example, in books and movies they always use silver chains to restrain the vamps. Turns out that silver doesn't work when the vampire possesses your best friend. The silver can't soak through the human skin to get to the vampire, and because silver is relatively weak, it breaks too easily. Instead, a plain old rope soaked in holy water will do. The rope restrains, and the holy water keeps the vamp inside the human. As an added bonus, with Marcus' fangs trapped in Michelle's human mouth, a regular gag was all we needed to shut him up.

"I think it's best that we keep Marcus bound until after the ceremony. It will be dangerous," Rick said. He leaned over my best friend's body on the couch in his cottage and tested the bindings. "Marcus did this to force us to remove him from the enchantments of the cemetery boundary. He'll do anything in his power to free himself, and I warn you he'll be much harder to catch if he escapes on the outside."

"So, we don't let him escape."

"He'll try to take advantage of your inexperience." Rick shook his head like he was breaking bad news.

"Whoa. What? I thought this was wham, bam, memories back. Poof. I'm the witch."

"I'm afraid it won't be quite that easy, *mi cielo*. The power will come, but learning how to wield it will take some time."

I sighed. "And I thought I was done with school."

He brushed my bangs back and ran his fingers down my cheek to my chin. His gray eyes wrinkled at the corners with his smile. "You are more than capable of rising to this challenge."

His stare was too intense. I had to look away. Fidgeting, I dug my fingers into the holes in the afghan on the back of the sofa. "This is beautiful," I said.

"You knitted it more than one hundred years ago."

I yanked my hand back and wiped it on my jeans. It didn't help. The weirdness stuck to me. "Where does the, er, ceremony have to take place?"

"The attic. It is your seat of power," he said.

"Can we move a mattress up there, or do we have to do it on the altar?"

He lifted an eyebrow, and a sultry smile stretched across his face. My blood accelerated to a frantic pace.

Beast or not, he was incredibly attractive. "Didn't Prudence tell you? The attic adapts to whatever you need it to be. It is made of your magic. It can look any way you want it to look."

"You mean, like, I can change it with my mind? No furniture-moving necessary?"

"You might need Prudence's help at first, but yes."

"Let's do it." I tried not to think about the double entendre, but heat crept up my neck to my ears anyway.

Ever the gentleman, Rick pretended not to notice. "I think we should take my car. Even though it's the middle of the night, it would do us no good to have a citizen of Red Grove see us carrying a bound woman into your home."

"You have a car?" It sounded stupid, even to my own ears. "Sorry, that was silly of me. Of course you have a car. We live in the boondocks. You wouldn't be able to get groceries without one."

Rick frowned. "There are things about me you should know. Differences. I...I don't need groceries, unless I'm cooking for you."

I thought about the night I'd been over for dinner, how I'd never seen him eat. The liquid in his glass looked different from wine but somehow familiar. It *was* familiar. I worked with it every day. Blood.

"Logan said you feed off blood and other things. So that's all you need?"

"The magic that makes me immortal is tied to the evil I'm here to control. My strength is their strength, but I also inherited their hunger, their desires. It isn't always ideal."

My face was numb. I stood motionless behind our vampire captive, staring at Rick as if he had sprouted two heads. My thoughts immediately went to the practical. We would never share a bowl of ice cream. We could never go out for pizza.

"Oh, I *can* eat," he said, and I realized he was reading my thoughts. "I drank the wine at your house the night we met, remember?"

I nodded.

"But I don't have to. And sometimes nothing but blood will do."

"Oh," was all I could manage.

"There is much I should tell you about me, but we have years, maybe lifetimes, for that. There is something more important for us to talk about now." He walked around the couch to me and took my hands in his. "There will only be this one first time. In your last lifetimes, you married me before the ceremony. I would have it that way again, if you would let me."

Blink. Blink. Seconds passed, but he didn't break into laughter or say he was kidding. "Did you just ask me to marry you?" I asked incredulously.

"Yes." He walked to the bookcase on the far wall and opened an ornately carved ivory box. In it, a heavy silver ring with a lapis stone gleamed. "I have the ring you wore the first time. I planned to ask you in a more romantic way, but it appears we are pressed for time. If we don't get

Marcus out of her by sunrise, he will die inside her body for the day and she will likely not survive it."

"But Prudence said I only had to sleep with you to take back the power. She didn't say anything about marriage," I whispered.

"Technically, that is true but..." His face fell. "These are different times than when I once knew you. When you and I first fell in love, a lady would not do such a thing without being married."

"I'll become the witch, Rick, but I will not marry you. I haven't known you long enough. I'm not even sure I love you." My entire world was out of control. Wasn't it enough I was becoming the witch? Did he have to own all of me?

Facing the bookcase, he closed the box. His expression went stony. I didn't need our connection to know I'd hurt him.

"I'm sorry," I said, because that's what you say to someone after you rip their heart out.

"Do not apologize for honesty, *mi cielo*," he said toward the bookcase. "But know this. I *do* know that I love you. I've loved you for more than three hundred years. I will love you when the sun comes up in the morning and when it comes up on the three thousandth morning after that. I loved you on the day you died, and I love you now." He cleared his throat and turned to face me. "I am immortal, Grateful. I have an eternity to love you, whether or not you love me in return."

If I'd been forced to decide right then and there if I loved him, I would have said yes. I didn't know if the memories made me feel that way or if it was hard not to return such authentic and unearned affection.

He scooped Michelle into his arms and carried her toward the garage behind the kitchen. I opened the door for him.

"You drive a Tesla Roadster?"

"You sound surprised. Immortality makes one an environmentalist by necessity."

"These are, like, a hundred grand. How much does being a caretaker pay?"

"I invested wisely in the summer of 1945. Plus, you left me a large life insurance policy."

"So you mean this car is really mine, since I'm alive again."

"The life insurance policy belonged to my wife. I'll let you drive it when you hold that title once again."

I couldn't respond to that, so I concentrated on helping to shove Michelle/Marcus into the passenger's seat. "No backseat. I'll walk home." I turned to leave.

"Come, *mi cielo*. Don't waste time. Sit on my lap."

I didn't argue. He lowered himself behind the wheel, and I slid in after him. I had to practically lie down across his body to fit. I slipped my arm down the side of his seat and fit my chin into the groove of his clavicle. I wrapped my other arm across his chest and snuggled in. The dark smell of him, the spice of nightfall, filled my nose. With my best friend possessed by a vamp in the seat next to me, you'd think I could control my libido, but I caught myself inhaling Rick and wishing I had more than his scent inside of me.

He sensed my attraction immediately. I heard his breath draw in, and his face turned into my neck, nuzzling me behind my ear. "When we were married," he whispered, "you loved this."

I found out what "this" was when he bit my earlobe gently then licked up the back of my ear. Yep, even in a new body, that move rocked my clock. I shivered in the circle of his arms. His black eyes sank into me, and my core tightened decadently in response.

"We've got to go," I said. "We have only a few hours until sunrise."

"Yes. Let's go."

Turns out those Teslas really can haul ass. Rick's car was tucked in next to mine in the garage before you could say "foreplay." The hardest part was getting up off Rick's lap. Or should I say, I got up off the hardest part of Rick's lap. Surprise, surprise. I was looking forward to this ceremony.

CHAPTER 20
We Make Magic Together

Mercifully, Logan wasn't in the attic. I didn't ask Prudence where he'd gone as I thought his absence was in his best interest. Instead, I threw myself into the task at hand, preparing for the ceremony that would help me save Michelle.

"Your magic is amplified by the night," Prudence said. Her nurse outfit was gone, replaced by a sequined green gown that reminded me of the Oscars. I guess this was a big deal for her. "With concentration, you can mold this attic to your will, but when the sun rises, all you have created will disappear. You won't be strong enough to maintain it in the daylight."

I nodded. "We need a place for Michelle. I don't want her to be afraid if she wakes up in a strange place."

"Concentrate on the room you would like to create for her. Picture each object and will it here. You must visualize it, exactly, in your head. Any uncertainty and it won't come through."

The walls themselves were easy enough. I created them behind a door in the north wall. The apartment mystically expanded the size of the attic, an instant room addition. But the rest was more difficult. Don't get me wrong; the best part about having a magical attic is the decorating. Don't like the color of the linens? Just think of something new, and poof—there it is. I didn't have to move any furniture or go to any stores. Everything was free and exactly as I wished it. Only, even though I'd spent plenty of time at Michelle's, trying to picture her apartment down to the throw pillow was almost impossible. I made the room as close as I could to the real thing and placed Michelle/Marcus inside.

Then I started preparing for the ceremony.

"Are there any rules? Or do we just, like, do it?"

"It's your party, Grateful. You invite the caretaker into the attic, your most personal magical space." She stepped closer to me and placed her ghostly hand on my elbow. "Rick's magic is internal. It is part of who and what he is, in his very cells. Your magic is external; it is what you choose to be. The ceremony is in the choosing. You will choose to be the yin to his yang. Your power rests in him and in this house. He is the vessel."

I closed my eyes briefly. "I think I know what to do."

"One more thing. You will need this." Prudence approached a large wooden trunk near *The Book of Light* and retrieved a sword as long as my torso, the same sword as in my memory. "According to legend, the sword was made from the femur of St. Callistus, the patron saint of cemetery workers. It is as sharp as steel. You conjured it for yourself when you first came into your own power. Because it is a holy object, you can't touch it until you've accepted the responsibility that goes with it. If you do, it will burn your hand. However, once the sword knows you, no one else on earth or in the underworld will be able to wield it."

"Cool," I said, dumbly staring at the faint blue glow of the blade. Prudence held it out toward me. I conjured a small wooden table for her to rest it on.

"Now I will give you some privacy." Prudence winked at me and dissolved.

I focused on the empty room. From the moment we'd met, I'd thought of Rick as a matador. I'd supposed that I was the bull. But I was wrong. We both were the bull, and we both were the bullfighter. Sex is akin to death in a way. It is the end of one stage in a relationship and the beginning of another. Something is given up when you have sex, and something is given to you. It's why I don't believe there is such a thing as casual sex.

Nothing about sex is casual. In the best situation, sex can create life, but more often it ruins lives. And so, it is a dance of trust. It is a dance of beauty and humility. It is a dance with death. Tonight, who I thought I was would die, and I would become what I was meant to be.

I wore a red cape and nothing else. The floor was sand. The bed was red silk and velvet. Candles encircled the room by the hundreds—red glowing things that provided the only light. A table next to the bed held the sword Prudence had placed there. When all was prepared, I invited Rick in.

He'd dressed in a T-shirt and jeans, but as he walked through the door to the attic, my magic changed him. Now he wore a blood-red matador outfit, complete with beaded jacket and skintight pants that left nothing to the imagination. He wrinkled his brow as he looked down at himself.

I shrugged. It was my fantasy; I pulled the strings. His sultry smile told me he'd willingly resigned himself to his fate.

Rick strode into the arena with the grace of a dancer, a Baryshnikov in bullfighting gear. He circled me slowly, never taking his eyes off me. I backed away, the red cape wrapped around my body. When we'd completed the circle, I faced him head-on, wrapped one of my arms in the side of the cape and with a large, quick circle, flourished the fabric in front of my body. The effect was that Rick could see only portions of my nude flesh as the cape fell—the line of my neck, a shoulder, my breasts, my stomach, a hip, and the length of my leg—all before the red fabric swallowed me again.

Power flooded the room, a wild, tangible thing. Rick's tongue ran across his lips, and he started toward me, tentatively at first, but then his steps quickened. He reached for me and his fingers grazed the space between my breasts. I dissolved and appeared behind him on the other side of the arena, panting with desire. The move was effortless. The magic, part of me.

He turned toward me like a predator, lowering his chin and meeting my eyes through his lashes. His lips parted, and the corner of his mouth rose in a way that made me long to kiss the grin away.

I circled the cape again, slower this time so that each part of my body was etched into his memory. In the blink of an eye, he traversed the arena, his hands at my waist. Every cell in my body wanted to sink into his embrace. But not yet. His fingers passed through me as I faded. Across the arena, I appeared again, circling the cape as fast as he could turn to see it.

Rick was on me in an instant. This time, I allowed it. I kissed him, my tongue searching his mouth as I stroked him through the thinly stretched fabric at his groin. I noticed again how huge he was, definitely longer and thicker than any man I'd had before. Intimidating as it was, the feel of him in my palm made my heart race and my body clench with anticipation. I broke apart and reappeared across the arena, in front of the bed.

This time, when I circled the cape, I swept it off me and tossed it aside. And then I was flying. My feet had left the floor before the cape hit the sand. Rick's arms were around me, and we were falling, falling toward the bed. He rolled in the air, taking the impact of the fall and catching me on top of his body. I had a glorious moment of feeling my weight stretched out on top of him. Then he smiled and showed me a set of razor-sharp, elongated teeth. His jaw had lengthened, and his eyes were coal-black disks. This half-shifted state was the caretaker at his most powerful.

For a moment, it threw me, made me question my choice. But what had I expected? I'd known he would take blood. He waited patiently for me to make the next move, waited for me to process what was happening. I lowered my lips to his, darting my tongue between those long canines.

Heart pounding, I crawled off him to the end of the bed. He tried to follow, but I had other things in mind. I liked control, and today I would have it. Arms shot out of the bed and gripped him to the duvet. Twelve of them. All mine, of course—echoes of my own. I crawled to the end of the bed and watched my magic at work. My echo hands grabbed handfuls of his shiny red matador outfit and, at my command, ripped it off and cast it aside. He tried to reach for me, but my magic was stronger than him here, and I was enjoying every second of this game.

"Mmmm. What shall I do with you now that I've caught you?" I whispered. The candles blazed higher, fed by my lust.

Languorously, I worked my real hands up his legs from his feet, dipping down to lick his inner thigh. He growled.

Power so thick it was like we were under water filled me and connected us as it had before. Every kiss, every caress registered in my body as if it were done to me. I lapped up his hard shaft, toying with the heavy weights at the base. I circled the tip with my tongue, then sucked harder, taking him deep into my throat.

He moaned and arched into me.

I released him slowly from my mouth as I prowled up his body, brushing my breasts over the smooth expanse of his chest. My eyes caught on his scar. I'd put it there when I'd made him my caretaker. I traced my finger over it, noting that it no longer hurt for me to see it. Whatever magic unraveled within me had cured me of that malady. I raked my nails gently down his arms and flicked my tongue over his right nipple. His breath caught.

"*Mi cielo*, please. Please," he begged.

When I finally reached his mouth, I spilled my hair over my shoulder to keep it out of the way and allowed my lips to linger over his. With my nose and cheek, I traced the sharp line of his jaw, warm skin on skin. I ached to have him inside of me, but owning him like this was exquisite torture. I rolled my hips against him until he moaned my name, and I couldn't take it any longer. I positioned him at my entrance. My echo hands retreated into the bed as I lowered my hips.

Slowly. Slowly. I had to go slow or I feared he would split me open. Truly though, the pleasure was unbelievable. I felt my own but then I felt his as well. Up and down, I worked him into me inch by throbbing inch.

He held himself back, patiently waiting for me to get comfortable with his size. But once he was completely in me, he began moving, kissing me, my neck, my ear, rubbing his hands down the length of my body.

Then he flipped me up. It was effortless, like I weighed nothing. He folded his lower legs under and rose to a kneeling position on the bed, grabbing me under my butt, so we were chest to chest and hip to hip. In this position, he was so deep it was almost painful. He thrust into me, worked his hand up my stomach, cradled my breast. I arched backward, and he sucked my nipple. The rhythm of our bodies caused the pleasure to build, greater and greater until I was at the edge.

"*Mi cielo*," he moaned, closing his eyes and tilting his head back. The words echoed warm and sweet inside my head. "It's time. Pick up your blade."

I did as he said, and it did not burn my hand. I allowed him to guide the blade to the right side of his neck and pressed the sharp bone into his flesh. Just as the orgasm overcame me, he moved my hand, slicing open the skin over his jugular. His other hand palmed the back of my head, pulling my mouth to the wound.

The thought of drinking blood had never intrigued me before, but Rick's blood was liquid orgasm. Pleasure flowed from my lips to my toes. I rolled with it, coming again and again. His release mirrored my own, and I milked Rick of what he pumped into me as the warm blood coated my throat. The power bound us together, made each orgasm feed the next.

His teeth sank into my neck and shoulder, a wide bite that drew blood but wasn't painful. My flesh moved aside to allow him access. Warm and wet, blood dripped down my back, washed into his mouth. I sucked from Rick while he drank from me, pleasing each other in every possible way.

I was vaguely aware of a wind circling us, stirring up the sand in the arena, gentle at first but then with a terrible force. We were in the eye of a hurricane, a cyclone of power.

Time stopped. I raised my head. A trail of Rick's blood dripped from the corner of my mouth to my chin. I wiped it away with the back of my hand. The grains of sand from the arena hovered like static in the air. Rick was motionless at my neck. The candles were frozen mid-flicker. Everything had stopped but me.

"What the fuck?" I said, watching as the ceiling opened up above me.

A ball of light appeared and plowed into my chest with such force, it took my breath away. I gasped, and time knocked back into its flow. The sand fell and so did we, onto the bed.

Panting and spent, Rick pulled out of me, rolling to his side and wrapping me within a cocoon of his body. He burrowed his face into the back of my hair. "I love you," he said into my ear.

I wanted to respond in kind. I wanted to say I loved him too. At that moment, I even felt like I did. But I wasn't sure if it was the magic or the memories or the fantastic sex. So I didn't say it. He didn't press for a response. He held me until it was obvious that we had to get back to business if we wanted to have any hope of saving Michelle.

But I found myself longing for five more minutes in his arms.

CHAPTER 21

I Perform My First Exorcism

I willed the arena to dissolve into the attic's sanded wood floor, and Rick left to check on Marcus/Michelle.

That's when Logan returned. For a long time, he stared at me with the hollow expression of someone who'd completely lost hope. My heart broke to see him like this, and I opened my mouth to say something, anything to comfort him.

He cut me off. "Not now, Grateful. You're running out of darkness. Save your friend." He glanced toward *The Book of Light*.

I walked over to the tome and used two hands to open it. In my last lifetime, I must have been a freak about organization. It was tabbed like an encyclopedia. Exorcism-Vampires in the E section right after Exorcism-General and right before Exorcism-Wraiths.

The spell seemed simple enough. Forcing the vamp out was the easy part. Keeping him out was the greater challenge. A puree of honey, sage, and lemon balm had to be poured over the victim. The concoction acted as a one-way membrane to keep the vampire out of the victim's body. Salt, sprinkled in a ring around Michelle and me, would act as a boundary to contain the vamp once released.

"Logan, can you make this puree for me? You're the best with the food processor." Anything to get him to stop staring at me like I'd killed his puppy.

He nodded and disappeared. A moment later I heard cabinet doors open in the kitchen and the scrape of the food processor being loaded onto the kitchen island.

Rick returned, grimacing in the direction of the sound, like Logan was a rodent in the walls. I shook my head. I had other problems.

"We can't leave Michelle in the bindings. Marcus has to be able to get out during the spell. But if we take the ropes off, he could attack me, using Michelle's body. You'll have to hold her down."

"I can't," he said, matter-of-factly. "I'll upset the balance of power within the ring."

"Crap. We have to contain her body." I flipped pages in my massive spell book, looking for answers.

"A paralyzation spell?" Rick offered.

I thumbed over to *P*. "It's complicated. It says it takes an hour to brew." I looked toward the darkened window.

"We don't have that kind of time," Rick said.

Paralysis. We needed to cause paralysis. The answer hit me. I snapped my fingers. "Propofol. We put her to sleep with medicine, not magic!"

Rick stared at me blankly.

"Trust me." I conjured a bottle of propofol, aka milk of amnesia, and some IV supplies. I put her under on the couch in her apartment-styled attic room. I didn't think the medication would have any effect on the vampire, but he'd be trapped within an uncooperative body.

The door squeaked open. A mixing bowl and large container of salt floated to the coffee table. Logan formed by my side. "What is all this?"

"Anesthesia. Rick, help me remove the bindings." Her heavily sedated body was dead weight as Rick and I untied Michelle and removed her gag. I checked the drop rate on her IV.

"I'll clear a space for you." Rick tugged the coffee table back against the wall.

"Prudence? Are you here?" I yelled at the ceiling.

She formed next to Rick. "I'm here. You can do this. Just like riding a bike."

"In my past life," I mumbled. Per the book, I sprinkled the salt in a large circle around Michelle and me, closing us into my ring of magic. Step two was the balm. It felt sticky and thick when I stuck my hand into the mixing bowl, but I layered it as evenly across her body as possible. Afterward, I wished I could wash my hands, but I couldn't leave the circle.

The power came when I called it, like an ocean wave crashing to shore. Only, I was the shore, and the force of it almost knocked me over. It's hard to explain what it was I did to call the power or where it came from. I just know that when I made love to Rick, some part of me connected to it. Afterward it was there, waiting for me as if I had grown another appendage. But like a new appendage, it felt awkward wielding it, and I didn't have the benefit of a team of physical therapists to help me. All I had was Rick and Prudence trying to coach me from outside the circle.

"You have it, *mi cielo*. I can see it pulsing around you. Throw it into her chest, and your magic will drive the vampire out."

"How do I throw it?" I asked.

Prudence answered. "I've seen you do it before. You bring your hands to your chest, focus on the object, and then thrust them toward your target."

I folded my hands in, concentrating on Michelle, and then pointed them at her. Nothing happened.

"The power is around you, not a part of you. You must collect it with your arms. Gather your aura, then throw it in her direction," Rick said.

I tried again. I closed my eyes and reached out my hands to the power. It circled me in a thick cloud like cream soup. With my eyes closed, I could sense a pulse collecting in my hands. When I brought them to my chest this time, the magic came with them. A great, glowing ball of energy formed in front of me. I opened my eyes, focused fully on Michelle, and pushed with everything I had.

No way was I prepared for how quickly Marcus would emerge from Michelle's body. He leaped on me in a flurry of slashing teeth and claws. As planned, I stepped out of the circle just in time for his face to slam into the magic barricade I'd created with the salt. Only I hadn't thought it through. Michelle was still sedated within the circle with Marcus. She couldn't step out because she was unconscious. Sure, he couldn't re-enter her body because of the balm, but that didn't mean he couldn't hurt her. A couple of minutes of ricocheting around my magic ring and he turned his attention on her.

"No! Leave her alone!" I yelled.

"I'm sorry, witchy poo. I can't hear you from within this circle. Let me out and then maybe we can communicate." He bit down on the last word, turning it into a threat.

Rick paced the edge of the salt ring, a low growl bubbling up his throat.

"Oh, please. Caretaker, you are so out of your league. Even now the vampires are growing in number. Soon our army will be large enough to circumvent your defenses. You'll never be able to keep us in the underworld." He walked over to Michelle's IV and placed his hand on the clamp controlling the rate of administration.

"Stop!" I yelled, but he began to turn the dial. The propofol flowed too quickly. If I didn't do something, she could go into cardiac arrest.

"Rick, what do I do? It could kill her."

"You control its existence. Take it away."

I willed the remaining drug to vanish, but it was too late. Marcus had opened the valve and allowed the anesthesia to flow into her vein as fast as her body would take it in. Her breathing slowed. She was in dangerous territory.

"I need to get to her."

"Very well, *mi cielo*. Break the circle and I will fight Marcus."

He didn't have to ask twice. I wiped away a section of salt, and the vamp blew by me, a black wind that smelled of sulfur. I ran to Michelle's side and took her pulse. Slow but steady.

"I need to stay with her," I called, but Rick and Marcus were already circling each other. I removed Michelle's IV and put pressure on the site, trying to watch what was happening in the room behind me.

Rick dove for Marcus in fast-forward. Marcus dodged, equally fast, sending Rick somersaulting across the floor. Marcus hustled toward Rick, positioning himself to deliver a kick to his gut. I willed a concrete wall between the two and watched Marcus' foot crash through it as if it were paper. Rick dodged to the side, grabbed Marcus' foot and lifted. I willed a row of wooden stakes behind Marcus, hoping he would fall backward, but he cartwheeled to the side and delivered a punch to Rick's ribs. I winced, but Rick barely flinched. Instead, he thrashed a half-shifted hand and shredded the front of Marcus' chest.

I was sure if Rick had the time and space to shift into his beast, Marcus would be history, but the vamp was strong, quick, and more intelligent than I had given him credit for. While I was thinking of ways to distract him to give Rick time to change, he spotted the attic window. Marcus dove through headfirst, sending a shower of glass into my front yard. Rick lunged after him.

I ran to the window and watched the chase continue toward the bridge. I thought Rick had him, but Marcus turned into fog and melted into the night. Rick followed, dematerializing. Deep inside, I knew we'd lost him. Marcus was free from the cemetery.

He'd escaped and with him any delusions I'd had of feeling safe.

CHAPTER 22
The End of a Rough Night

"The sun is rising. He'll have to go to ground," Rick said as he re-formed inside my attic window. He paced, fists clenching and jaw tight.

"You mean he'll have to dig a hole to sleep underground." I was such a rookie.

"Yes, our best chance is to wait and find him during the day. Once he rises, he'll try to find a free coven to protect him."

"Free coven?" I asked, shaking my head.

"Vampires you haven't sentenced to the underworld," Rick clarified.

"What? Living among us?"

"You didn't think they were all behind the gate?"

I scowled. "Yes, actually I did." Now that I thought about it, Prudence mentioned that Marcus had help from the outside, but the notion that there were supernatural beings living among us, outside the graveyard, hadn't registered until just now. Even when that *thing* attacked me at Java Jane's, and I found it wasn't human, I'd assumed it was an exception, an escaped convict of the supernatural world, not a creature living freely outside the cemetery. There was so much I didn't understand.

Hands on his hips, Rick snorted, and shook his head. I didn't think he was being critical. More likely, he was frustrated at the turn of events. So was I.

"So how do we find him? Can you hunt him down?"

"We can do it together. If you can cast a spell to determine his general vicinity, I'll be able to track him once we're close."

"Damn, I don't feel good about him being out there."

Rick gave a sideways nod, like any husband in America might give his wife. "I am sorry, *mi cielo*, that I failed to kill Marcus. This is twice he has evaded me."

"It's my fault. I should have thought of a way to keep Michelle safe. *Holy crow!* Michelle!" I raced back to the room I'd disguised as her apartment where I'd left her with Prudence. Prudence was gone, but Michelle sat on my replication of her Pottery Barn sofa, sipping ice water and looking extremely confused. I quickly closed the door to her pseudo-apartment behind me.

"What is going on?" Michelle asked, her head tilted.

"What do you mean?" I squeaked nervously.

"Well, unless I've had the worst nightmare of my life—your house is haunted, your boyfriend is a shape-shifter, and I just survived being possessed by a vampire."

"Worst nightmare of your life," I offered, nodding.

"Hmmm, I don't think so. I'm covered in something gooey that smells like turkey stuffing, and I'm sitting in a room that looks exactly like my apartment did six months ago."

Oh, crap. Michelle had decorated her apartment the same way since college, in neutral tones. But now I remembered that six months ago she'd broken down and redecorated. She'd kept the couch but thrown in some sari print pillows and a jute rug. She'd draped some gauzy stuff over the windows. I'd been to her home. I'd seen the changes. But in the stress of the situation, my brain simply reverted back to the apartment I'd spent most of my college years living in.

"How's this?" I closed my eyes, and the new items appeared in their places.

"Holy shit!" Michelle cried. Her mouth opened and closed several times. "It's really disturbing, like one of those 'find what's different' games. I know this isn't my apartment, but I can't tell you exactly what's different. Tell me what's going on while I try to get my head around what you just did."

I told her. I spilled my guts about everything—Rick, Logan, Prudence, my history, and Monk's Cemetery. I told her because she was my best friend, and I trusted her more than anyone. Plus, she already knew most of it and, for her own safety, needed to understand the rest. When I was done, she sighed deeply and took my hand in hers.

"So, Rick and Logan are the two guys you were talking about at Valentines?"

"Yes."

"Damn. You know, if I hadn't seen this with my own eyes I would have thought you were crazy."

"Uh-huh."

"I suppose that's why you weren't completely truthful?"

"Yep."

"I forgive you." She gave me a tight hug. "But no more lies, okay? I believe you now, so there's no reason to keep this from me anymore."

"Absolutely. But Michelle, I think we should keep this between us. Don't tell Manny. It's too weird." Not telling her husband would be hard for Michelle, but I needed this to stay between us.

"Of course," she said. "Anyone else would either think we were insane or plot some way to use this to their financial advantage. And Manny doesn't need the stress. I love you, Grateful. I wouldn't do that to you."

"Good," I said.

Our conversation was interrupted when Prudence walked in. "Excuse me, but the sun is about to rise, and I was hoping you could name me before it breaks the horizon. I'm not excited about spending another day in this attic."

"What do I need to do?"

She brought me a silver bowl. "Concentrate on me, and who I was will come to you. When you know where I belong, say 'Prudence Meriwether, I release you' and where you release me to." The last part she said in a whisper. "Then you provide a sacrifice of blood, and I will go."

"What do I sacrifice?"

Prudence looked down at her feet. "The bowl needs blood. You used your own in your past life. A sacrifice to open the portal."

"Oh, I see."

I picked up my sword and positioned it on a small table that I conjured. Prudence bowed her head. I took her in. When I say I "took her in," I don't mean the normal way, when you see someone on the street and scan the person from head to toe. My magic seemed to bloom and envelop her. Her life played out before my eyes, from her simple beginnings on a farm to her death in this house. Prudence had lived a good life. She'd always been there for others, and becoming a nurse was simply an extension of the altruism inherent in her character.

"Prudence Meriwether," I said in a strong, clear voice, "I release you to heaven." I sliced my forearm with as small and gentle a cut as possible and watched a drop of blood drip into the silver bowl.

Prudence's head shot up. With a smile as bright and warm as the sunrise that pressed against the horizon, she broke apart into pieces of light that swirled toward the ceiling. In a funnel cloud of positive energy, she ascended and disappeared beyond my attic to a place I knew somehow was everything she'd wanted it to be.

"Logan," I called, "it's your turn."

He appeared in front of me, looking less excited about the process than Prudence had. "Are you sure there's enough time? We could wait until tomorrow."

"Now, Logan," I said. "Don't put this off."

I concentrated on him. I saw his life in a series of images. He was running through bright green grass in a yard as large as a park. A woman I understood was his mother ran after him, swooped him up and planted a kiss on his cheek. I saw him as a teenager swinging a bat on a baseball field. He was in high school and a girl, maybe seventeen, was under him.

Pictures flashed one after the other, but it was the feelings that came with them that told me about him as a person. I wasn't surprised when I saw him in culinary school and then cooking in a restaurant. A string of relationships flashed through my brain. As thoughtful as Logan had seemed with me, he'd been a selfish lover in the past. But there was another side to him. He could be exceedingly generous with his time and money.

I took Logan in and what my magic told me was that he was balanced—some good, some not so good. But he wasn't evil. He didn't belong in the underworld. If I had to say anything about his soul, it would be that he was unfinished. He was in-between.

But I was the witch, and I needed to send him home. I'd named him Logan, but I sent my magic into him to find his real name. I'd decided. I would send him to heaven, not because it was clear to me that he belonged there but because it was clear he didn't belong anywhere else.

Nothing came to me. It was as if his soul had forgotten its own name. Was this what Prudence warned me about? Was this the great forgetting? Was I too late to save Logan?

My magic receded, spitting Logan out as if I'd rolled him in my mouth like a candy. I wasn't sure what was happening until I turned my head and saw the first rays of light cascade in through my broken attic window on the crest of a warm breeze. The light washed over Michelle's living room, and as it did, my illusion disappeared. My magic evaporated in the light of day. All that was left after the light touched it was a sanded wood floor and chipping white walls. And then it was just me, Michelle, Rick, and a filmy version of Logan, standing in an ordinary attic.

"Sunrise," I said. "I'm sorry, Logan. I'm too late."

Logan was barely visible in the light, a human-shaped outline, but he turned toward me and shrugged, the type of gesture that indicated he was okay with what had occurred. Then he dissolved completely into the light. He was still there somewhere in some form. Wearily, I looked toward Rick with no idea what to do next.

"Do you have plastic to cover the window until I can fix it?" he asked.

"In the kitchen, but don't we need to go find us a vampire?" I approached my spell book, which thankfully had not disappeared but rested on a stand at the center of the wood floor, near an antique wooden trunk. The book, at least, was a physical thing that would survive the day. I walked over to it and flipped to Locating Paranormal Entities: Vampires. The spell was complex, and I was fresh out of eye of newt. "How do I create a spell to find Marcus without my magic to conjure these ingredients?" I asked.

"I have all of these at my house," Rick said, "but I think you should get some rest first. You've been up for more than twenty-four hours."

"No. We can't lose Marcus."

"Marcus is dead until sunset. You have time, *mi cielo*. It will be safer if you face Marcus well-rested."

Michelle, who was now sitting on the wood floor since her couch had disappeared, blinked sleepy eyes at me. The salve on her clothes and in her hair made her look as pitiful as the bags under her eyes.

"Okay, I think you're right. It's time we call it a night. Or a day. Hell, I don't care what you call it. I just need some sleep. Michelle, I'll show you to the shower."

"Thank God," Michelle said.

Rick nodded, then used his super speed to retrieve the plastic wrap and duct tape from the kitchen. While he sealed my broken window, I descended the stairs and put what had happened in a hole in my mind. I shed my magic for a cloak of normalcy like one might change clothes in the morning. I settled Michelle into the guest bathroom with some soap and fresh towels, then flopped onto my own bed. I didn't object when Rick crawled in next to me and wrapped his body around mine. In the safety of his arms, I slept.

CHAPTER 23

Remorse

Anxiety checked into Hotel Grateful the moment I woke up. When Michelle's life was at stake, becoming the witch seemed like the obvious thing to do. But now in the light of day, I realized what I'd done. Let's just say I could forgive myself for having sex with a virtual stranger by intellectualizing that I'd been married to him in a past life, and we shared each other's thoughts. The sex was incredible, after all, and people had gone further on less.

But even if I could set the sex aside, I did magic that involved cutting myself. I drank Rick's blood. Even for me that was pretty racy. I hadn't done anything *evil*. On the contrary, I'd cast out a vampire and sent Prudence to heaven. But what did becoming the witch mean for my soul? I was in uncharted territory here.

What now? If I wasn't able to send Logan back, I'd be obligated to include him in my life. It wasn't like either of us could move out.

But it was obvious Rick wanted more from our relationship. Hell, he wanted to get married. I was twenty-two years old. I wasn't ready to be married. To be honest, I wasn't sure I was ready to have made such a lifetime commitment as becoming the witch.

Speaking of lifetime commitments, there was something I needed to know about Rick—the sooner, the better. I turned over within his arms and was startled to find his eyes open and watching me. "Oh, you're awake!"

"Yes," he whispered. "I don't need to sleep like you do."

"You don't sleep?"

"I do, but I don't need the amount that you do. Not if I'm well fed. A few hours a week is sufficient."

I thought he was joking, but his face gave no hint of humor. The light filtered through the lace curtains and washed over the hard bones of his jaw, the crooked line of his mouth, sharp cheekbones, and clear gray eyes. Without thinking, I ran my hand up his body, from his stomach to the scar on his chest. My fingers lingered there, teasing the raised flesh as if it were the most natural position in the world. His gray eyes widened.

"I need to ask you something."

"Then ask, *mi cielo*." He leaned into me, tracing his nose up the side of my face. He buried his lips in my hair.

"We had sex last night."

"Yes, we did," he breathed. "But that isn't a question." He nibbled my ear.

I pressed my hand against his chest, trying to fight the lightheaded feeling that was quickly overcoming me. "Unprotected sex."

He pulled back to meet my eyes.

"How worried should I be?" I asked.

"I can't impregnate you. Unfortunately, this immortal body is unable to procreate."

"Actually, I'm on the pill, so I wasn't so much worried about the possibility of pregnancy. I was asking more for peace of mind about your history. You know, STDs?"

"STDs? You're worried about sexually transmitted diseases?"

"I'm a nurse, okay? It is everyone's responsibility to be worried about STDs. Let's face it, you are tall, dark, and handsome and have had more than a lifetime to be with who knows how many women. You may be immortal, but I'm not. I want to know if I should be worried."

Rick placed his finger under my chin and his pupils expanded crowding out the gray. I thought I would drown in those black pools, like the darkness would swallow me up. The thought should have been frightening, but it was oddly peaceful.

"The only person I have ever made love with is you," he said.

I blinked a few times in his direction while that piece of information sank in. "What?" I asked dumbly.

"I was a virgin when I married you, and I could not bring myself to be with anyone else after your deaths."

"Wow." The word slipped out of my mouth. In front of me was a man with a face and body that would fit as the lead heartthrob in any blockbuster movie. Rick was a man who could make women swoon, and he'd waited for me, not once but multiple times.

"You need to know that I've been with other people."

"It was before you knew of me. The times are different now. It is to be expected."

I cocked my head to one side. "We're not married, Rick. I haven't promised you that I won't be with anyone else ever again."

"Then marry me. Make that promise."

"I'm not ready for that." As much as I wanted to avoid the tension building between us, I forced myself to maintain eye contact. He needed to know I was serious.

His expression darkened. "It's Logan. I smelled him on you. You've been with him, and you want to be with him again."

"I don't think I need to remind you that Logan doesn't have a body."

"What of it, Grateful? Will you tell me, honestly, that you haven't had sex with him?" He scowled.

When he put it that way, I supposed that being possessed by a ghost while I masturbated was a type of sex. To call it anything else would be fooling myself. "Yes, we did."

Rick leaned over me, his arms on either side of my body and his face too close. The position made me claustrophobic, and I pressed my head into the pillow to maintain some distance.

"No more," he commanded. "You are mine now. Mine." The smell of pine, earth, and water filled the room, strengthening with his emotions.

"Excuse me, but the only person I belong to is me." The words floated oddly calm from my lips, partly because I knew he wouldn't hurt me and partly because I was expecting to have this conversation.

His face contorted as if I'd punched him in the gut. His head jerked back, and for a moment, I thought I saw tears in his eyes. Then his entire body began to convulse. I watched his black eyes close as the spasms reached his head.

When the seizure ended, Rick opened his eyes. The irises flashed green.

"What the hell?" I wiggled under his arm. In a clumsy and very unsexy fashion, I spilled over the side of the bed and onto the floor. "What's going on, Rick?"

"Rick? Guess again, Grateful." Rick's lips moved, but Logan's voice came out.

"Logan, what are you doing? Get out of his body!" I slapped Rick's shoulder as if I could knock Logan out of him.

"Isn't this what you wanted? A little bit of both of us? Not to have to choose?" Logan's voice was venomous.

"Logan, this is wrong. *Get out!*" I tried to thrust my power into him but what was a hurricane last night came out of me a tiny puff of air.

Logan laughed. "Sun's still up, sweetheart. It takes practice to be able to use your power during the day, or so Prudence told me. Besides, if you really want me out, all you have to do is ask."

"Please, Logan. Please get out of Rick."

A cloud of dark smoke filtered from Rick's mouth until a transparent Logan stood beside a very pissed-off caretaker.

"I will send you over myself, foul vapor!" Rick growled. He raised his hand, preparing to strike.

I placed myself between the two of them and held up my hands. "Everyone, relax. I will do the sorting in this house," I said to Rick. I turned toward Logan. "No matter how much a certain soul deserves the underworld."

"I would prefer the underworld to watching the woman I love be with another man for eternity. It's torture, Grateful, torture. You let me taste you. Not just the sex but our conversations, our dates. Did you think I'd be happy to live forever in this house, watching you come and go with…with *him*? Don't threaten me with hell. This *is* hell." He flickered out and receded into the corner, nothing but a glowing orb.

"Easy enough to do as you please," Rick seethed. "I'll send you to the underworld and put you out of your misery."

"Rick! Stop! Logan isn't a bad person. He doesn't belong in hell. I saw that much last night." I pressed my hand against Rick's chest, his bare-naked chest. I couldn't help myself. I glanced down his body, to the heavy length between his legs, and a current of desire zinged through me.

"Oh, spare me," Logan said.

Rick backed off, taking forced interest in the window.

"Look, Logan, I'm sorry. I do like you and have enjoyed your company." I placed my fists firmly on my hips. "But as I've said before, I consider what happened an accident."

Logan groaned. Rick sputtered something under his breath that sounded like "no accidents."

"Besides, now that I'm the witch, a romantic relationship with you would be inappropriate. It would be like a teacher dating a student. I'd be taking advantage of you in a way."

"You've got to be kidding. Is this the spiel you tell yourself to get to sleep at night?" The lights in the room flickered.

"You heard the lady. She's not interested," Rick said through his teeth.

I rolled my eyes at the dramatics. "I'll try again to send you home, Logan, but I can't make any promises. Until we find a way to sort your soul, I think we'll just have to make the best of it."

"What does making the best of it mean for you and me?"

"Honestly, I don't know, and I don't think I should have to decide right now," I answered.

Logan shook his transparent head in exasperation.

"Even if you were alive and standing in front of me, a flesh-and-blood man, I wouldn't know what our future would hold. So how can I give you any guarantees when we don't know for sure where you'll be tomorrow?"

Logan didn't get a chance to respond. A knock at the door heralded Michelle's entrance, her eyes skipping around in her best attempt not to look at Rick's assets.

"I'm gonna hit the road, Grateful. Thanks for the memories," she said.

"You're not upset with me about this, are you?" Why would she be upset? What's a little vampire possession between friends?

"Manny's going to be pissed I didn't come home last night, but I definitely don't blame you. For Pete's sake, you have enough to worry about."

I threw my arms around her and hugged her tight. "You're the best. Let me know if I can help you with whatever you decide to tell Manny."

"Oh, you can help. In fact, he may hate you once he learns you made me work a double for you last night."

"Fair is fair." I smiled and walked her to the door.

"See you tomorrow."

I started to close the door behind her.

"Oh, and Grateful?"

"Yes?"

"The thing about Manny is that I know even now that he'll forgive me. Marriage is about trust. You have to trust the other person more than anyone, even yourself sometimes, or the relationship doesn't stand a chance. Promise me you won't rush into anything on my account. I'd never forgive myself."

"I promise. But thanks for the reminder."

She nodded and headed for her car. I marched back upstairs to tell Rick I was ready to find Marcus. I didn't have time to analyze my feelings for Rick and Logan. I needed to kill the vampire who'd possessed my best friend and murdered me a lifetime ago.

CHAPTER 24
Move Over, Buffy

After a shower, and throwing on the most comfortable sweats I owned, I returned to the attic and copied down the spell for Locating Paranormal Entities: Vampires from *The Book of Light*. Rick had left to make preparations to execute the spell at his cottage. When I leaned over the book, pen and notebook in hand, the antique trunk near my feet hummed to me. I crouched down and lifted the lid. My sword, all ivory bone wickedness, waited there for me next to the silver bowl, candles, salt, and other witchy paraphernalia. I hadn't picked up after the fight with Marcus, and I was the only one who could touch my sword. I guess my attic had magically organized itself. Cool.

Near the back, the sword's sheath was tucked away. The crisscross of the straps reminded me of my death at

Marcus' hand. I'd worn this sword on my back that night. The memory *The Book of Light* had shown me played vividly in my head. I clenched a fist, remembering. I owed Marcus. I'd have my revenge.

I yanked off my T-shirt and slipped into the harness. It took me several minutes to sheath the blade while it was on me. Donning my shirt again, the hilt poked out at the neck. I practiced withdrawing the sword a couple of times and rotating it, clumsily, through the empty attic.

If I had to use this, I was doomed.

Stiff and awkward, I walked to Rick's cottage.

"You found the sheath," he said.

"How did I ever fight with this thing on? It feels like I have a steel beam strapped to my spine."

The corner of his mouth lifted impishly. "Give her a name."

"Excuse me?" I flashed him my most confused look and paused under the wind chimes.

"You always name her. She responds better to a name." He shrugged.

"Of course *she* does. What magical sword made from the femur of a dead saint doesn't?" I stepped backward into the yard and pulled the sword from its sheath. The bone reflected the sun, its white blade taking on an almost blue glint. Memory or raw emotion flooded me with awe for her—so magnificent, so powerful. But what would I name her? "Nightshade," I said. A twang like singing metal rang out around me.

"Same thing you called her last time," Rick murmured, stepping from the porch.

I re-sheathed Nightshade and immediately noticed the difference. She seemed smaller and lighter on my back, almost as if she was an extension of me. An extra limb.

"You mentioned you had the ingredients for this spell," I said.

He nodded. "The herbs that grow around the house are yours. You planted them in your last life. Everything from goldenseal to lungwort on this property and in the wooded acres to the back."

I gazed at the wild field to the side of the cottage. "How do I know what's what?"

He slid his hand into my back pocket, temporarily rendering me mute with desire. I rolled into him and landed a kiss on his mouth, but he pulled back.

"There's an app for that," he said, grinning just a little too widely.

"Yeah, we have work to do," I said. "Keep your hands off me."

He winked. We got busy gathering the ingredients I needed, using my phone to verify I had the right plants. By the time we had everything, it was already one p.m. and the sun was due to set at six forty-five. I followed him through his front door, anxious to get started.

The skulls were back, as were the candles and the creepy paintings.

"That first night, when I ran to your door, I wasn't just seeing things."

"No," he said. "This is caretaker magic. Not as strong as yours, but it will help strengthen the spell. We'll need all the help we can get, considering the time of day." He placed a cauldron on the floor between the skulls. I started mixing the herbs I'd collected with the wet ingredients from the pantry, which Rick brought to me as I asked for them. When it was done, I'd made a salve that smelled like eucalyptus.

"It says I'm supposed to spread it on the closed eyes of the searcher and that when I wipe it away, the spell will reveal the path to the vampire. It doesn't say specifically how it works. Should I wipe it on me or on you?"

"You'd better use it, *mi cielo*. That way I can protect you as you follow the path. Some of these spells are rather compelling, incapacitating the user to anything but the chase until the object or person is found."

"Sounds logical," I said. I smeared each eyelid with the stuff, thankful that I hadn't worn makeup that day. I waited a minute or two and then wiped it off. At first, I didn't notice anything different, but as I stood up and turned in place, a red dot appeared in the northwest corner of the room as if someone was shining a pointer in that direction.

"He's that way," I said, pointing at the wall.

"Let's move outdoors and see where it takes us."

I followed Rick out and toward the rear of the house. The red dot hovered in the trees, beckoning me to follow it into the woods. "He went through the forest," I said.

We picked our way through the brush and trees, the thick forest floor tripping me more than once.

"Marcus was wise to come this way. The forest provides shelter from the sun. He may have been able to continue after the sun came up, if he wasn't exposed directly."

"How far do you think he could've gotten?"

"I'm not sure. Marcus seems to get stronger every day. The way he fought last night…" He shook his head. "I won't underestimate him again."

I tripped again, this time face-planting into a fern.

Strong hands helped me to my feet. "You are thinking too hard, *mi cielo*. Trust your instincts. Your power element is the air. When you run, imagine that you are blowing over the ground and through the trees."

I wasn't excited about the idea, but I tried again. Instead of watching my feet, I looked straight ahead and trusted my instincts. At first my feet plodded forward, deliberately. But then I picked up the pace. Accelerating until the trees blurred, I ran toward the red dot, Rick following close on my heels. He was faster than me, but stuck by my side since I knew where to go. After an hour of running hard, my thighs ached, and I stopped to rest. The witch gave me speed, but she didn't give me new legs. I was going to feel that in the morning.

"Damn. Did you ever think he'd make it this far?" I asked Rick.

"No. I confess I didn't." He inhaled deeply through his nose. "I believe we're close, though. I smell something coming from there." He pointed to a place where the trees parted. The red dot glowed.

"The spell agrees. Let's move." I forced my sore legs to jog toward the clearing. Rick followed at a walk, which must have seemed painfully slow to him. The spacing between the trees widened with each step until I was certain we were on a man-made path, and then the forest opened into a small clearing. At the center was a shack made from roughly hewn logs and branches that looked like they were broken manually from their source and crudely cemented with mud.

"He's here. I can smell him." Rick pointed at the shack.

"Do you think he built that last night?"

"I don't think so. I've seen hunters build these to hide in during deer season. I think Marcus was lucky to come by this."

"So he's inside?" The thought of being so close to my killer made my blood run cold.

"Yes."

"What's the plan? How do we kill him? Stake through the heart?"

"That only works in movies. There are three ways to kill Marcus—your blade, my teeth, and the sun."

Great. No pressure or anything. If I wasn't exhausted from the run and hell-bent on revenge, I might have been terrified. As it was, fear was a luxury for the safe. I was not. This vamp had killed me once already. I pulled Nightshade from her sheath and started toward the shack.

"Are you going to shift, or am I going to have to do this alone?"

"If I shift, I won't be able to fit inside." He touched my shoulder and smiled like he had a brilliant idea. "I will pull him out of his grave, and you cut off his head."

I swallowed hard. The head-cutting off part didn't thrill me. Even if it was a vampire I hated, I wasn't sure I could do it.

Clearly Rick picked up on my thoughts because he frowned and narrowed his eyes. But he didn't say anything. Smart man.

I thought back to last week, before I'd moved into the new house, before I was expected to know how to sort the dead or kill vampires. My, how things had changed.

Repositioning my blade, I reached for the door.

The darkness of the shanty made me temporarily blind, but I was not deaf. I heard a shotgun cock. The back of Rick's arm slid in front of my waist, pushing me behind him before the room came into view. Curled on the dirt floor, a man rocked cross-legged, staring at us through the sight of his rifle.

"Get out," he rasped. His left side was covered in blood. A bite mark on his neck still oozed onto his shirt. Hmm. Marcus had a snack before going to sleep for the day. A bead of sweat dripped down the hunter's forehead onto his shoulders. Shaking. Sweaty. Pale. He was hypovolemic from the blood loss and close enough to going into shock to make me wonder how he was still sitting up.

"What's your name?" Rick asked.

"Shut up," the man said.

Rick held out a hand. "You've been infected. The thing that bit you has poisoned your blood. We can cure you, but you need to come with us, and we have to kill the one who's buried beneath you."

The man shook so hard I thought for sure the gun would go off in his hands. Tears streamed down his cheeks. "Just go away," he pleaded.

Marcus is controlling his mind, Rick thought into my head. *The man may be as good as dead. If Marcus forced him to drink some of his blood, he might be a changeling, a servant of the damned soon to become a vampire himself.*

How do we know if we can fix him or need to kill him? I asked.

Check if his heart is still beating.

And just how am I supposed to get past the gun to take his pulse?

I'll take care of the gun. Rick shot forward, lightning-fast.

Crack. The gun fired, and Rick curled over.

CHAPTER 25
Something About Myself

The shell blew through Rick's chest. In the spray of blood and thicker things, I didn't stop to check if any of it was mine. After all, the bullet that passed through Rick could have struck me, standing behind him. I didn't think about myself at all or reach for the man's neck to check if his heart was still beating. None of those things crossed my mind until after the sight of Rick with a hole in his torso elicited a reflex in me. Nightshade came around and decapitated the man before Rick could hit the floor.

I stared, heart pounding as his head rolled to the side of the hunting shack. His body collapsed to the earth in a pool of his own blood.

"I wasn't sure you had it in you," Rick said.

I snapped my head toward the Rick I'd thought was dead, only to see the hole in his chest stitch itself. The wound, once clear through his torso, was now a shiny pink spot on the skin behind his mutilated shirt.

"I thought you were dead," I yelled.

Rick's heady laugh filled the room. "I'm immortal, Grateful. You know that." He reached for me, hands running down my body, checking for injuries.

"Ow," I said as he brushed over my left shoulder. I looked at the source of the pain. The shell had clipped me. Blood soaked my shirtsleeve.

Rick stepped in close to me, his eyes locked on mine, eyebrows knit together in concern. He pulled the neck of his shirt aside. "Your knife, Grateful," he said.

"What? Why?"

"My blood will heal you," he whispered. The grave look on his face made me think he wouldn't take no for an answer.

I unsheathed my blade and sliced the skin over his collarbone. I sealed my mouth over the blood that bubbled there, and the hot fluid ran down my throat. The raw taste of him reminded me of the night before, and my pulse picked up its pace. My hands found his body, my fingers dancing over his newly healed chest. The world around me melted.

He pushed me away, breaking the connection. "Forgive me," he said, his voice cracking.

I wiped my mouth with the back of my hand, blushing at my lack of self-control. My shoulder was completely healed. "Will your blood heal anyone?" I asked.

"No. Just you. I am the vessel of your soul. My blood renews you and only you."

I nodded, my face still hot with embarrassment.

I turned toward the hunter's body. His blood had puddled over the dirt floor, and a thought came to me. "Do you think that blood is getting to Mar—"

An explosion of earth blew through the shack, stripping my skin where it made contact. I was lucky Rick was slightly in front of me. I'd been shielded from the worst of it. But I choked on the cloud of dust that followed, closing my eyes tight against the abrasive grit. It was more than the little shack could withstand; the roof collapsed and then the walls fell in. Rick tried to shelter me with his body.

Marcus stood in the rubble, eyes red and stomach bulging with the hunter's blood. Through the gap between the wall and the fallen roof, the sun's setting rays cut through the woods. Where the light touched Marcus' shoulders, his skin steamed ominously. I raised my blade between us. Rick kicked out the remaining wall and folded over next to me, his skin splitting as the beast burst from within.

I lurched forward, placing myself between Marcus and the woods. The vampire seethed and ran toward me at a full run. I tried to bring Nightshade around, but I was too slow. Marcus body-slammed me. One of his knees hit me in the gut, knocking me to the ground. My back slapped the earth. In a blur, he ran for the shelter of the woods.

Rick finished shifting and attacked, taking to the air for a better view. I caught my breath and followed on foot. The vampire pinballed from tree to tree with superhuman speed, then suddenly...nothing. I halted just inside the tree line. I'd lost him.

Do you see him? I thought, testing my connection with Rick's beast.

No. He's gone.

Do you know where he's headed? I asked.

I'm guessing Carlton City. There's a free coven of vampires there.

Do you think we'd have a better chance of heading him off than catching him here?

Considering vampires are most at home in the woods, and he's fortified with human blood, I'd say yes.

I ran back out into the clearing. He landed next to me.

Come, we need the car if we're going into the city.

Why can't we fly?

I'm fairly certain a dragon over Carlton City would cause human panic. Come, I'll fly you back to the cabin, and we'll take the Tesla.

I climbed on his scaly back, tucking my knees behind his wings. With three running steps, he took to the air. I gripped his shoulder blades as he climbed above the trees, soaring toward his cottage at breakneck speed. When he dove for the yard, my stomach dropped. I thought I'd be sick. He landed roughly, beginning to shift before we even stopped moving. I yelped as I slipped off his back, but he twisted his folding body and caught me in his arms before I hit the grass.

His eyes were still black as he carried me into the house. Always the first and last part to change, I watched, enchanted as they bled back to gray. He set me on my feet inside the back door. In a flash, he was dressed and had pulled the Tesla around. I climbed in. Rick floored it just as the last remnants of the sun sank behind my house to the west.

I tested my seatbelt a few times once I saw the speedometer top a hundred. To take my mind off the blur beyond the windshield, I decided to start some conversation. "Do you know where the vampires are staying?"

"TiltWorld, down by the river."

"TiltWorld? The amusement park?" I turned in my seat to face him.

"It's closed for the season. There's a barn near the back of the property where they have a fun house in the summer. The windows are blacked out, and there's a basement. It's the perfect place for them to stay during the day."

"The Barn Blast. I've been there. You walk through a maze of fun mirrors and joy buzzers."

"Hmm, I'm sure they've redecorated."

"Wait, if you know where they are, why haven't you taken them out?"

"They're free, and they're not breaking any laws."

"Is harboring a fugitive enough for us to put them away for good?"

"You are the judge and jury. It's for you to decide. But in the past, you were hesitant to condemn anything that hadn't harmed or killed a human."

"What was my reasoning?" I asked.

"The last thing we want is a supernatural rebellion. We're not strong enough to take out the entire coven. Wielding your power sparingly is the best way to keep balance and control."

I shook my head. "We can't let Marcus go free."

"You're right, of course. But diplomacy may be in order."

"What good is having a bone sword if I'm not allowed to use it?"

His previously serious composure broke, and he flashed me a half-smile.

We hit traffic on the exit to MacArthur Avenue. Still, we made it to the parking lot of TiltWorld in ten minutes—less than half the time it usually took me to drive to the hospital. Rick paid no attention to the *Closed for the Season* sign as we rumbled up to the gate. A plywood cutout of an alien torso jutted out of a tilting spacecraft above the entrance, its grin indifferent to our arrival. Rick pried the lock open with his bare hands and swung open the massive chain-link door. Climbing behind the wheel, he drove through and then closed it behind us. We drove all the way to the back of the amusement park, the roller coasters and midway games eerily abandoned.

The sun had finished setting, and the darkness outside the car window reminded me of Marcus' advantage. He could see in the dark and I couldn't. Not to mention he was probably three times as strong now from the hunter's blood. I wasn't sure how big this coven was, but Marcus definitely had the upper hand here.

We reached the Barn Blast, but for some reason I didn't think this fun house would leave me laughing. "I'm scared," I said to Rick. "He's killed me once. I don't want it to happen again."

"I'll keep you safe, *mi cielo*."

We exited the car and scanned the woods to the west of the warehouse. I didn't see anything. "No red dot. Maybe we beat him here."

"Come," he whispered. Rick motioned for me to follow him to the back door of the barn.

The red dot glowed to life again. "Here. The door. He's gone through here," I said.

He reached forward and twisted the knob. It was locked, but with a slight push of his hand, Rick broke the mechanism, and the door swung open on its hinges. The dark inside was thick, blinding.

"Stay with me," Rick said. "I can see in the dark."

I drew Nightshade, hooked my fingers into Rick's T-shirt and followed him over the threshold. A suffocating smell filled my nostrils—earthy sweet copper I was all too familiar with. *I smell blood*, I thought to Rick. Better to use our connection than to risk calling attention to ourselves.

Then again, Marcus had fed thoughts into my head last night. Maybe it didn't matter.

Not when you have Nightshade, Rick thought. *She protects you from vampire mind tricks.*

Oh.

The blood you smell is from the animals. There are carcasses hanging from the ceiling. It looks like they've been draining the blood. This is a good thing. It means they're not using humans.

My shoulder bumped something that felt like meat and bone. I could hear the clink of chains above me and an awful image of a strung-up deer filled my brain. I had serious trouble thinking of this as a good thing.

Be vigilant, mi cielo. I'm not sure I'll be able to smell Marcus over the stench.

We turned a tight corner, deep inside the barn now. *Crack.* I lost contact with Rick. My skull hit something hard and bounced. *Boof.* A sharp pain erupted in my ribs. I slid across the floor, Nightshade slipping from my hand. Head throbbing, I patted the gritty, sticky concrete, frantically scanning the darkness.

I heard scuffling in front of me. I had to find my blade! Searching more aggressively through the filth on hands and knees, my hand landed on bone. Nightshade. Her energy sang to me. I gripped her hilt, rolled my legs above my head, and flipped to the balls of my feet. *Shit!* That was new. Had I ever moved like that before? *Rick? Rick?* I called with my mind.

To your right!

A fist or some other body part hit me, and the whole right side of my face exploded. I sailed sideways, my left shoulder slamming into a wall I couldn't see. Luckily, my suddenly tough and nubile body seemed to know how important Nightshade was, and I landed with her still in my hand. I forced myself to stand, the pain in my shoulder, ribs, and head making me gag. My face hurt like he'd broken my jaw, and my left arm hung useless at my side. Luckily, I was a righty.

The scuffling grew near. I circled my blade around me in a move that must have been remembered from my past life because it surprised my conscious mind. I hit nothing.

I closed my useless eyes in the dark and focused on my other senses. Fists hit flesh. Growls. A shuffle across the floor in front of me. I smelled blood but also the sulfur scent of vampire. I had to do something, but how?

Use my eyes, Rick thought to me.

Like it was obvious or something that I could do that. I reached out of myself with my power, into Rick's head. Behind my closed eyes, images flickered, a zoetrope of choppy action washed in red. The motion made me nauseous. I broke the connection.

Rick growled. Teeth snapped near my head. Disoriented, I took a deep breath and tried again. The images came back and, this time, I concentrated so hard sweat dripped down my face. I could hold this. I could see what Rick saw.

Half shifted, Rick grappled with Marcus. The vampire had grown three times larger since the hunting shack, engorged with human blood. Rick's fist shot at Marcus, who turned into thick black smoke at the point of impact. Whirling, Rick saw the vamp re-form behind him, and pulled his own vapor act, narrowly escaping the vamp's slashing claws.

From my front row seat inside his head, I felt Rick's teeth extend from his mouth in the partially shifted way I'd seen the first night we were together. He was resisting the full change. In close combat, it would make him vulnerable. A split-second hesitation and Marcus would have the advantage.

Rick tackled Marcus and the two rolled head over heels across the floor. But before Rick could sink teeth into him, Marcus went up in smoke and rematerialized again, lifting Rick by the neck and pounding him against the wall. I had to do something. If Marcus was going to die, it would be up to me.

Heart pounding, I adjusted my sweaty grip on Nightshade. I tried to take a deep breath, but the air rattled in my throat. I only managed a shallow fill of my lungs. Using the image in my head, I walked forward ten big steps, broke my connection with Rick and opened my eyes. In the darkness in front of me was the reddish splotch. Marcus noticed me. I sensed him turning to take me out. But my blade was already around. The part of me that was the witch sprang into action. My sword glowed like a supernova as it sliced through Marcus' neck. Blood sprayed. His head dropped and rolled in the ethereal light. The vamp's blood hissed acid-like on the floorboards.

Black ooze pooled near my toes. I stepped back. Slowly, the light from my blade began to fade.

"Nice work," Rick gasped.

Clapping echoed through the barn. The buzz of electricity flowing into cold bulbs reverberating through the large space, and fluorescent light glowed from above. I blinked, trying to force my eyes to adjust. The blood stench seemed to grow stronger as I saw the source. Cows, deer, and even a bear hung strung up from the ceiling near where we'd entered the barn, dripping blood into ruts in the floor that drained, presumably, into the basement. The system was messy. I looked at my hands and saw the remnants of blood, grit, and animal hair I'd crawled through searching for Nightshade. *Gross.* Rick and I had slain Marcus in a section deeper within the barn, near a stage with a paneled screen instead of a curtain.

The panel slid aside to expose the source of the ongoing applause. In a suit that draped across his muscular frame like it was some sort of living material, a man approached. His hair was slicked back, movie-star style, a deep chocolate color you rarely see in real life. I could tell immediately that he was a vampire, not just because his swagger was smoother than any human could pull off, but also because his eyes were too big for his head, like they belonged in the skull of a nocturnal animal. His pale features had a chiseled appearance, down to the straight white teeth that filled his mouth.

He approached me with a sardonic grin. "Very nicely done, Hecate."

"Julius," Rick hissed. The name might have been a curse.

The vamp ignored Rick and moved toward me. "Allow me to introduce myself," he said with a voice that was both masculine and honey sweet. He held out a hand to me, closing the distance between us. "I am Julius, leader of the Carlton City free coven. It is a pleasure to make your acquaintance." He bent to kiss my hand and his eyes flicked up to meet mine. His irises were as yellow as a candle flame and luminescent.

I pulled my hand away before his lips could touch my skin.

"Marcus was here to meet up with you. Why?" I asked.

"I have no idea." He looked accusingly at Rick. "Why was he out of the graveyard? Padnon and I have been away until just this moment."

Padnon? The man I'd battled in the parking lot of Java Jane's stepped forward, his wrinkled face sending an icy current through my nervous system. Instinct took over. I launched myself forward, flipping onto the platform, Nightshade coming around toward Padnon's neck. The blue glow from my blade told me the demon was as good as dead.

A lightning-fast blur came from my right. *Thunk.* I flew backward, caught by the waist. Julius! His other hand wrapped around mine, restraining Nightshade. Fangs grazed my neck.

He turned me to face Rick, who was crouched, ready to pounce. "Don't move, Caretaker. I'll drain her like a blood bag." Julius's tongue licked up my jugular.

Rick didn't move, although I could feel his frustration through our connection.

A firm hand thrust me forward, sending pain shooting through my shoulder. I tripped off the platform into Rick's arms.

"You must have manners, Witch, if you come into my house," Julius hissed.

I turned to face him, Nightshade still in my hand.

Julius tipped his head and pointed toward Marcus' remains. "I only wished to congratulate you on a fine kill. You are a natural, my dear. I'd introduce you to my associate, but it seems the demon Padnon has already made your acquaintance."

How close Padnon had been. And now, how easy it would have been for Julius to kill me. Why hadn't he? I gripped Nightshade tighter, but Rick's hand on my elbow stopped me from a repeat performance. Probably wise. My intuition was doing cartwheels. Rick squeezed my elbow. I glanced up toward a hayloft above us and saw no less than fifteen sets of yellow eyes looking down on me from the shadows. This was a big coven. A very big coven. A very big, pissed-off coven.

"We need to go," I mumbled to Rick. He nodded and widened his eyes at me as if to say, *no shit*. My jaw still wasn't working right, and with the adrenaline wearing off, the pain in my shoulder was almost unbearable. It was dislocated for sure and maybe broken. Plus, I was exhausted. Two beheadings in one night was a lot for a girl.

"Rick is a lucky man to have won you so easily," Julius said, his tone cryptic. "Padnon and I thought you would wait before joining yourself again."

"Watch yourself," Rick snapped.

"Why, Enrique? Should I not tell her the whole truth about who she is? Would you prefer she live believing only your version of the truth?"

"Let's go." Rick took my good arm.

"Wait. What's he talking about?" I narrowed my eyes at the vamp.

Julius had the look of someone you couldn't trust. When he smiled it seemed like there were more teeth in his mouth than there should be. He was shifty, and he was a vampire. Still, I was curious like any person might be about a particular piece of gossip. It probably wasn't true, but I wanted to know anyway.

"The truth is that you, my dear Hecate, are much more powerful than Rick could ever be. You didn't need him to access your magic. He didn't make you what you are. You made *him*. He used caretaker magic to trick you into joining with him again. You didn't need him at all."

"That doesn't make any sense," I said. Why would Rick be guarding the cemetery if I didn't need him?

"Don't you think it odd, Hecate, that you were powerful enough to reincarnate yourself but needed to join with Rick to gain that power back?"

It *was* odd, now that he mentioned it. But I bled all emotion from my face, refusing to give him the satisfaction of a reaction. "And what benefit is it to you to inform me of this?" I spat at Julius.

"I am interested in a long, free existence. It is in my best interest to win your good graces. What better way to earn your trust than to unveil this deception to you?"

Wow. He was good. My hackles were up. He definitely had that used-car-salesman vibe. But some part of me wondered if there wasn't a shred of truth among the lies.

"Message received," I said, starting toward the door again with Rick by my side. I stepped over Marcus' head and moved into the forest of carcasses.

"Before you go," Julius called, "I'd like to introduce you to the newest member of our coven." Over my shoulder, I watched Julius sweep his hand toward the left. A door opened. I halted abruptly.

"*Gary!*" I gasped as my ex-boyfriend walked forward. He'd changed. His blue eyes bulged, and his skin was so pale I could see the map of his veins on his forehead. With a stiff gait, he limped to Julius' side. "What? You're a vampire? You're a *vampire.*" I lowered my eyebrows and peered at him as if an explanation would bloom across his forehead.

"Grateful," Gary said, his nocturnal eyes finding my face. "I'd like to apologize. As you can see, I've gone through some changes."

I managed to close my gaping jaw. "You stole my money!" I accused. After I said it, I questioned whether it was appropriate. I'd just discovered he was the undead. Was it polite to focus on the money rather than the loss of his humanity? I was too tired to think about it.

Julius grinned. "Gary will be paying back his debt to you. I'll make sure of that. As I said before, our coven wishes to maintain a long and prosperous relationship with you, Hecate."

Rick grabbed my arm and forced me toward the door. He wasn't gentle about it.

"Next time, then." Julius laughed wickedly. "I'll remember the pleasantries if you will."

"Rick, stop pushing me. What is the matter with you? Ow!"

"You are injured. Julius is trying to distract you, to delay you, because if we stay much longer, healing will become…complicated. We will be vulnerable."

He was right. Once we were outside, the pain hit full force.

"Help me," I cried to him.

He walked around to my left side. "This will hurt, *mi cielo*. I can't heal you until your bones are in the correct alignment. I will have to put your shoulder back in first."

I gritted my teeth. I'd seen this done in the ER and, if patient screams were any gauge, it was excruciating. "Go," I said.

He made it quick, lifting and slamming my arm into my shoulder in one smooth move. Still, I screamed until his wrist plugged my mouth and blood gushed over my tongue. The more I drank, the better I felt. Warmth spread through my body, healing my jaw, my bones, and my bruises. With the pain gone, I stopped drinking and started thinking. I pushed his arm away.

"Is it true?" I asked, the taste of his blood still in my mouth.

"Of course not," he said. "Julius' greatest desire is to come between us, to weaken us."

"But how does he know how I got my power back?"

"He knows because of the timing. Julius said you'd met Padnon before?"

"Yeah, the wrinkled shit attacked me at Java Jane's a few days ago."

"That is how. Julius knows how it is done."

"That makes sense," I said, feeling tired. I chided myself for doubting Rick, even for a minute. Hadn't he risked his life for me enough times to earn my trust?

I crawled into the passenger's seat of the Tesla. Rick pulled out of TiltWorld and headed for home. I dozed the entire ride, only waking when the car stopped in my driveway. Once alert, the uncertainty still had me in its clutches. A train of thought I couldn't stop took control.

"Rick?" I asked before I climbed out of the car. "Why did you let me go into that barn? You must have known I wasn't ready. I'd never fought a vampire before, and I'm not immortal like you. We were vastly outnumbered. Why didn't you warn me?"

"I needed you. You are stronger than you know."

"But you couldn't have known I would kill Marcus." It dawned on me the moment the words were out of my mouth. "You were using me as bait. You knew Marcus would smell my human blood and come running."

"It was necessary," he said, refusing to meet my eyes.

"Does my life mean so little to you?"

"*Mi cielo*, you were never in danger. I was with you the entire time."

I raised my hand to my face, to the place where the pain had radiated through my jaw before his blood had healed me. "My shoulder and jaw disagree."

He frowned. "Perhaps I should've been more cautious. Forgive me."

"Yeah," I drawled.

I waited, but that was all the apology he offered. "Did you know my ex-boyfriend was a vampire?"

He looked away, toward his cottage. "No."

My gut told me there was more to the story, but I didn't know what questions to ask to uncover the truth.

"Do you need more of my blood?" he asked, and there was the promise of sex in his voice.

"Not tonight. I'm going home." I climbed out of the car and started toward my house.

Rick knew better than to come after me.

CHAPTER 26
Try, Try, Again

The door to my home was a welcome relief, a promise of sanctuary from this life that was quickly getting away from me. Although I felt the familiar weight of Logan's presence in the foyer, I did not greet him or call him out. I jogged up the stairs to my room and slammed the door behind me. I stripped out of my clothes, removing Nightshade and propping her in the corner of the bathroom. Then I stepped into the shower and turned on the water as hot as I could stand it. The spray ran off my body red and black, remnants of my first kills swirling the drain. I braced myself against the cool tile and sobbed.

When the hot water ran out, I slipped on my coziest flannel pajamas and flopped into bed. What day was it? Thursday. Days and nights had tangled together until nothing made sense anymore. Rick had used me as bait.

Even though somewhere deep inside I thought he might have done the right thing, the logical thing, in my heart I felt betrayed. What did I expect? I had to learn somehow.

I drifted to sleep thinking about Gary. *Fuck*. Gary was a vampire. When had that happened? Was that why he disappeared? In my dreams, I asked him these questions, but I could never make out his answers.

I woke late and hurried downstairs where hot pancakes waited for me on the counter.

"Thanks, Logan," I said.

"You had a rough night."

"And today I have to work. Phone nurse."

His presence vanished from the room without saying goodbye.

"I'll see you tonight," I called toward the attic. He was still mad.

The buzz of my cell phone vibrating on the counter popped me out of my seat. I hit the answer button.

"Hello?"

"It's Dad. I got your message. I'm showing a house on Sunday. Would you be up for dinner tonight?"

"Sure," I said, thinking of Logan. "Maybe we could make it an early one. I've got to catch up on some sleep."

"Valentine's?" he asked.

"Actually, I'm working from home today. Could you come here?"

"See you at six?"

"Sure," I said. "Bring food if you want to eat."

Dad laughed and said goodbye.

I logged into my cracked-screen laptop and started taking calls, thinking about the first time I'd done this here, the night Prudence had called and my life had spiraled out of control. But today there were no supernatural inquiries. Today, the routine of my work lulled me into a false sense of normalcy.

* * * * *

Dad arrived promptly at six with his arms full of Valentine's food. Roasted chicken and pasta salad with asparagus spears. I set the table in the dining room and doled out the food while Dad droned on about the uptick in the real estate market. I wasn't really listening until he said, "So, how do you feel about that?"

"Sorry, I spaced for a minute. What were you saying?"

"How do you feel about moving to an apartment in the city? I have some folks who might be interested in this place."

"No!" I said too quickly. After all the nights I'd prayed for a way out of this house, out of my responsibilities here, suddenly the thought of losing it made me sweat. The house was my seat of magic. It was mine now and had to stay that way.

He grimaced. "I thought you hated this house! The dead people. The distance from work."

"Actually, it's kind of grown on me. I was thinking, maybe, I could buy it."

He shook his head. "Where is this coming from?"

"I'm not sure. I'm just really attached to the place. It feels like home to me."

The fork in my dad's hand dropped to his plate. "Well, I wasn't expecting this. I'll be honest, Grateful. I've got a buyer on the line. He's new in town and needs a place. Asked specifically to see this house even though it's not listed."

A chill ran through me, my intuition jumping up and down and waving her arms. "Do you remember the guy's name?"

Dad pulled a card from his pocket. "A Mr. Helleborine."

Helleborine was the herb Marcus had used to kill my last incarnation, Samantha. On reflex, I stood up and reached for Nightshade. She wasn't even on my back. I'd left her upstairs. "I will get the money, Dad. Please. Tell him the house isn't for sale. For me. I'll do anything."

Dad frowned. "I don't understand your sudden infatuation with this place, but okay. If you think you can get your financial situation together enough to put in an offer, do it. I'll give you six weeks. Otherwise, I gotta let it go."

Six weeks. Could I get a mortgage loan in six weeks? "Why? Don't you owe it to Prudence to keep it, after what she did for you?"

He rubbed his forehead. "Ah, I see. You're attached to this house because you connect it to your personal history. But Prudence isn't here anymore and neither is your mother." He placed his hands on mine. "It's time for both of us to move on."

I scrambled for what to say. "I want the house, Dad," I said, pulling my hands away. "I'll get the money. I will."

He nodded his head. "Okay."

We finished dinner in silence and said our goodbyes. After he left, I paced the foyer, feeling helpless. How would I ever get the money to buy this house? Could I trust Rick? Would I ever find a way to send Logan on? My body was exhausted, my mind a jumble of discontent. I paced while I thought about things. What I needed was a taste of success. I needed to scratch something off my list, to get my hands around one of these nebulous puzzle pieces. I needed to prove to myself, once and for all, that *I* was the witch. I had the power. I controlled my own destiny.

At midnight, I climbed the stairs to the attic, Nightshade in hand. I called for Logan. Reluctantly he materialized, crossing his arms in front of his chest.

"Don't block me, Logan. I feel strong tonight. This is happening."

"You mean you hope this will happen so you won't have to deal with me anymore."

"We don't have time for this." I flipped through my spell book and found some notes on amplification of power. I opened the canister of salt from the night before and drew a large pentagram in the middle of the attic. Pentagrams are powerful symbols. I used to think they were evil but according to *The Book of Light*, they simply strengthened the power of the person using them. Since I wasn't evil, my pentagram wasn't evil.

I coaxed Logan into the center. He wasn't happy about it, but he followed my instructions. I picked up my bowl and blade. With a deep breath, I centered myself and threw my power into him. I was so strong, I bounced inside his head like light in a mirrored room. I saw everything, from images of what he ate for breakfast in the morning when he was alive to how many times a day he went to the bathroom. I saw what color underwear he had on the day the car hit his motorcycle and the darkness swallowed him. I saw everything, every moment. But every time I experienced a memory that included his name, it was obstructed. I could see every test he took in high school, but a black bar marred the top of the paper. When he earned his driver's license, the name was unreadable. I learned he was a chef, which explained his unbelievable cooking ability, but in my vision, his nametag was blank.

More than the missing name bothered me. The feeling that he was an unfinished soul was undeniable. I searched his life thoroughly, but unlike Prudence, the answer was nowhere to be found. I worked at it until fatigue caused my power to spill out of him. I'd failed him, again.

I leaned forward, catching myself on my knees, and allowed Nightshade to clatter to the floor. "I'm sorry, Logan. I don't know why, but I can't sort you. I can't find your name in any of your memories. It's like you're not supposed to move on." Inside my circle of power, I was suddenly powerless. Under Logan's scrutiny, I came apart.

"This isn't supposed to happen. It's my job to send you on. If I can't do this, what does it say about me? How will I fight off Julius when I can't even sort a soul?"

He cocked his head to the side, his body so solid in the midnight power of the attic that he might have been human. "Maybe I was sent here for you the same way you were sent for Rick, to support you. Maybe it's not supposed to be the same this lifetime."

If I couldn't send him on, I was obligated to include Logan in my life. The thought was both comforting and suffocating. He was a good friend, but the crush he had on me would only get worse if I was his only social outlet. Logan needed to get his own life, a notion complicated by the fact we lived under the same roof, and he didn't have a body. Well, unless my dad sold this place. Then I'd have to move, and he'd be living with Mr. Helleborine. *Ugh.* I couldn't let that happen.

I ran my hands down the electrical charge of his arms. "I don't know why I can't sort you, but this isn't over. There has to be something in the book. I'm going to find a way to send you on."

Rick's beast howled beyond the attic walls. I scurried to the window, scattering the salt pentagram in the process. I couldn't see anything through the darkness. I lunged for Nightshade and sheathed her on my back.

"He might need me," I said. I was still licking my wounds about being used as bait, but I wasn't about to leave him alone out there.

"Of course. Go do your job," Logan whispered, shaking his head. "I'll be here when you get home."

I spilled out of the house into the night and made my way toward the cemetery. Rick's beast was circling above the gate but landed on the road in front of me as I neared. The oozing limb of a partially eaten zombie bounced from the corner of his mouth as he jogged toward me. I pointed toward the remains, and he flipped the chunk between his teeth, crunching the bones and licking up the black blood that leeched out from between his lips. When he was finished, he lowered his head to my level.

Close up, he looked so much like a large dog that I couldn't help but scratch the tuft of hair behind his ear. The beast closed its eyes and did that leg-thumping thing dogs do. I had to stop scratching to avoid damaging the pavement. Red Grove didn't need to deal with a pothole because of me.

One large black eye blinked in my direction before the beast's skin began to boil. The thing folded in on itself, bones cracking. Rick once said it didn't hurt when he shape-shifted, but as he unfolded himself, naked in the street, I thought he looked tired. I wondered if he'd made it out to be less than it was for my sake.

He walked up to me, his face grim.

"Do you need my help?" I asked.

"It's taken care of," he said. His jaw clenched. He looked away from me.

"Is something wrong?"

"I can smell him on you, Grateful. You've come from Logan."

"I tried to send him on, but it didn't work. There's something blocking his name. I could see everything about him but his name. It's like I wasn't meant to see it."

"Or he's blocking you. Don't be naïve. He wants to stay. He wants you."

My first impulse was to tell him he didn't know what he was talking about, to deny that Logan would do anything to avoid his final journey. But some part of me knew Rick was right. After all, Logan had admitted to me that he was afraid to be sorted.

I placed my hands on my hips and sighed. "So, how do I send him on if he's blocking?"

Relief passed over Rick's face. He took a step toward me until he was so close his chest almost brushed against my breasts. "There is another way. With your permission, I can *force* his soul to move on."

"I'm not going to let you make a snack of Logan," I said firmly.

"No. This is caretaker magic. It forces the soul in one direction or another."

"But I thought I needed to decide which direction he was supposed to go?"

"With this spell, the soul decides. It forces the soul to judge itself."

I thought about Logan, about the balance of his soul. I was certain this spell would end well for him. Logan's soul didn't seem finished, but his lifetime was. I couldn't sit back and watch the Great Forgetting take him memory by memory. Something had to be done.

"Yes, Rick. I think you should do it. I give you permission."

To his credit, Rick kept his happy dance on the inside, although our connection made it impossible for me not to notice his gleeful anticipation.

"I learned something else tonight." I placed my hands on my hips and looked out over the graveyard.

"What?"

"I think a vampire is trying to buy my house."

Rick's skin began to bubble again, and his eyes turned black as coal. "Your house isn't for sale."

"A Mr. Helleborine contacted my father and asked to see my address. "

"Helleborine was what Marcus used to—"

"Kill me. Yes, I know. And it doesn't grow in the cemetery, which means someone on the outside was helping him."

"Someone who wants you to know he isn't happy about Marcus' death."

"And isn't happy about my return. Do you think it was Julius?"

Rick shook his head. "I do not know. Julius is very old and very evil. But he could have killed you last night, and he didn't."

I narrowed my eyes. "Why didn't he?"

"That, I do not know, *mi cielo*."

That made two of us.

CHAPTER 27
Wanted Dead or Alive

When you're doing magic until the wee hours of the morning, six a.m. comes appallingly early. I yanked on my scrubs and ate the breakfast Logan made for me, complete with coffee. At the same time, guilt ate me. Rick and I had planned every detail of sorting Logan last night, and I'd made my peace with him going. The spell had to be a surprise to Logan so that he wouldn't have time to resist the magic, but keeping the fate of someone's soul from them seemed wrong. My dad always said that sometimes you have to choose the lesser evil. I told myself the omission was necessary.

I climbed into my Jeep, resisting the urge to say one last goodbye to Logan. Sometime around noon, Rick would let himself into my house with the key I'd given him. The sun would be at its highest and Logan at his weakest. Rick would set up a ring of candles resting in human skulls—something he called the ring of bones—and begin chanting the spell that would send Logan home. At sunset, he'd call the soul by bleeding a live chicken into a wooden bowl. Logan would be trapped within the ring of bones until his soul decided its fate or until the candles burnt out. If that happened, the magic would read Logan and decide for him.

According to my phone app, the sun would set minutes before my shift ended at seven. Chances were good that before I got home from work today, Logan would be gone.

As I pulled out of my driveway, I tried not to cry or to think about the finality of it. This was only natural. People died, moved on. It was part of life, and Logan's time had come. So why was I still thinking about the unfinished feeling I got from his soul?

I slowed down as I passed Rick's house, but he wasn't outside. He was probably preparing the spell for this afternoon. The first time I'd driven up this street, a vivid fantasy had gripped me—Rick in the shower. I was convinced now that it was, in fact, a memory, probably from just before I died. I still wasn't sure if I loved Rick. I was definitely not ready to marry him. But I wanted him. We were at the beginning of something that might be bigger and more important than anything I'd experienced. I just wasn't sure what it was.

St. John's parking lot was relatively empty, but I parked in the back of the lot anyway. Some doctors and nurses parked up front, but I've always felt that those first spots should be left for the sick people and their relatives. I was healthy. I could walk. As luck would have it, Michelle was operating under the same idea, and I caught up with her halfway to the front door.

"Well, if it isn't our friendly neighborhood soul-sorter," she said. "You ready for a day among the living— or mostly living?"

"I think so. We're sending Logan on today."

"I thought you said he couldn't be sorted."

"Rick figured out a way."

"Do you trust him? Isn't Rick jealous of Logan? Aren't you afraid he might get a little overzealous and, you know, chomp-chomp?" Michelle made a biting motion with her hand.

Watching her fingers close around the air did make me think about the possibility that Rick might resort to offing Logan his usual way. I believed Rick would try the spell, but if Logan didn't decide right away, would he take matters into his own hands or wait for the magic? I wasn't sure, and the thought of him taking the easy way out did bother me. Logan wasn't a perfect soul by any means, but he didn't deserve the underworld.

I sighed deeply. "I trust Rick," I said. I didn't sound very convincing, even to myself.

"Hmmm," Michelle said, staring me down to let me know she wasn't buying it. To her credit, she didn't push the issue. "Will you meet me on Neuro today during lunch?"

"Why Neuro?"

"I told you, Rhonda needs our opinion on a patient."

I snorted. "Still? Are you sure he's even there anymore? It's been weeks."

"She says yes. No change. He's off the vent, but the lights aren't on and nobody's home," Michelle said.

"What problem could this patient possibly have that you and I need to consult on after all of this time?" I asked.

"Rhonda can't decide which celebrity he looks like," Michelle said.

"Are you serious? You've been bugging me about this because you want to *ogle* a patient?"

"I wanted to ogle him *with you*. It's no fun to do it by myself."

We'd reached the fishbowl corridor to the ICU, and I stopped at the double doors. "You do know you're married, right? Does Manny know you're ogling patients?"

"It doesn't count if they're unconscious. And it doubly doesn't count if a single friend is with me. Wink, wink."

Resistance was futile. "Okay. Lunch it is."

Unfortunately, lunch it wasn't. The ICU was short-staffed, and my three patients were needy. An eighty-year-old male who was recovering from surgery threw a clot, and I ended up performing CPR. I told his soul to get back into his body, and it obeyed. The code staff might have thought it was a little creepy—after all, they couldn't see his soul hovering above his body—but they didn't say anything to me when his heart started beating again. I think they just figured I was overly passionate about saving him. What else could they think?

Anyway, the time flew by. I subsisted on toaster pastries and soda from the vending machine until almost six. That's when Michelle called me.

"I'm giving up on you and heading down to Neuro to see sexy Mr. Unconscious. Last chance to join me."

"Sorry, my friend. Can't leave until my relief gets here. I almost lost a guy today."

"Sounds like it's been a rough one. Okay, you're off the hook. I'll give you the scoop tonight."

I wasn't expecting to hear from her again, which was why I furrowed my brow at the floor secretary when she motioned for me to pick up the phone fifteen minutes later.

"You need to get down to Neuro, stat," Michelle yelled into my ear.

"I told you, I can't."

"No, Grateful. Listen to my words. You *need* to come down to Neuro and *sort* some things out, *now!*" She hung up the phone.

I waved down my charge nurse and begged her to cover for me for my last forty minutes. I told her I was sick, which wasn't exactly true unless you counted severe anxiety as an illness. She said it was okay. I took off down the hall and across the atrium to the east wing. Neuro was on the fourth floor. I jogged into the elevator and waited as the pathetically slow doors shut, and the Muzak version of "Gold Dust Woman" played annoyingly in the background. The song was nearly over by the time the doors opened on four.

Michelle met me, pacing.

"What's going on?" I asked, but she grabbed me by the arm and led me into a room on our left. She ushered me to the end of the bed and pointed at the patient. The man had bushy blondish hair and a beard. His muscles were wasted, but that was to be expected when you'd been in bed for more than a month in a coma. His bandages looked okay. The feeding tube and IV were operating as intended.

"What am I looking at?" I finally asked.

"Grateful, concentrate!" Michelle turned the man's head with her hands to face me and pulled up an eyelid to expose one green eye.

My brain refused to process what I was seeing. There had to be an explanation. This wasn't how it was supposed to work. "It couldn't be him. A cousin? Maybe a brother?"

Michelle handed me a piece of paper, a handoff report we used at the hospital to bring caregivers up to speed on a new patient. I read through it and knew without a doubt that it was true.

The man in the bed was Logan.

CHAPTER 28
We Steal A Body

"Holy hell! Fuuuck, we've gotta stop Rick!"

I whipped out my cell phone and dialed the house, then kicked myself for not buying one of those old-fashioned answering machines. Rick wouldn't pick up my phone, and there was no way for him to know that it was me on the line. I tried our mental connection but got nothing. I guess my power didn't stretch that far.

"He's not answering."

"Try his cell."

"He doesn't have one. He's more than three hundred years old. Technology isn't his thing."

"I guess when you spend your nights sending the unholy to the underworld, a cell phone isn't a priority."

"What are we going to do?"

Michelle and I turned toward Logan and blinked. The room was so quiet I could hear the fluid dripping in his IV. I pivoted toward the window and saw the sun low in the sky. We had roughly thirty-five minutes to stop Rick's spell. I wasn't sure what would happen if Rick tried to force Logan over, considering he wasn't exactly dead, but I didn't want to find out. One thing was clear to me: we needed to rejoin Logan to his body.

"We have to get back to the house, and Logan has to come with us."

"Are you kidding me? Grateful, he's been on continuous tube feeding for a month. If you disconnect it, he's going to go hypoglycemic on your ass." She was right, of course. People had to be weaned from the stuff slowly, over days and weeks. The machine had to keep running.

"We need an ambulance."

Michelle's face went stoic. "Oh my God. You're serious."

"As a heart attack." *Or a coma.*

"We could lose our licenses."

"Yes, we could. I don't expect you to do this with me."

"Are you kidding me? I'm totally in." She flipped open her cell phone. "I know an EMT who might be able to help."

While she talked to her friend, I moved to the nurse's station. It was shift change, so it was deserted; the nurses were in the rooms getting reports. I wondered for a minute why no one had been in Logan's room but then realized they would probably visit him last, considering he was stable and unconscious. It's true what they say, that the squeaky wheel gets the grease, and comatose Logan was not squeaking.

I found a computer that one of the floor nurses hadn't logged out of. I felt guilty doing the dirty work under her name, but hell, if you couldn't train yourself to hit the little lock when you were done in the system, you deserved to be messed with. Also, if all went well tonight, I'd be using magic to reverse what I was about to do. I brought up Logan's file and marveled again that I had chosen the right name.

All that time I'd been searching for his name in his memories, and it was right in front of me—Logan Valentine, owner and chef of Valentine's, my favorite restaurant. I'd even seen the restaurant in his memories. I just didn't realize it was Valentine's. Somehow, the part of me that was the witch had known his name, even before I'd fully accepted my role.

I added a CT scan to his orders and scheduled it for now. That way, when the body was missing, the nurse would think radiology had come and taken him while she was away. That should give us enough time to get him home.

By the time I returned to the room, Michelle had found a gurney and was butting it up to the bed. "Help me move him."

"Sure, but we've gotta be quick. His nurse will be here any minute."

I moved to the other side of the bed and helped shift him onto the gurney. Moving his fluids over, I checked the drip rates. We had several hours before he'd run out. We were rolling him out the door when his nurse came barreling down the hall. Luckily, she was new and didn't recognize either of us.

"Where are you two taking my patient?"

I tucked my ID into my pocket. "We're from Radiology. He's got orders for a CT."

"'Kay. You guys need help getting him in the elevator?"

"Nope. We've got it," Michelle said. With a cheesy smile plastered on my face, I held my breath until the doors closed.

I let it all out in a whoosh once we were alone.

"Should I be concerned she seemed almost excited to have one less patient to take care of?" Michelle asked.

"Wouldn't you be? I mean, it's not like people steal grown men in comas every day. She thinks he'll be back in an hour," I said.

"It's surprising, really, that more people don't get themselves a comatose guy. There's no better way to keep birds out of the garden."

I tried unsuccessfully to stifle a laugh.

"So, who is this EMT friend of yours, and how are we going to get Logan to the ambulance?"

She shrugged. "The less you know, the better. Trust me."

The elevator doors opened on the ground floor. I swung my head out and looked both ways.

"Clear," I whispered, and we rolled Logan out.

The hall seemed to stretch on forever as we proceeded toward the double doors to the back lot. Halfway there, trouble came around the bend in the form of Dr. Wellington. I winced. Dr. Wellington was St. John's resident windbag. This could take a while, and each passing minute could mean Logan's soul.

"Grateful Knight, I'm glad to run into you. I've been meaning to ask you about your opinion on the effects of low glycemic diet on controlling inflammation." Dr. Wellington walked right by Logan and Michelle as if they didn't exist and came to stand in front of me. Without looking up from the file in his hands, he continued to talk.

"Um, we're in the middle of something—"

"—this month's JAMA research seems to indicate…" Dr. Wellington droned on and on, motioning for me to follow him as he walked.

I complied, hoping to steer him away from the gurney and Logan. I knew better than to try to stop him. Dr. Wellington would not take a breath until his entire thought was aired in a verbal string of logic and statistics. I followed along until we stopped in front of the emergency room doors.

"So what do you think?" he asked me. I had no idea what he'd said.

"I think you are absolutely right about that. Insightful as ever, Doctor."

"Good. Then you'll help me chair a cross-disciplinary committee to make the change?"

"Um, sure," I said. Surely there was a spell in *The Book of Light* that would erase this conversation from Dr. Wellington's memory. I hoped.

He gave a little nod and disappeared into the emergency department. I raced back to where I had left Logan, but Michelle was gone, as was the gurney. As fast as I could walk without drawing attention to myself, I moved out the doors into the back lot and toward the ambulance. I hoped Michelle had made it without me, but the vehicle was dark and quiet. I looked in the window and saw the keys were in it.

"Psst," Michelle's voice came from the back. "Get in. You need to drive so I can stay back here with Logan."

I climbed behind the wheel and took off for home.

I've always loved sunsets, especially the orangey-pink ones that happen low in the sky on a cool fall night. But as I raced for home, I cursed the setting star that would without a doubt reach the horizon before we reached Logan. I sent up a silent prayer that Logan would wait to decide his fate, that he would resist Rick's spell.

Then I yelled to Logan in the back, just in case some part of his subconscious got through to his soul. "Logan, if you can hear me, don't choose. Please don't choose."

By the time I reached home, the sun was completely behind the horizon. I tore through the front door. Logan's ghost hovered over a bowl of blood in the foyer. Rick, in some kind of a trance, chanted in front of the circle of bones.

I did what any woman would have done. I slid, screaming, across the wood, crashing into the skulls and pushing the bowl out from under Logan. To be honest, I had no idea what the consequences of my actions would be. I could have forced him on right then.

But whether by magic or fate, I got lucky.

CHAPTER 29
For The Best

"Grateful, what is going on?" Logan's molecules separated and rejoined. "This A-hole says you agreed to this."

"We did agree. Explain yourself, *mi cielo*." Rick pointed at the spilled blood on the floor.

"You stay out of this, dirt jockey." Logan turned, pointing a finger in Rick's direction. "Do you know what this bastard almost did to me? I might have never seen you again!"

"It was for the best." Rick spread his hands.

"Logan, I…" My eyes drifted from his.

"You knew, Grateful? How could you agree to this?" Logan's voice blasted at me, shaking the walls and making the hanging pots in the kitchen clink together.

"I didn't want you to spend eternity forgetting yourself in my attic," I yelled. "I thought it was for the best."

"Why did you stop me?" Rick asked. "Have you changed your mind?"

"Of course she's changed her mind! Grateful and I have something. She wouldn't do this to me." Logan's orb form floated closer to my face.

"Actually, Logan, it would have been for the best, if I hadn't found what I did."

"What did you find?" Logan and Rick asked in unison.

I walked to the door and opened it for Michelle, helping the gurney's wheels over the threshold. Logan floated over to his body, and Rick stepped closer. After a moment of awestruck silence, Rick jerked.

Logan took longer. He hovered over his body until I wondered if I'd caused some type of metaphysical shock. Eventually, he re-formed in front of me, looking like a younger, healthier Logan than the body on the gurney. With a glance toward Rick, he nodded in my direction and said, "Can you put me back in?"

"I hope so. I don't know yet. I need to check the book."

"Can I suggest we move Logan's body to the attic and get cookin'?" Michelle said. "I mean, we do need to sneak Logan back into the hospital tonight if this works. He's already been gone a long time for a CT scan."

"I agree. Rick, can you carry him up the stairs?" I asked.

"What? I don't want that guy touching my body," Logan protested.

"You should have had such qualms when you possessed me, you insolent ball of gas!" Rick threw up his hands in disgust.

"Rick has a point, Logan. And furthermore, there is no way Michelle and I are making it up those stairs with this gurney. If we're going to do this, we need Rick's help."

Logan frowned, placing his hands on his hips and pacing around his body. "I don't look good. Are we sure I'm not going to die anyway?"

"Logan! Are we going to try this or not?"

"Okay, okay. He can carry me up the stairs."

"Good. Let's go."

Rick lifted Logan's body in his arms and carefully moved toward the attic. Michelle and I followed with the liquid nutrition and his IV fluids. As we turned the corner at the second floor landing, Logan's head bumped into the banister. I didn't think Rick did it on purpose. I really didn't. But Logan was not happy.

"Hey! Do you mind?"

"Sorry," Rick said, but I caught the tiniest of smiles flash across his face. I gave him my best death stare.

We all spilled into the attic, and I conjured a hospital bed for Logan's body. Once he was settled in with his fluids safely hung, I hurried to *The Book of Light*. I started with *P* for possession, but the only spells in my book were to force a ghost out of a living body. I found some promising spells under *H* for healing, but while they would make Logan's body stronger, they wouldn't bind his soul to it. After an hour of searching, I slammed the thing shut and turned toward Rick.

"Before I die, I'm upgrading this thing into a searchable database. I can't find anything useful. What do you know? Any caretaker magic that can put him back?"

"No. Caretakers usually exorcise ghosts, not the other way around."

"Maybe we're making this harder than it needs to be." I moved to the hospital bed. "Logan, try to possess your body."

Logan floated to himself and placed a hand over his body's heart, but before he proceeded, he looked at me with something close to panic in his eyes. "I don't think I want to do this. Look at me. Will I ever be normal again? I don't even know if my limbs work. Did I break anything in the crash? Will I be in pain?"

Michelle piped up. "You have a broken femur and collarbone. They should heal eventually, but you've endured a nasty bump on the head."

"The bottom line is that we don't know, Logan," I said. "There are no guarantees, but it's your life to live, whatever there is left of it."

"Maybe I don't want to live it. Maybe it would be better if I let this body die and didn't have to go through the horror of seeing myself waste away every morning. I'm not sure I want to grow old and crippled. I'm not sure I want to live again."

Fear is a poor decision-maker. I saw it strangle all of the logic out of my friend, felt the weight of it on my shoulders. The terror of crawling back into a broken body was a feeling I would never want to experience, but the worst part was doing it alone. Logan was a chef, a restaurant owner, an avid biker. But the one thing he wasn't was a husband and father. His next of kin was a cousin who lived in Albuquerque. Recovery was bad enough when you had a support system, but when you were alone, every day could be a struggle.

"Logan, I know you're scared. I'm not sure what condition your body is in right now or how long it will take for you to get better. But I can promise you this. I'll be there for you. I won't let you do this alone. I'll help you with your recovery."

Michelle had known me long enough to pick up on when to chime in. "Hey, when Grateful promises something, she does it. I'll help too. We'll be your support system."

Hovering over his body, he seemed to consider this. He looked from me to Rick, as if weighing the costs and benefits of what it would mean to have his body back, his life back. I couldn't help in that moment but to question what my life would be like without Logan. I'd quickly become accustomed to his presence in the house and wondered how empty it would feel without him. But like a lost dog, his life did not belong to me. I couldn't keep him.

"I'm going to hold you to your word," he said to me and then sank his hand into his heart. His body jerked as if we'd hit it with a defibrillator. Logan sank in deeper until there was no more ghost. The body's green eyes fluttered open.

"How do you feel, Logan? Can you wiggle your fingers and toes?"

I saw his finger twitch and then the sheet over his feet move. He opened his mouth. No sound came out.

"That's good," I said.

Logan sat up out of his body. "It's not that bad in there. I think I can move everything, but my throat feels weird and, obviously, I'm not sticking. I mean, I can't just possess my own body, right? I need to somehow join with it."

"Yes, of course." I frowned and rubbed my chin. "Let's try one more thing—although, I have no idea what will happen. I've never done this before."

"What the hell. It's just my soul."

"I'm sorry, Logan. I don't mean to use you as my guinea pig, but I think this is our best bet."

"Shoot."

"Lay back into your body."

He did as I asked. I retrieved the canister of salt, making a mental note to buy more, and emptied the remainder around Logan's bed. I stepped into the circle with my bowl and blade. The concentration it took for me to center my power within Logan's body and soul was more than when he was a ghost. A bead of sweat formed on my temple as I pushed my power into him. Like forcing Jell-O into mashed potatoes, fingers of power oozed into the space where his soul was supposed to be. When I had an imprint of his metaphysical energy, I raised the blade, opened my eyes, and said, "Logan Valentine, I release your soul into your body." I sliced my arm; blood flowed into the bowl.

The seizure that hit Logan shook the entire bed. I rolled him onto his side and held him so he wouldn't hurt himself. Michelle tried to help, but she bounced off the salt circle I'd drawn as solidly as if it were made of glass. Luckily, the shaking didn't last long.

"Logan! Logan!" I called. "Are you okay?"

The body under me opened its mouth, and a raspy whisper floated to my ear. "Are you stupid? Of course not."

I rolled him back and squealed.

"I'm me again," he said. As weak as his body had become, for a moment Logan's face looked positively radiant.

CHAPTER 30
Come Daylight

Sneaking Logan back into his room at the hospital was easier than you might think. Nightshift nurses are woefully overworked and aside from a cheery hello from the unit secretary, no one questioned us about why Logan was missing for so long. The hardest part was bringing him into the hospital without going through Emergency. We ended up rolling him through a service entrance.

Michelle and I did allow ourselves one tiny pleasure before going home for the night. We waited in an empty room next to Logan's for his nurse to do her assessment. The wail of joy she emitted when he opened his eyes was priceless. We climbed on the elevator smiling. We'd just created a medical miracle.

"It's been quite a night, Grateful," Michelle said.

"Yes, it has. Did you ever think we'd be up to our armpits in magic and immortals?"

"Only on Halloween."

We laughed.

"Seriously, girl, you know your life just got a hell of a lot more complicated," Michelle said.

"Why? My attic is free of ghosts, I have a boyfriend—sort of, and I think I'm handling this witch thing pretty well."

"Logan is alive and has a body. When you say you have a 'boyfriend—sort of,' are you talking about Rick or Logan? Judging by what you've told me, you're attracted to both."

"I'm with Rick. It's practically part of my job description."

"A relationship shouldn't be a job. Can you honestly admit that you don't feel a connection to Logan?"

I couldn't lie to Michelle, so I remained silent. Lucky for me, the doors opened, and I escaped into the hospital atrium.

Michelle didn't let it drop. "Mmmm-hmmm. I thought so. Your offer to help Logan recover was your subconscious way of maintaining a connection to him. You weren't ready to say goodbye, not really."

Thank you, mental health nurse, for that unsolicited diagnosis. "Is it wrong to not be sure? I'm not married to Rick, after all."

"It's not wrong as long as you're honest about where things stand with both of them. Does Rick know how you feel?"

I stared at my coupled hands.

She gave me a hug and headed for her car.

I said a silent prayer that Manny wouldn't give her a hard time about being so late again.

The ride home was the perfect time to think about the last week and the way my life had changed. I hadn't agreed to marry Rick, but making love to him was a life-altering decision. It meant that I accepted my role as the Monk's Hill witch and believed I'd lived before as Rick's wife. It was a commitment to Rick, even if there wasn't a license involved. But I couldn't deny what Michelle said. Logan and I had a connection that was forged in this lifetime. As much as I thought I could love Rick, I didn't think he was in love with the real me. It was much more likely that he was in love with a memory.

I pulled into his driveway, resolved to set Rick straight. With the number of disastrous relationships I'd left in my wake, it was important for Rick to understand what he was getting himself into— I couldn't promise him monogamy. Prudence had said that he needed to feed on me. I wasn't sure how that worked. What if my noncommittal heart altered the amount of energy I could give him? Honesty was the best policy.

Dawn lurked on the horizon. The night's icy fingers slid from my ribs, darkness lifting from my skin, scurrying from the impending sunrise. This was a new skill, a magical thing. I'd been a witch for all of forty-eight hours, and already I was changing, my cells tuning in to the force of things around me. Suddenly, I missed Prudence and wished I'd asked more questions while she was with me.

I rapped on the wood door to Rick's stone cottage. The wind chimes tinkled softly in the gentle breeze, and the smell of herbs wafted through the waning dark. The door opened, and light filtered around Rick's body. He was shirtless and barefoot, wearing only loose, straight-legged pants that hung low on his hips. Maybe he'd just shifted back. Was it a dangerous night? How many undead had he sent back to the underworld?

In the shadow of his sexy silhouette, all I could squeeze out of my mouth was, "Hello."

He didn't answer my salutation. My feet left the stone slab and I was whirled inside, his mouth finding mine under the arch of the doorway. The kiss was hard and wanting as if he were trying to drink me in. I concentrated on our connection. He was weak. He needed me.

I wrapped my legs around his waist. He planted my back against the wall and ground his hips into me, trailing his nose up my neck. The pounding of his heart came through our connection, quickening my pulse. I rode waves of palpable desire, a decadent ache blossoming deep within me, begging to be soothed. He was the only medicine for my malady.

His body stilled, pressed against mine, and he met my eyes, his need filling their hollow blackness. An unspoken question lingered there. He was an honorable man, not at all like any other man I'd ever been with.

"Yes, Rick. Yes," I whispered.

His mouth found mine again, and he leaned his weight into me, the hard bulge in his pants rubbing in just the right place. I moaned.

"The sounds you make. It lights a fire within me."

"Ditto," I said, sliding my hand between us. Down between my legs, I rubbed him through the thin material of his pants.

Rick gripped me under the butt and carried me into his bedroom, tossing me on the bed. The sunrise filtered through the filmy window dressings and gave me an impressive view of his expansive chest. God, he was gorgeous. All lean muscle and tanned skin. My heart broke from the gate and galloped around my psyche. As he crawled on top of me, I opened for him, more than ready for anything he had in mind. I untied the string at his waist and yanked his pants down to his knees. In one graceful move, he pressed his lower body toward the ceiling and kicked them off. His knees slowly descended on either side of me in a move I'd only seen male gymnasts perform on television.

I had some moves myself. I slid down between his legs and licked a wet trail up his shaft. I circled my tongue around the head, tasting him. Lightning bolts shot through the length of my body. What I was doing was a turn-on, but through our connection, my world became lips, tongue, and wet heat.

He growled. In a heartbeat, my scrubs landed in ribbons on the floor. I crab-walked backward on the bed, watching Rick remove what scraps of fabric still clung to me. The added space gave me room to appreciate the view. He was glorious. Dark and dangerous. I traced the scythe-shaped pattern of his scar—the scar I gave him. The thought was highly erotic, and I leaned in to lick the raised skin.

I worked my hands down his abs and was suddenly airborne. When I landed, he was under me.

"Oh," I said, feeling the head of him pressed against my slit. His hands circled my waist, thumbs caressing my bottom ribs. I sank deeper, taking the tip of him into me and watching his breath hitch in his throat. His jaw lengthened at the tease, the animal within fighting for the surface.

He leaned his head back, closed his eyes, and raised his hips, plunging himself deeper into me. The pleasure was so intense, I could have come right then, but I was afraid if I did it would bring him to orgasm and cut this short. I wanted more, much more.

Instead, I rolled off him and the bed, landing on the balls of my feet. I glanced over my shoulder and grinned. "When you catch me, you can have me."

With a squeal, I ran out of the bedroom and to the opposite side of the couch. He was there in a split second, playful and hard. He circled after me to the right, and I dodged left. He changed direction, but so did I. Then in a leap that was humanly impossible, he was over the couch and behind me. His right hand wrapped itself in my hair, pulling almost to the point of pain. His left circled my waist from behind. He lowered his lips to my ear.

"I have caught you, *mi cielo*. You are mine." He bent me over the back of the couch and entered me.

Even though I was still wet, I inhaled sharply as he stretched me to my limit. Slowly at first, he worked his shaft in and out, raking his fingers through my hair, down my back, around and over my breasts. He found a rhythm and reached around my hips to stroke between my legs.

His size and strength was almost painful. I was sure I'd have bruises, but all I could think about was how I wanted every part of him inside of me. The pressure built until I burst apart at the seams, screaming his name, and still he worked me until I'd come so many times my mind could form only incoherent thoughts, most revolving around pleasure and Rick.

Finally, he bucked, shivered, and draped himself across my back. A wet kiss landed on my neck, followed by a sharp nip. I stiffened. My blood poured into his mouth. Slowly, he started stroking again. The decadent tension built within me once more. I was hungry, so damned hungry. I turned my head and bit down on his inner arm, breaking the skin.

He moaned against my neck.

A mind-blowing orgasm ripped through both of us as his blood washed into my mouth, fueled by the magic that bound us to each other. I came again and again, shattering around him.

When he finished, we lay there, a heap of flesh on the back of his couch. He pulled out and offered me his hand.

"I'm not sure I can walk," I said honestly.

He beamed, tossed me into his arms, and carried me to his bed.

CHAPTER 31
Versions of the Truth

Waking up in a lover's arms is one of the great joys of life. I turned in the circle of Rick's embrace to find him watching me.

"It's unsettling how little you sleep," I said.

"I could pretend for you if you'd like?" he replied in a voice as intoxicating as the body stretched out next to me.

"No, I'd rather know the truth. Speaking of, there are things I need to tell you about myself. Things you should know about my past if we are going to try to make this work."

"You forget, I was part of your past."

"Not my past life. I mean my romantic past."

Rick frowned. "You are only twenty-two, yes?"

"Yes."

"How much history could there be?" He laughed, nervously.

I grimaced. "You represent my foray into the double digits."

His brow wrinkled, and he scooted back as if to get a better look at me. "Are you saying, Grateful, that you have had intercourse with more than ten men in your short life?"

"Well, yes. Normally, I wouldn't admit to it, but because you have waited for me, I thought you should know."

"And you did this why?"

"Don't think that I just slept with these people. I'm not a slut or anything. Every single one of them was a meaningful relationship."

Rick jumped a little as if I'd shocked him, and I realized that he might not consider a string of serious relationships any better than anonymous sex.

"I lived with the last one—er, Gary—and I dated the others for more than a month each. I just can't seem to stick with someone for more than a year. Technically, I've never made it to a year, but you know what I mean."

"Marry me, Grateful. Put the past behind you."

"Don't you see what I'm saying? I'm terrible at this stuff. My relationships never last. I can't marry you because I don't want to be divorced in a year. Let's face it. We hardly know each other. If this is going to work, we need a firm foundation, something to build a life on. Let's take it slow and get to know each other."

Rick bounded out of bed and paced the floor, running his hands through his hair. "I know you, Grateful. Sometimes, I think, better than you know yourself. You are stalling, waiting for certainty in a life that offers no guarantees. You say to take it slow yet here we are, and what we have just done is anything but taking it slow. What are you afraid of?"

I scrambled for an answer, anything to put him off. The feelings I had for him were too overwhelming. They scared me. I'd already risked too much. "Why don't we just live together?" I suggested, although I knew my father would be upset at me jumping into the arrangement so soon after Gary. "Wait a minute. If we were married in a past life, why do we have two separate houses? Why didn't we live together then?"

Rick's features sagged. He was hiding something from me.

"We were married but didn't live together. Why?" I asked again.

"You needed your space—a space to do your magic."

"You said 'you needed your space' at first. Did we have our problems when we were married?"

"Every couple has problems."

"But ours were enough to keep us living in separate homes?"

He placed his hands on his hips. "You don't understand. There are extenuating circumstances. Each of us has our own seat of magic. Mine comes from the earth. Thus, my home is made of stone and wood. Yours comes from the air, thus the attic arrangement. It is natural for each of us to have our own places."

I thought about that for a while. Truthfully, it wouldn't do to fret over a past life I didn't even remember. But this meant I couldn't rely on some past happiness to confirm if I was supposed to be with Rick for the rest of my life. I needed to find out for myself, in this life. And I needed to change the subject because I was seriously ticking him off.

I lowered my eyes and waited a few heartbeats for the silence to drain the energy from the room. "What do you think we should do about Julius?"

"You're changing the subject, *mi cielo*."

"I don't believe he didn't know about Marcus. He's up to something. If he's raising an army of vampires, we have to stop him. Too many, and they will be impossible to control."

"I counted fifteen in TiltWorld. We may have already reached the tipping point."

"Do you think he was in contact with Marcus before he escaped? Is Julius Mr. Helleborine?"

"I don't know, but I'm staying vigilant. I believe we should keep a close watch on Julius. It's our best chance of maintaining the peace."

"Peace. I'd prefer an excuse to kill. The only good vampire is a dead vampire," I said.

"That's a harsh attitude, even for you." Rick peered at me through hooded eyes. "Be careful who you say that to. We don't want to alienate the supernatural community."

Who would I talk to? "Julius is up to something. If he changed Gary, that has to be against the rules, right?"

"Not if Gary consented."

"But it's obvious he's building his coven, and Marcus knew just where to go when he escaped."

"We have no proof of that."

I narrowed my eyes. "Yeah…not yet, anyway. Maybe I can get some dirt on him from Gary, but then if I didn't trust him before, I certainly don't trust him now that he's undead."

"Don't take this the wrong way, but perhaps you should brush up on your magic before taking on Julius. He's very old and very powerful."

"No offense taken. I know I have some things to learn." I pressed myself up from his bed. "I should get going. I have errands to run today, and I seriously need a shower."

"Are you going to see Logan?" he asked, resentment making his words short and sharp. Standing over me, the sheer size of him was intimidating, but it was this look of possessiveness that made me uncomfortable.

"Actually, no. I need to go grocery shopping and clean up the bloodstain in my foyer. But since you brought it up, I'm visiting him tomorrow. You should come. He needs all the support he can get right now."

Rick's head fell. I couldn't deal with the jealousy shit, not when the person he was jealous of currently was so weak he couldn't get out of bed by himself. I walked to his chest of drawers and pulled them out one by one. I found a T-shirt and some sweats to wear home.

"Oh, and Rick, if we're ever going to do this again, you need to stop shredding my clothes. Those were my favorite scrubs."

I left through the front door, more pissed off than I should have been, with Rick staring after me. His arms were crossed over his chest, and he wasn't smiling. It was a shitty way to leave things between us. But Rick wouldn't be happy until Logan was a distant memory, and I was married to him, to boot. I couldn't talk about it anymore. The answer was no on both accounts, and I wasn't going to cave. No way.

CHAPTER 32

I'm True To Myself

Cleaning bloodstains from hardwood might be easier when the blood is fresh. Dried as it was, I had to mop it up in layers. I used an old string mop I found in the broom closet and watched it taint the clear water in my bucket with every swipe. When I was done, I flushed the blood and water down the toilet and threw away the mop.

I collected all of the skulls into a large black garbage bag and left them on the side of the porch. I thought about walking down to tell Rick they were there but decided against it. He was a grown man. He could take care of his own skulls. Plus, I wasn't ready to talk to him again. Whenever I was within three feet of him, my feelings became a confused mishmash of past life memories, uncontrollable lust, and his personal hang-ups pouring through our metaphysical connection. And let's not forget the thick layer of jealousy Rick had added over the Logan situation. I needed space and time to sort out my feelings.

With my foyer back to normal, I microwaved some water and mixed in hot cocoa from a packet. It was a far cry from the kind Logan used to make for me. I sat on my stoop, sipping the unpalatable concoction and tried to sort out the tangled mess of emotions inside my head.

I missed Logan.

I'd promised to help him through his recovery, and I intended to follow through. But what would happen when he was better? Could I honestly dismiss him from my life? We'd shared a deep connection, friendship for sure and more. How would our relationship change now that he didn't live in my attic? Would friendship even be possible when I could still feel the way he'd slid under my skin? I wasn't sure. And what did that mean for my relationship with Rick?

Rick was my...what? "Boyfriend" wasn't strong enough, but I wasn't married to him. I wasn't sure exactly where that left us. I did love him. At least, I thought I did, but it was hard to sort out which feelings were his and which were mine. What did love mean, anyway? One thing was for sure: I needed him. If I was going to fend off Mr. Helleborine from my house and keep Julius and his quickly expanding coven in check, I required Rick and his beast. Beyond the help he would give me to understand my power, his muscle and the strength his blood gave me were essential to my survival. Love or not, we were connected in a symbiotic dance of magic and wills.

Which made me think how little I understood about all of this. I wished there were more witches like me—a mentor who could take Prudence's place. On some fundamental and cosmic level, I trusted Rick more than I'd ever trusted Gary or anyone else besides my father. But trusting someone didn't mean I had to hand over the reins of my life to him. I had to learn *The Book of Light*. It was my sole objective source of information about who I was and what I could do.

As I watched the sunset, the sky painting itself in pinks and purples, I came to terms with reality. I couldn't control who I was before, or the challenges hidden in my future. All I could control was today. Today—well, tonight—I was going to begin reading *The Book of Light*. I was going to start to plan how Rick and I would stop Julius. And I was going to find a way to buy this house from my father. Because if one thing was for certain, my attic did not belong in the hands of someone else.

The rumble of a heavy vehicle on imperfect pavement drew my eye toward the road. A FedEx truck navigated my driveway, parking only halfway up. The driver jumped out, retrieved a package from the back, and headed toward me.

"Delivery for Grateful Knight."

"I'm Grateful," I said, accepting the signature pad from him.

"That's an unusual name, Grateful Knight."

"Well, I'm an unusual girl." I handed him back the signed form.

The man eyed my house and the deep, dark woods across the street. "Almost didn't find the place. GPS in the truck doesn't have you on the map. What's a young woman like yourself doing living all the way out here in the boonies, anyway?" He said the words through a playful smile.

I accepted the box, which was heavier than I expected, before I answered him. "This is home."

He grabbed the bill of his cap and gave me a little nod before retreating to his truck.

I juggled the door open as the last rays of light sank behind the tree line, realizing this would be the first night I would spend in this house alone. Prudence and Logan were gone, and although a soul could visit my attic at any time, so far tonight there was no one. Considering Logan had been the first in two years, I supposed I'd better get used to being alone. And maybe that was for the best. I needed to know more about who I was to be ready for something more.

Kicking the door closed behind me, I placed the package on my kitchen counter and dug in my junk drawer for scissors. I cut the tape holding the box together, exposing another box, gift wrapped. Someone had sent me a present! A card taped to the side had my name on it. I tore into the envelope to find a picture of a puppy lying on his back in a gigantic bowl of food. Inside the card was blank except for a handwritten note: *An early birthday present. Thought you could use this. Happy birthday. Love you, Dad.*

Under the paper was a new MacBook Pro. Aww, Dad. My birthday wasn't for another month. He must've seen my cracked screen when he was over for dinner. I whipped out my phone and texted him a quick pre-thank-you-card thank you. He had no idea what this meant to me.

I lifted the box and headed for the attic. The key turned easily in the lock, and I walked into the light, using my magic to change the layout to my needs. Today I conjured a desk in front of *The Book of Light* and placed the laptop on it. I'd buy a real desk as soon as I could afford one so that it would be here during the day. Entering my spells into a database would be a great way to learn them, not to mention find them quickly. I even had a database app on my phone I thought might come in handy on the run.

Judging by the size of the tome, learning my own magic could take a lifetime. Of course, Prudence had said I'd live longer than most. My stomach twisted, thinking about the practicalities of not growing older, having the world continue on without me, watching everyone I know die. Rick said he was sterile. I'd never have children. I shook my head. I wasn't ready to go there.

A growl outside brought me to the back window overlooking the cemetery. The scales of Rick's beast glinted from between the headstones. I smiled, reaching for Nightshade.

Love was scary. It made you vulnerable. I couldn't trust my romantic feelings for Rick yet, but I could trust he would do his part as my caretaker, no matter what.

I had come to this house wanting to stand on my own two feet, to grow into the responsible adult I knew I was, and take back control of my life. I'd blamed myself for what happened with Gary and felt inadequate and naïve. But I'd come a long way. I was stronger, levelheaded. I'd killed. I'd taken risks and succeeded for my cause. And I would accept what life and fate had in store for me. I might have surrendered myself to Rick and to the role of witch, but somehow I felt like I'd finally come into my own skin.

I was Hecate. I was the Monk's Hill witch.

KICK THE CANDLE (EXCERPT)

Book 2 in the Knight Games Series

Chapter 1

A Familiar Tale

"Hey, Grateful, why are zombies entered under Wayward Magic instead of Supernaturals?" Absentmindedly, Michelle leaned back from the computer monitor, hands cradling the base of her head.

"Because they're animated dead bodies," I explained to my friend. "The body itself is natural, as opposed to ghouls or fairies who were born and raised Supers." I flipped to the next page in *The Book of Light,* which featured an eavesdropping spell that enchanted a bee to listen in and relay information to the spell caster. *Sigh.* As if a vampire wouldn't be suspicious of a bumblebee persistently circling its head. Still, an earlier reincarnation of myself thought this spell was important enough to put in the daddy of all grimoires. My book of magic had been with me for multiple lifetimes; I needed to trust in its wisdom. With a tap of the return key, I started a new database entry.

Michelle lifted her cup of coffee from the desk and took a deep swig. "But what about vampires and shifters? They were human once. Why are they under Supernatural?"

I stopped typing and gave it some thought. I'd only been the Monk's Hill Witch for two months. Magic and supernatural monsters were new to me too, even if I was a Hecate, aka sorceress of the dead.

"I think it's because with zombies, someone else is pulling the strings. Whoever animates them controls them. They're soulless, for lack of a better word. Vampires and shifters can make their own decisions—well, as long as it meshes with the orders of their coven or pack leader."

"Hmm. Who controls the ones you've imprisoned in the cemetery?" She stood and walked to the window overlooking my front yard. The glass still sported the Anderson Windows sticker from when Rick replaced it two months ago after the vampire Marcus shattered it while escaping us.

"The zombies? They're possessed by a type of vaporous demon from the underworld. In my last life, I sentenced them to hell for possessing humans. Of course, the demons were expunged from the human bodies, so…ah…they possess corpses to come out at night. They can't come out of the underworld without one. The fresh air is toxic to them."

"Oh."

I didn't want to be a bitch or anything, but I wished she'd get back to work. I'd slayed Marcus, but Julius was still out there. As vamps went, Marcus was child's play compared to Julius. I'd only met the vamp once, but once was enough. Julius was ancient, insidious, and had a following. I suspected Julius was behind the murder of my last incarnation, and now was growing his free coven to dangerous sizes in hopes history would repeat itself. The spells in *The Book of Light* offered my best hope for protecting myself against Julius, and this database promised fast and easy access on the move. The book itself wasn't going anywhere. The tome weighed hundreds of pounds.

I truly appreciated Michelle volunteering to help me with data entry, but when she got like this, questioning, it really slowed us down. We'd only put in about four hours. I wanted to get another hundred entries done before sunset and all the witchy responsibilities that came with nightfall. Thankfully, she walked back to my iMac and sat down. "At least we can work during the day now. Real, honest-to-goodness desks," she said, knocking on the wood.

I shrugged. I'd found two big desks at Elmer Bishop's estate sale for next to nothing, which was everything in my checking account. I butted them against each other and networked my new computer, a birthday gift from my dad, with my old laptop. We could both make entries to the same database. Plus, *The Book of Light* was large enough that if we opened it across the two desks, Michelle could enter one spell while I entered another. It was a nice setup.

"Not that your magic isn't totally cool, Grateful. I mean, conjuring shit out of the ether is wicked awesome, but you have to admit, it's nice not to have them disappear when the sun comes up."

"Yeah." Unfortunately, the magic of my attic was tied to the night air, and everything I conjured disappeared when the sun rose. It sucked, but I suppose everything has to have limits. Otherwise, I'd be conjuring myself a million dollars up here.

The soothing rhythm of vigorous typing filled the air between us...for all of thirty seconds.

"Did you hear about Logan?" Michelle asked, blowing away any delusions I'd had about her getting back to work.

"Hear what? I saw him at physical therapy yesterday. He's walking pretty well with a cane. Put some weight on too."

"He's starting back at Valentine's. Just a few days per week at first, but he's planning to work up to full-time."

Valentine's was Logan's pride and joy. He'd started the restaurant from scratch, and it was one of Carlton City's best rated. In my opinion, Logan was lucky his assistant manager had kept the wheels on while he was missing. Another employee might have closed shop.

"That's good news," I said. "Logan needs somewhere to focus his energy."

"You mean on something other than you."

"No," I said defensively. "I mean on something other than the pain of his recovery." Logan had been in a coma for almost a month after a truck plowed into him on his bike. He'd been damaged bad enough to knock his soul out of his body and leave him unrecognizable to his rescuers. It was sheer coincidence he ended up in the hospital where I worked as a nurse, and serendipity that I was the one who could put his soul back into his body. His recovery had been a long, hard journey.

"So, you're saying that Logan hasn't tried to rekindle those old romantic feelings now that he has a body?"

"What Logan felt when he was a ghost was just a misunderstood metaphysical attraction to me as his soul sorter."

"Nice story. How do you explain what you felt for him?"

"Logan knows I'm with Rick now."

"Yeah," she drawled. Her eyes drilled into me.

I wasn't sure what she wanted me to say. Rick was part of my job description. He was my caretaker, the immortal vessel for my soul between lifetimes. Hundreds of years ago, the first me, Isabella Lockhart, had made Rick her caretaker. At the moment of her death, she stored a piece of her soul inside him, which he'd returned to her when she was reincarnated. I was a reincarnation of that same witch, and I'd taken back the immortal part of my soul from Rick in a ceremony that included blood, magic, and sex.

Pursuing anything with Logan didn't make sense for a number of reasons. Aside from the superhuman level of understanding it would require of him to allow me to continue to be the witch and have sex with Rick as needed, my feelings for Logan had changed since he was reunited with his body. As far as I was concerned, the night we shared when he was a ghost had been an accident. I was seeking comfort, and he'd accidentally slipped inside my body and given me an orgasm. Ancient history.

"Logan's my friend. That's all." To signal I was done with this particular avenue of conversation, I flattened my page with my palm and returned to typing vigorously on my laptop.

Michelle raised an eyebrow and pursed her lips inquisitively. "How is Caretaker Rick, anyway? You guys still trying to start a fire by rubbing your crotches together?"

I fought a smile but only half of my mouth obeyed my command. "Nice, Michelle. You know, it's not like it's tawdry or anything. We *have* to do it. It strengthens our powers."

"Power sex. Right. He gets all charged up and you get..."

"Multiple orgasms and sometimes his blood."

"Yum." She grimaced.

"It heals me. Last week, we were bringing in a vamp we caught feeding on a human at a strip club in the city. The thing practically bit though my arm before I sentenced it to hell. A little sip of Rick and the wound healed right up. It's nothing short of miraculous."

Michelle shook her head and took another gulp of coffee, as if she could rinse the taste of blood from her mouth. The TMI convo was enough to make her turn back to her work. She focused on the page closest to her and poised her fingers over the keyboard.

"Hey, here's something interesting," she said.

"What?"

"It's a spell to call a familiar."

"A what?"

Michelle scooted closer to the book and read to me. "*Familiar, Spell to Call. A familiar can be summoned to amplify Hecate's power by performing the following spell. A willing spirit will arrive in the form of an animal possessing those traits the current incarnation is deficient in and supporting optimum natural balance. Through mutual respect and bonding, a familiar can become a trusted and powerful companion.*"

"Cool. Like a black cat or whatnot."

"Or maybe you'll get an owl like Harry Potter!"

"Oh yeah, those things are wicked awesome." I stood and leaned over the book to get a good look at the spell.

Michelle tapped the yellowing page. "Hey, there are some notes here in the margin. *Tabitha 1721, Abraham 1823, Gertrude 1898*. Grateful, I think this is a list of past familiars. Is that how many times you've lived?"

I shrugged.

"Well? Are you going to do it?"

"Maybe. Does the spell look difficult?" I tried to read it through myself, but Michelle's head was in the way. She was practically crawling into the page. My friend seriously needed glasses.

"You tell me. It says you have to meditate. Once your mind is clear, you make an offering in your silver bowl and a willing spirit will come to you."

"What kind of offering?"

"It doesn't specify."

"As long as it's not blood." I'd learned the hard way that blood—my own—was required to sort a human soul to the afterlife. When I'd put Logan back into his body, I had to slice my arm and bleed into my silver bowl to make his soul "stick." The cut itself healed magically, but the blood loss on top of the mystical effort involved left me exhausted.

"I guess it can be anything that's valuable to you," she said.

I nudged her out of the way and read through the spell myself. "Look, this symbol in the corner means I can do it during the day." I pointed to a yellow circle next to the title.

Michelle nodded and looked at me expectantly.

"It might be nice to have a pet," I said.

"Grateful, this isn't just a pet. This is a *familiar*, the perfect pet to balance you. It's like petmatch.com but better. This little guy will make you more powerful. Hell, all I've got at home is a pug with flatulence."

"You love Bosco."

She giggled. "He was an impulse buy that grew on me."

I sighed and plopped back into my chair. "I don't know, Michelle. Do we have time for this? I really wanted to get more done today."

Tipping her head to the side, my friend folded her arms across her chest. "Really? The pages aren't numbered, but this thing has to be five thousand long. We've been at it all month and have barely made a dent."

With attitude, I combed my fingers through my hair and rolled my eyes. "All the more reason to buckle down and get to work."

She jabbed her open hands toward the mammoth book. "Hello? It's going to take us a year to enter all these spells. It's not like we don't both have full-time jobs. This is like moving a bucket of water with an eyedropper."

"Now you're exaggerating."

She folded her arms across her chest. "What's the rush?"

Crossing the attic, I leaned against the window frame and watched the naked branches of the oak tree in my front yard twist in the late November wind. Less than six weeks until Christmas. I was sure Michelle had better things to do with her day off than enter spells into my database. My chest sank thinking about the burden I'd been to her the last several months. I was the reason she'd been possessed by a vampire.

But I *was* in a hurry. Besides the danger of Julius's growing coven, and the fact that he probably wanted me dead, Julius said that Rick had lied to me, that I didn't need a caretaker to regain my power. Julius was a vampire and almost certainly deceiving me. I had no reason to trust him. But ever since he'd said the words, I'd questioned my connection to Rick and the boundaries of my power. In my gut, I had the tiniest needling that Rick was keeping something from me. I'd tried time and time again to put the feeling aside, but it wouldn't leave me alone.

My past incarnation had the wherewithal to name a guardian of my magical attic, Prudence. She'd helped me learn about what I was. Unfortunately, when I accepted my role, Prudence moved on to her eternal reward. With her gone, if I couldn't trust Rick, the only source of power, protection, and information I had was *The Book of Light*. I was sure all the answers I needed were within its pages.

I didn't want to trouble Michelle with all the details. She'd done enough to support me already. This was my boat to row. Besides, I was willing to bet obsessing about it was exactly what Julius wanted me to do.

"It could save my life, Michelle. The book weighs hundreds of pounds. This is the only way I can take it with me while I'm learning. I may need one of these spells in an emergency."

"Really?" She leaned across the book. "An eavesdropping bee is going to protect you against a vampire attack on the fly?"

"You've got a point," I mumbled. "But it's still my best hope."

Michelle rubbed her palms together. "I'm not saying the database isn't important, but it isn't everything. It's going to take time. No matter what you do, you're going to have to learn how to use this magic. There are no shortcuts."

I sighed. "You're right. This is just the workaholic in me coming out."

"Exactly. It will all get done eventually. A little a day and by the time you're thirty, you'll be done." With one arm, she hugged my shoulders playfully.

I suddenly felt compelled to entertain her. She'd earned it. "You wanna watch me summon a familiar, or what?"

"That's the spirit."

We jogged downstairs to look for something to offer the familiar's spirit. Unlike when Logan lived here, the house was a mess and there was nothing in my pantry but coffee grounds. I opened the refrigerator to check if food had mysteriously appeared there while I was in the attic. It hadn't. The contents consisted of a box of baking soda, a half-empty bottle of ketchup, and the remains of Valentine's takeout from two weeks ago with dodgy-looking fuzz growing under the lid. I tossed the takeout but grabbed the coffee grounds. Michelle appeared in front of me with a bottle of wine from the cellar.

"This should work," she said.

"Wine? Is that necessary?" I asked, not thrilled about wasting a bottle.

"The book said you needed an offering. The connotation is that you sacrifice something important to you. You don't want to use blood, and there's nothing more important to you in this house than wine and coffee, except maybe me, and I'm not sitting in that bowl."

"Wine and coffee it is."

We returned to the attic, and I pulled out the wooden trunk containing my magical paraphernalia. On top was my blade, Nightshade. Made from the femur of the patron saint of cemetery workers, Nightshade could only be wielded by me. I set her aside to dig beneath her space in the trunk. Under her was a silver bowl, salt, candles, a few shrouds, and a bell. My predecessor had left the witchy toolkit, and I was becoming more comfortable with it day by day. I selected the bowl.

Cross-legged on the floor next to the wine and coffee, I closed my eyes and tried to clear my mind. I flexed my shoulders toward my ears, inhaled, then released the breath, slumping forward. I tried to relax as much as possible, concentrating on the flow of breath at the back of my throat. When a thought threatened at the corner of my consciousness, I pushed it aside.

They say when you enter deep meditation that you visualize a light of some sort moving toward you. I did. A green light that seemed flat at first until I reached it and then expanded into a tunnel. The light branched out and formed leaves. And then, in my clear mind, I was in a garden. Even though I logically knew my body was sitting in my attic meditating, I *was* physically there, nestled in blades of cool dewy grass with my bowl and offering beside me. The sun was warm upon my face, and the leaves of the plants rustled in the sweet-smelling breeze.

From a grove of trees, a naked woman stepped toward me. Large dark eyes and silky black hair contrasted sharply against the light that shone behind her head. She stopped just short of my bowl.

"Hecate," she said. "Welcome to my garden. Make your offering."

I wanted to know more about this woman and this place, but my intuition warned this was not the time to ask. Maybe it was the way her skin glowed like it was radioactive and the light broke around her torso. Reflexively, I reached for the wine and poured half of it into the bowl. I sprinkled coffee over the top.

The woman laughed, a sound as pure and clear as a choir of bells. My eyes started to hurt so I looked away from her, back at the bowl. It was empty.

"Yes, I know who you seek, and I send him to you with my blessing. He is yours and will teach you what you need to know."

The woman opened her hand. A black butterfly bobbed toward me, growing fast and spreading out until it barreled into me. I somersaulted backward from the impact, eyes closed against the onslaught. Everything—the garden, the woman—disappeared in a wash of darkness.

"Grateful!" A hand slapped my cheek. "Grateful, snap out of it!"

I opened my eyes to see Michelle hovering over me.

"D-Did it work?" I stammered.

The corner of Michelle's mouth tugged upward. "Um, yeah. It worked."

"So what is it? A cat? An owl?"

"Maybe you should see for yourself," she said.

She helped me up to a sitting position. Behind my silver bowl was a huge black ball of feathers. I reached for it and a pair of beady black eyes popped open to peer at me. A large hooked beak snapped the air and two shiny black wings stretched on either side of a lissome black body.

"It's a crow," I said with distaste. On the spectrum of magical creatures, I hadn't expected a yard rat. The thing looked like something I'd shoo off the garbage cans.

Michelle took a step back. "That's not a crow, Grateful; it's a *raven*. And I think it just pooped on your floor."

ABOUT THE AUTHOR

Genevieve Jack grew up in a suburb of Chicago and attended a high school rumored to be haunted. She loves old cemeteries and enjoys a good ghost tour. Genevieve specializes in original, cross-genre stories with surprising twists. She lives in central Illinois with her husband, two children, and a Brittany named Riptide who holds down her feet while she writes.

Visit Genevieve at:

http://www.GenevieveJack.com
https://twitter.com/Genevieve_Jack
https://www.facebook.com/AuthorGenevieveJack
http://instagram.com/authorgenevievejack
http://www.goodreads.com/author/show
/6477522.Genevieve_Jack

ACKNOWLEDGEMENTS

I am indebted to the following people for their help, support, and inspiration:

To my husband, A, thank you for supporting and encouraging my writing.

To my friend MM, who survived nursing school with me and is always willing to share her experiences, thank you for the inspiration.

To the women of Random Moon books: Laurie Larsen, Laurie Bradach, Katy Lewis, and Leta Gail Doerr, thank you for your friendship, constant support, and helpful advice.

Printed in Great Britain
by Amazon.co.uk, Ltd.,
Marston Gate.